Montage Publishing
Texas

The Dragon Whistler

The Secrets of the Soul Treasures

Kimberly J. Smith

For Steven, Harrison and Ben,
who make every day musical.
And for Mom,
who taught me so much more than the notes.

PART ONE

CHAPTER 1

THE MUSIC WAS everything and everything was the music. The lilting, hypnotic tune consumed Willow, freezing the world as if someone had pushed the pause button on reality. Notes poured out of the tiny whistle, hovering in the air around her like magical bubbles that floated up into the cornflower blue Colorado sky only to be popped by sharp rays of morning sunlight. She'd never felt a peace like this before, so serene and clear and focused—

And then the dragon blasted through the mountainside and everything became chaos.

Broadmoor Crest Park was a good five miles across the valley from Cheyenne Mountain, but the view from its plateau was spectacular, so Willow had a clear view of the massive explosion of rock and rubble as the enormous silver dragon escaped the mountain. It was all she could do to tear away her gaze to share shock with her cousin Ben. Both he and the unfamiliar teenage girl seemed just as stunned by the dragon's appearance as Willow, if the way their mouths hung open was any indication. Willow studied the girl's face, but she'd never seen her before. Her clothing was odd, like a costume, and her appearance was just as mysterious as the dragon's, even if not quite as dramatic. She had yelled at them as she ran up, though. Now that Willow thought about it, the girl had been yelling at Willow. Yelling at her to stop.

Stop what? She'd only been playing that whistle she and Ben had found in the old hotel near summer camp. What was so bad about that?

The dragon's bellow drove everything else from Willow's mind, the roar bending the air from foothills to park where the three of them stood in the dewy grass transfixed with horror, terror and, if Willow was honest about it, kind of a thrill, actually.

Two months short of her thirteenth birthday, Willow was too old to believe dragons existed outside of storybooks, movies or video games. But there was no doubt that a real, live, honest-to-goodness dragon flew over the valley below them, turning in graceful, terrifying circles.

Her brain zapped and sparked like a live wire, trying to reject what her eyes took in. One bellowing roar later and she surrendered to the truth.

It was there. It was real.

A DRAGON!

Willow wasn't sure if she actually screamed the words because, seriously, she couldn't even breathe and oxygen in your lungs was essential to screaming. Unfortunately, her lungs felt packed with some kind of thick icy substance, like maybe that oozing stuff inside those blue ice pack things. It sure didn't feel like summer anymore, although the morning was a warm one for Colorado.

The dragon moved its wings forward, then back toward its long, spiky tail, propelling itself through the air like a missile. That's really not how I expected a dragon to fly, Willow thought. The movements reminded her of swimming more than flying. Except, of course, that the thing was flying. Except, of course, that the thing wasn't supposed to exist in the first place.

The air vibrated with another bellow. Willow clutched the thin, bone-white whistle hanging from the silk cord around her neck. "Noooooo! This can't be happening, it just can't!" the stranger moaned. She looked like she was probably in high school, maybe a little older. The girl buried her fingers in her long, dark hair like she might yank handfuls from her scalp, totally freaking out. She whirled on Willow. "This is your fault!"

Willow's stomach turned to water. "Me? Wh— what'd I do?"

The girl's expression shifted to grim determination. Her light brown skin flushed with angry red splotches. She glared at Willow with dark brown eyes, nothing but pupils. Instead of answering Willow's question, she grabbed her arm and shook her. "You did this. And you have to fix it."

"Get your hands off me!" Willow squawked, but the girl grabbed the whistle out of her hands. Something was going on with the black markings on its underside — glyphs Ben had called them. Whatever they were called, they now glowed a harsh, volcanic red. "Where did you get this?" the girl demanded.

"Leave Willow alone!" Ben spat, pulling at the girl's other arm. Willow had to admit, she was impressed. In the short time she'd spent with her cousin, she'd never heard him raise his voice before. Not like this, at least.

The girl turned her piercing gaze on Ben and he shrank back. So much for his protective side. "You have no idea what you're talking about." Her gaze returned to the whistle in Willow's hand, eyes closing in defeat like those glowing red glyphs confirmed her worst fears.

Then her eyes snapped open, flashing with anger. She spun Willow around, pointing her at the dragon soaring over the valley. "That dragon is awake because you woke her. Which means Willow here is the only one who can put her back to sleep." Heaving a deep sigh, the girl backpedalled, dialing it down from fury to plain old seething anger. With a hint of regret, she said, "Congratulations, Willow. You're a Dragon Whistler."

10

CHAPTER 2

ONE WEEK BEFORE a real, live dragon exploded out of Cheyenne Mountain and forever changed her life, not to mention the world, Willow pushed her back against the brick wall of the Shop N' Sell a few blocks from her house, hiding from the shop's owner, Mr. Botana.

She peeked around the corner of the building as Mr. Botana tossed a tattered cardboard box into the enormous metal dumpster. The old guy did this a few times a week: tossed unsold items from his pawnshop to make space for new items that had a better chance of selling. Willow grinned, hearing the box thump to the bottom of the dumpster. She'd arrived at exactly the right time to rescue the treasures from the landfill.

Willow had discovered a few gems among his trash in the past, like the leather-bound book of Grimm's fairy tales, and that set of vinyl albums by some old rock group named Led Zeppelin—not that she had a turntable to play them on, but her cousin Marcus told her vinyl was making a comeback, so she'd kept them. And what about that beat up, blue California license plate from 1974? How could Botana have tossed that one? It was practically an antique! Leftovers from other people's lives fascinated Willow. Who knew what amazing journeys had led those items to Mr. Botana's place? Willow loved imagining their stories.

Willow's mom didn't understand. She called it "poking through the trash" but in Willow's opinion the woman had no vision. No taste for adventure, either. The only spontaneous thing Amanda McLain had ever done in her life was marrying Willow's dad after dating him for under a month. Look where that got her: a quick trip to life as a single mom.

At least when Willow's dad left them he only moved across town. Not like the father of her bestie and treasure-hunting partner Emma. Her dad had moved to California. And now Emma was spending the summer away from her friends. At least Willow didn't have to do that.

She pulled open the side door of the dumpster but the box was too low for her to reach, so she was going to have to climb in. Not her favorite part, but sometimes necessary. She grabbed onto the dumpster's top edge, careful of where she put her fingers, avoiding any sharp, rusted metal. She swung herself through the opening and landed in a puddle of sludge, catching herself before she slipped and fell. How annoying. What was this slimy, nasty stuff, anyway? It stunk. Great, and now it was smeared all over the sides of her new black Chucks.

Mom would not be happy.

Willow pulled the box toward her, disappointed to find only a few sets of ripped-up sheets and some old tattered blankets.

"Great. Just … great," she muttered.

Her cell phone rang in her back pocket, her mom's ring. Ever since she'd had an allergic reaction to a bee sting when she was seven, Willow's mom wouldn't let her out of the house without a cell phone and an EpiPen. The phone, so her mom could track her down if she was kidnapped or got lost, the EpiPen to save herself in case of anaphylactic shock.

Bees were most definitely not on Willow's list of happy things. And unfortunately, they tended to hang around dumpsters. Just one more reason Mom hated her treasure hunting. But it was an occupational risk Willow was willing to take.

She adjusted the sports bag strapped across her back and tried to use her fingertips to remove her cell phone from the back pocket of her jeans. As careful as she was, she still ended up smearing a dark and oily patch on the hem of her red jersey. Dang it! The Bulls shirt was one of her favorites—a classic Michael Jordan, #23. Hopefully that nasty goop would come out in the wash. She flipped her long, strawberry-blonde ponytail to her opposite shoulder, and delicately held the phone to her ear with a grimace. "Hi, Mom," she said like she had no idea why her mother would be calling.

"Why are you not home?" The chiding voice on the other end of the line demanded. "It's nearly 12:20! Your father will be here to pick you and Ben up for camp in forty minutes and you haven't even eaten lunch. And when are you planning to get your practicing done?"

Willow closed her eyes and sighed. "Sorry, Mom. Lost track of time."

"I have told you a million times, that excuse is not going to fly anymore, young lady. Five minutes. If you're not washed up and at the table in five minutes …" She dangled the threat.

"On my way." Willow crammed the phone back into her pocket, smearing even more goop. Climbing up on the box of sheets, she was able to reach the opening in the dumpster. Her mom was serious this time, she could tell. She'd find some "consequence" for Willow if she didn't make it home in the allotted five minutes, no doubt.

Willow dropped to the ground, and sprinted out of the alley. She jogged down the cracked, uneven sidewalk, veering around the tall prickly weeds sprouting up through the concrete. Willow had made the ten-block run in two minutes before, but it was right before lunch and Willow's energy tank was low. Running in sludgy Chucks was brewing a nasty blister, too, which wasn't helping.

She should have been more careful about the time, especially after last night's meltdown. Even after they'd made up, Mom had still tucked her with the "I spent the last twelve years of my life putting up with attitude from your father and I refuse to put up with it from you" speech. Yes, Willow had inherited her smart mouth from her dad but why was a little attitude such a big deal? It sure wasn't a reason to blow up the whole family. Seemed like when you said "for better or for worse" that meant you realized you were going to have to put up with a few things about the other person that might drive you nuts. Nobody was perfect, right?

If she went too far one day would Mom kick her out, too?

Music Camp was the first thing her mom and dad had agreed on in years. Dad was so proud she'd made first chair in Honor Orchestra and thought music was her "calling," just like making movies was for him. Willow wasn't so sure. Music Camp seemed like a waste of time since she was going to quit violin anyway. At least, she was going to as soon as she worked up the courage to tell her parents.

And then there was the whole Ben thing. Making him going to camp too just made the whole thing worse.

Willow's Chucks pounded the sidewalk. She ran faster, her knees feeling every jolt.

Willow still hadn't told her mom how she really felt about her uncle and cousins moving in with them. She barely knew them! And as if having two unfamiliar boys and their dad in the house wasn't awful enough, now she had to spend a whole week at camp with one of them. It didn't even seem like Ben wanted to go, but it was hard to tell because he was so darn quiet. Mom thought that since he played the drums he should go to Music Camp, too. He played the kettledrums. Who played the kettledrums in the sixth grade? He didn't even seem that into the drums anyway. All he ever did was read his stupid fantasy books. Elves and warlocks and dragons. Ugh.

Such ugly thoughts made Willow feel horrible, but she couldn't help it. Especially considering why her mom's brother and his kids had to move in with them. But Willow didn't want to end up babysitting her cousin, someone she barely knew, all week long. At home, she could avoid him pretty well, but she had a feeling it wouldn't be that easy at camp.

Poor Ben. She really did feel sorry for him, what with Aunt Sarah dying and all. Hard to believe that was only a month ago. Getting over something like that would take, what? Forever? As much as her mom drove her mad, Willow couldn't imagine life without her.

Uncle Josh was willing to rent the rooms and they could use the money right now. Plus, Uncle Josh could help out with Great Aunt Matilda, so the nurse only had to come half days. Willow knew home nurses cost a lot, but there was no way her mom could watch after Great Aunt Matilda and keep up with her job without some help.

Willow raced through the neighborhood, picking up speed the last block despite the painful blister on her right heel. When she reached the front steps of her house, she collapsed onto the grass, sucking air as she stared up at the blue sky.

Her house was so suburbia, but she loved it. Flanked by four tall pines, it felt cozy and warm. Sure it was smallish, but it had a second floor and a big front porch tucked beneath the roofline. A carpet of lush grass covered the front slope of lawn and a series of barberry bushes grew at the far edges of the porch. Her family had lived in Denver for a bit when she was a baby, but this house in Colorado Springs was the only home Willow had truly ever known.

Willow counted to three, steeling herself before bursting through the front door. "I'm home!" she called, making a beeline for the stairs. She'd beat the clock, now she just had to get cleaned up before her mother saw her messy clothes. Willow was almost to the top step when her mother appeared at the bottom. "Freeze!" she hollered. Willow froze and turned. Her mom held a fistful of paint swatches. About the size of bookmarks, the strips of paper showed a variety of shades of paint colors. Willow's mother freelanced for a bunch of companies, one of them a paint company. Naming paint colors was her latest assignment.

Jaw clenched, her mom's lips disappeared into a straight line. "What. Happened." It was a question, yet a statement. Willow was 100% certain it wouldn't matter one bit how she answered.

She was so busted.

"I … fell?" Not her best attempt.

"Into the sewer?" Her mom's words sizzled the air.

"Not exactly …"

Her mom waited for Willow to go on. "Your haircut looks great," Willow said, beaming a toothy smile. Her mom had had an appointment that morning, and it really did look good: bobbed at her chin with long bangs that flowed back from her forehead in luxurious blonde wisps. She'd begged Willow to go with her, but Willow refused to cut her hair until it got so long that she was sitting on it. "Okay, all right? I climbed into the dumpster behind Mr. Botana's place."

"Willow! You promised me you wouldn't go crawling into that germ-infested slime hole again!"

"I know, I know, but I missed Thursday because of all the camp shopping and packing and—" Willow's mouth snapped shut. Arguing was pointless. Her mother folded her tanned arms across her chest, a sure sign she was ticked off.

"No." The glare grew more intense, which hardly seemed possible. "No. No! NO! No more Mr. Botana's dumpster. No more Mrs. Eldberg's trash can. Or the Winstead's trash can. Or the entire neighborhood's trash can!" Mom was headed for a full on freak out, and Willow knew only one thing would stop the madness—the thing that always worked, every single time, without fail.

Cue the waterworks.

Willow considered it a talent, her ability to cry on demand. Complete with real tears. Her nose even got all red and snotty, the key to making the performance truly convincing. Given how mad her mom was today, Willow threw in a few hitching sobs for good measure.

In seconds her mom was apologizing. "I'm sorry, sweetie. Sometimes I forget how much like your father you are." Willow slunk down the steps into her outstretched arms, trying not to smile. With a squeeze, her mom released her, whipping the dishtowel from her shoulder to dab at Willow's face. "Look … the tears helped clean you up," she cooed.

Willow allowed a timid smile, just enough to smooth things over. "They did?"

"Yes, see? Everything is fine. I'm sorry for yelling."

"I forgive you. And don't worry. Dad will understand."

Her mom's eyes turned cold and Willow felt the sinking rush of an epic fail.

Crimson crept up her mother's neck and across her cheeks like in one of those old cartoons on Boomerang.

Stellar, Willow. A+ job.

"Shower, young lady. NOW."

Young lady. That was never good.

"I didn't mean I was going to tell him," Willow protested.

"Oh no, of course not." Her sarcasm popped like ice water on a hot frying pan. "Get moving. Ben is already packed and ready to go. Your dad will be here in thirty-five minutes. You haven't practiced and you still have to eat. What kind of mother sends her daughter off to camp without food in her belly?"

Willow couldn't let the opportunity pass. "A great one?" she said, summoning a hopeful smile to her face.

"No sucking up allowed," her mother shot back, but Willow could tell she was fighting back a smile. "And make sure you packed your EpiPens."

"Yes ma'am." Willow pounded up the stairs. She didn't understand why she had to practice today. She was going to Music Camp—she'd be practicing there all the time!

The room Ben shared with Marcus was at the top of the staircase, making it impossible to avoid him. He sprawled across his bed reading that ratty old book just like he did every day since he'd moved in. Willow could tell by the expression on his pale, freckled face that he'd overheard their entire conversation. The look in his eyes said he thought Willow was a horrible person who didn't deserve to have a nice mother who cared about her whereabouts—a mom she didn't appreciate, when his mom was gone for good.

Guilt squeezed Willow's heart; a lump clogging up her throat, and the sick feeling in her gut had nothing to do with being late for lunch.

Her mom must have taken Ben with her to the salon because he had new hair. The cut was super short on the sides but long on top, flopping a bit over his hazel eyes. Sadly, it made him look even younger than his baby face already did. It was amazing the two of them were the same age. Ben had turned thirteen already and Willow would finally be an official teenager next month, but Ben looked two years younger than her. She towered over him by about a good inch and a half, and that had to drive him nuts.

"You're ready?" she asked, kneeling to untie the laces on her Chucks. They stunk something awful. A trip through the wash would most definitely be required before they'd be wearable again. Good thing she had a few back-up pairs. She pulled off the offending sneakers and tossed them into the hallway laundry chute. They clunked against the metal sides all the way to the basement. Willow imagined them landing squarely in the laundry basket but the plastic clatter that echoed up the chute told her they'd bounced out and tipped the basket over in the process. Another fail. She was on a roll this morning.

"Willow!" her mom yelled. "I told you not to do that!"

"Sorry, Mom!" she hollered down the stairs before turning back to Ben.

He stuck a finger in his book to mark his place. "Have any luck this morning?"

Guilt stabbed her in the gut again. She didn't ask Ben to go along because, well, she didn't think he could keep up and besides, it didn't seem like something he'd want to do anyway.

"Um, not really." Willow looked down at the mess on her shorts and jersey. "It looks more productive than it was."

Uncomfortable pause.

"Yeah, well … guess I better go get cleaned up." Willow forced a smile.

"Right," Ben nodded, eyeing the black smear on her hip.

"Okay then," Willow said, turning away.

"Okay," said Ben, returning to his book.

Lunch suddenly sounded awful. She slipped into the bathroom and shut the door. As she waited for the shower to heat up, she tried to convince herself it was a good thing that Ben was going to camp with her.

She tried … and failed.

Miserably.

CHAPTER 3

BEN COSGROVE KNEW his cousin Willow wished he wasn't going to camp with her. He wasn't exactly thrilled about it, either. He wasn't thrilled about anything life had served up lately. Losing his mom, moving to Colorado Springs from Texas, all of it made his head pound and his stomach ache. And now he was supposed to go away to camp for a week with someone who didn't really like him. What was Dad thinking?

After the funeral, he had sat Ben down and told him that, in time things would get better. Ben kept waiting for the getting better part to start, because it sure seemed like things had only gotten worse. He knew it wasn't easy on Willow either, what with the three of them moving in with them. But Ben had really tried to be friendly, even though he didn't feel like it. While she was almost always polite, Willow obviously wasn't happy about the whole thing. Those arguments with her mom happened all the time.

Things would be much easier if Willow and Ben hadn't been complete strangers to each other before now.

Dad wanted him to be patient; said he was sure to make tons of friends at camp and then at school come fall, but to be honest Ben didn't really want to make friends. Making friends meant talking to people, and he didn't feel much like doing that just yet. They would ask about his mom. What was he supposed to say, that some drunk idiot decided to drive the wrong way on the highway and ran straight into his mother's car? That would be a fun conversation. Then maybe they could talk about how he'd figured out that no amount of crying would bring his mom back. And that he missed her so much it was like acid burning a hole in his stomach every second of his life? He couldn't tell anyone all that. They'd think he was a crybaby. He'd probably get beat up or shoved into a few lockers to encourage him to man-up. Ben knew how these things went; he'd seen it happen millions of times to kids at his old school. If you showed weakness, the mean kids attacked. And right now, Ben was weak. Becoming invisible was his only hope of survival.

His dad, his brother Marcus, his books—those were the only things Ben had in his life that meant anything to him now. Reading helped him forget, if only for a little while. Especially *Widershins and the Angel*. The book was about an elf who falls in love with a fledgling angel fallen from Heaven. Accidentally fallen, of course. Actually, Ben had a little crush on the angel. She could change her appearance to look like anyone in the world. It would be so cool to be able to do that, just change your skin or your hair or your eyes or your nose whenever you wanted. Sure would be handy if you were a spy or in the witness protection program.

When the bathroom shower turned off, Ben slid off the bed and kicked Marcus' disgusting gym socks across the room toward the closet. Marcus was even more of a slob than usual, now that he'd gotten a job at the local Game Stop. He spent hours in the basement rec room, where his dad slept on a rollaway bed, "researching" the games he sold. Back in Texas, Ben would call that room a "family room" but here in Colorado— where Cokes were called pop and people looked at you funny for saying "ya'll" instead of "you guys"—it was called a rec room. It was cozy, though, with wood-paneled walls and a rectangle of thick carpet covering the cement floor. There was a worn couch and a wooden coffee table across from the old TV and Marcus' Xbox.

Ben heard Willow close her bedroom door as he tucked *Widershins* into the outer pocket of his duffle. Then he slung the strap over his shoulder and made his way downstairs.

Willow's lunch—chicken noodle soup and peanut butter toast— waited for her on the kitchen table. The soup had to be cold by now and the peanut butter was long past warm and melty. What a waste.

Great Aunt Matilda sat in her Lazy-Boy recliner in the den watching TV. She wore her standard nightgown and housecoat, but no slippers today. Ben quickly looked away from her wrinkled feet. Feet kind of grossed him out, and hers were horrible. Ben hadn't ever spent time around anyone as old as his great aunt. Her wrinkled skin hung from her bones and with her long, thin nose, she almost looked like a starving elephant. Her pure white hair was long and although Aunt Amanda usually kept it braided today it hung loose and messy. It made her look older and frailer than usual. Ben swallowed. Matilda made him sad. So he always tried to be really nice to her.

She rarely seemed to remember who he was, heck, most the time, she didn't even remember who she was. One day she'd be totally quiet and calm, the next she'd rant on about this or that, how she couldn't find something, or complain that Aunt Amanda was keeping her prisoner.

Alzheimer's was a pretty horrible disease. If nothing else, Great Aunt Matilda had taught him that.

Aunt Amanda walked into the kitchen, frowning at Willow's empty chair. Stupid Willow with all her back talk and running around that made Aunt Amanda worry. Sometimes Ben considered telling Willow she should appreciate her mom more, but she'd just think he was an even bigger nerd than she already did.

Willow bounced into the room, her hair slicked into a wet ponytail. A car horn honked out front and she groaned. "He's early!"

"Actually," her mother raised an eyebrow at her, "you're late. Throw that soup in a thermos and take it with you."

"Dad won't let me eat in the car!" Willow complained, but pulled a thermos from the pantry anyway. She cut her eyes at Ben before murmuring, "Oh well. Rules were made to be broken, I guess."

THE MILES SPED by quickly as Uncle Grant drove the black Audi at a speed that made Ben more than a little nervous. This was only the second time he'd been around his uncle, but Ben was again amazed by how different he was than his own dad, and not just because Uncle Grant was taller, tanner, and more handsome. He also looked younger, even though he was actually a couple of years older. He sure acted younger.

Uncle Grant had sandy blond hair that looked almost red sometimes, and friendly blue eyes, like Willow's. With his wide, white-toothed smile, slim jeans, and cowboy boots, he looked like he should be starring in movies instead of working behind the scenes.

"How's your dad, Ben?" Uncle Grant called over his shoulder as he turned down the radio.

"Hey!" Willow complained. "I was singing!"

"I know," her dad grinned.

Willow may be an accomplished violinist, but her singing was not so good and was making it hard for Ben to concentrate on his book. "He's okay, I guess. I mean, you know."

"Sure. I know." But he didn't know, did he? Of course not, how could he? Uncle Grant hadn't lost his wife. He'd left her. He chose to lose her, which wasn't the same thing at all. Ben felt a bubble of anger well up in his throat.

Thankfully, Uncle Grant turned his attention to Willow so Ben didn't have to say anything else. "And Great Aunt Matilda? How's she doing?"

Willow slumped against the window. "Same as ever. Impossible."

"Willow, be nice. The woman is sick. It's not easy being in your nineties, much less living with a disease like that for as long as she has," said Uncle Grant. "Most folks don't live to her age, even without Alzheimer's. It's quite the accomplishment."

Ben had overheard his dad and Aunt Amanda talking about just that the other night. The doctors didn't understand how Great Aunt Matilda survived all these years since her diagnosis. Her husband has passed away twenty years ago, but he must have left her some money, because they talked about it finally running out. That was part of the reason Aunt Amanda had taken Matilda in and hired a part-time nurse to help out.

Apparently it was cheaper than the place Matilda used to live. From what Ben could figure from what they said, Matilda's arrival was the final straw for Willow's dad. He left right after she got there.

Ben met Uncle Grant's eyes in the mirror, anger continuing to percolate in his heart. It really ticked him off when people ran away just because things got tough. Oblivious to Ben's scowl, Uncle Grant gave him a wink. "So, I'm scouting some locations for a new film and I need to ask Matilda if she remembers the old Canton Hotel. It was quite the place back in the late 1940s when she was a young lady."

Ben's scowl deepened. Was he joking? Ben looked at Willow, who frowned, too.

"Seriously, Dad?" Willow said. "If she *remembers*?" She shook her head and then looked out the window at the tall pines whizzing by. "And you get on my case about being nice."

Uncle Grant wasn't smiling any more. "Oh. Well, yeah. Right." He sounded embarrassed. He should be, but Ben couldn't believe he wasn't mad at Willow for talking to him like that. Ben would have been grounded for a month for such a smart mouth response.

"Why do you think she might have known about that hotel?" Ben asked after a moment of awkward silence.

"It was quite famous back in the day," said Uncle Grant, steering the car off the highway and down an exit ramp. "It was the place to stay around here a century ago. I'd love to get a first-hand account of what it was like back then. It's been shuttered up for over fifty years."

Silence fell over the car again as they pulled up to an intersection. "How close are we to camp?" Willow asked her dad.

"Pretty close," he said, glancing at the dashboard. "Actually, we're kind of early. Not supposed to get you there until 3:00 ... heh, heh. Guess I drove a little fast. We have half an hour to kill." The car idled at the stop sign. "You know, we could go see it ..." He hung the offer in the air like a treat to a hungry dog.

Willow glanced at her father, then at Ben. "We could go see the old hotel, you mean?"

"Yep. It's not far from here. In fact, the land backs right up to your camp."

"Really?" Ben had no doubt exploring an old abandoned hotel was right up Willow's alley. Ben closed *Widershins* and tucked it into the seat pocket in front of him. He had to admit, it did sound kind of interesting.

"Could we go check it out?" he asked and was pleased to see Willow shine a huge smile his way. That was a first.

Uncle Grant grinned. "I was hoping you'd say that."

20

The road leading to the Canton Hotel was more like two dusty tracks snaking through low-lying brush than an actual road. The Audi crunched along slowly, kicking up dust and debris. Uncle Grant grimaced as gravel dinged the side of his precious car. "I should have brought the production truck," he moaned.

As they inched along, Willow and Ben unbuckled their seat belts and rolled down the windows, eager to catch a glimpse of the hotel through the trees. Each turn revealed nothing but more trail. After a few twists and turns, Willow sighed heavily. "Where is it?"

"Should be right around the next bend," Uncle Grant said, and he was right. The next left turn revealed the most run-down, bedraggled, wreck of a building Ben had ever seen.

"What a dump." Ben said, panic lurching through him as he realized he'd spoken aloud. "Oh, I'm sorry, Uncle Grant."

"No apologies necessary, Ben. It is a dump. The place was condemned years ago," Uncle Grant said, a trace of awe in his voice like he admired the hotel's ability to defy time. "Yet, here it stands."

"I love it!" breathed Willow, opening the car door even before the Audi ground to a halt.

"Hey! Slow down!" Uncle Grant warned as Willow raced up the weathered front steps.

Ben emerged from the car more slowly, staring up at the ancient façade. The hotel looked more like a large mansion than a hotel. Scraggly weeds and overgrown shrubbery choked out any grass that might have once grown along the foot of its chipped stucco walls. Dozens of broken windows on upper floors sneered with jagged teeth. The deep red Spanish roof was pocked with shattered tiles.

The double front doors were made of dark wood, and Willow cupped her hands around her eyes, peering through one of the skinny panes of glass. "It looks like they left all the stuff in there when they closed it up. Everything's covered with sheets!" She knocked on the wooden door. The hollow thump echoed against the surrounding trees.

Ben felt a nervous flutter in his stomach. Being here felt wrong somehow. Sort of sneaky … like they were doing something they shouldn't.

Willow obviously didn't share his apprehension, as she gave the doors an experimental push. They swung open as if they'd been waiting for her to arrive.

CHAPTER 4

TIERNAN KETTLEMAN NOCKED the arrow, pulling the string taut. Steady, no need to rush. She had time. All the time in the world. Tiernan blew out all her breath and moved her fingers the centimeter it took to release her hold on the string. The arrow zipped across the monitoring station and thwunked into the tiny red circle.

That's right. *Bullseye.*

Lowering the bow, Tiernan sighed. She wished she could spend all day doing just this, but it was time for rounds. She wondered, as she always did, if it really mattered whether she starting her rounds on schedule or five minutes late. What would happen if she delayed? Not a thing, that's what. A big ole sloppy pot of nothing. Still, she had vowed to uphold the rigid schedule and she took those vows seriously.

The thing was, nothing was pretty much all that happened in Tiernan's life these days. Instead of making friends, playing sports, taping pictures of a cute boys on the inside of her locker door like most sixteen-year-old girls, Tiernan had a job. She'd spent her entire childhood training and studying for it.

It was a privilege to be a Guardian. An honor. She was special. And although no one outside her extended family and a few high-ranking government officials (whose identities were, of course, classified) knew what she did, Tiernan was considered a hero.

So why did she feel like such a loser?

Sometimes she questioned why becoming a Guardian was such an honor, anyway. This happened more often in those moments when she was dead bored, which were often. After all, Tiernan hadn't done anything to earn the privilege of becoming Guardian, other than be born before any of her cousins.

Luckily, Tiernan enjoyed the training. She had a natural gift for archery and was fascinated by ancient folklore. Her home schooling went far beyond any public or private high school curriculum to include Tae Kwon Do, weapons and other top secret subject matter taught in only seven places on the planet. It was an honor.

And Tiernan had studied hard for the day when she would become an official Guardian. Her sixteenth birthday. What she hadn't anticipated was how she'd feel when it actually happened. Now, three months later, she still wasn't sure she was the right one for the job.

With another sigh, Tiernan tugged on the hem of her khaki tunic, smoothing it beneath the black leather tool belt at her waist. Her hips had shown themselves this past year, and while she was pleased to finally get some curves, it didn't seem like any of the boys back in her neighborhood had noticed.

Tugging the arrow out of the target, Tiernan stored the quiver and bow in the cabinet near the door of the monitoring station and returned to the console. She scanned the series of screens; positive the readings would be the same as they were during rounds an hour ago. She was sure they'd be the same as they'd been that morning when she'd shuffled down the hall from the two-bedroom studio she would share with her Aunt Coreen until Tiernan's eighteenth birthday when Coreen would move back home to live with her husband and children for the first time in twenty years. After that, Coreen would return every other weekend to give Tiernan a break. Such were the lives of active-duty Guardians.

Tiernan stretched her long, thin arms over her head and groaned. When she bent over to touch her toes, her long dark curls brushed the ground. She flipped them back over her shoulders and sighed. Time to stop stalling.

She pulled open the thick Plexiglas door that led to the inner den, expecting the sudden rise in temperature, but something felt off. Her senses tingled and she paused, studying the wall thermostat. She narrowed her brown eyes. Hmmm. The reading should be 102°F. It was always 102°F.

Except now it read two degrees warmer.

As far as Tiernan knew, a temperature change had never occurred in any of the dens.

Ever.

Tiernan's heart kicked into high speed as she checked the cooling duct read-outs, but the air temperature inside was as it should be. She checked the air lock in the enormous steel exterior door in the far wall but it was properly closed, sealed tight and secure.

Worry twisted in Tiernan's gut, an unfamiliar feeling. In her world, change was more than unusual. It was unheard of. And of course it would happen when Aunt Coreen was in town at a doctor appointment. She hadn't been well lately.

Maybe the cooling system was malfunctioning. To simplify monitoring, the den maintained at a consistent 102°F using sophisticated systems to balance the amount of heat put off by its occupant with the air piped in. Any fluctuation in temperature was easily noticeable. Not that there was ever any fluctuation. Regardless, the consistency helped make the living conditions bearable. There were some benefits of being 21st century Guardians: the job sure hadn't been as comfortable for her ancestors.

Tiernan stepped down into the nest area. This section didn't have the sterile, white tile that covered the floors and walls in the main den. The exposed raw dirt and rock of the interior mountain made this part of the den feel more like a cave. Tiernan took a cautious step forward. Even though she knew she wasn't in danger, Tiernan's training taught her to put caution first: an essential rule when you were guarding a dragon, even if the creature in question had spent the past fifteen hundred years hibernating.

Tiernan slid her hand along Drynfyre's silver scales. The radiating heat tingled against her fingertips. She traced a finger along the raised swirl of the dragon's infinity mark. Located on the breastplate, this particular scale felt a bit warmer than the others. Tiernan removed the electric thermometer from her tool belt and tucked the long probe beneath it. Drynfyre's temp read two degrees higher as well.

A sweaty chill raised goosebumps on her arms. This was impossible.

Tiernan placed her ear against the infinity mark, listening to the pulsing roar of the dragon's inner fire. Was it a bit louder today or did it just seem that way because she was freaking out over the strange readings?

One phone call could quickly link her to Aunt Coreen, but she didn't want to ask for help just yet. Tiernan didn't want to be someone who panicked at the first sign of trouble. She'd figure this out on her own.

Back in the monitoring room, Tiernan grabbed her key ring from the hook, not bothering to lock the door behind her. As she jogged down the stark hallway, she couldn't help but think about the Guardians from previous generations. They walked a dirt tunnel lit by torchlight instead of this sterile, white florescent-lit hallway. But the job itself—the mundane existence—that part hadn't changed since the beginning. Nowadays, the den was more secure, with tons of steel built into the mountainside. Before 1954, the only way in or out was a hand-dug crater in the side of the mountain, large enough to be used should the Elders finally call for The Awakening. The massive wooden door installed in the 1800s, when gold seekers flocked to the Rockies, was replaced with steel in the 1950s when modern modifications incorporated new technology.

Tiernan trotted past her apartment, the workout room and the small kitchen. She unlocked the conference room door and flipped on the lights. At the vault in the back wall, she pushed her finger against the reader pad. The indicator light shifted from red to green and, with a loud clunk, the vault door opened in a slow, lazy swing. As always upon entering, Tiernan's first stop was to check the black velvet jewelry box that contained the Amulet, one of the set of two magical jewels used fifteen hundred years ago to send all the dragons into their long slumber.

Tiernan held her breath as she opened the lid of the box. Of course the jewel would be there. And it was, safe and sound, perfect and smooth, like a shiny black robin's egg attached to a silken cord.

Housing the Amulet was a huge responsibility, one that shifted from den to den with each decade, so that each Guardian family could partake in the responsibility. It was always a big deal when the Amulet was on premises. Even back when both Amulets were in the Guardian's possession, they were never stored together. They were too precious to keep in one place.

Tiernan relaxed, closing the box. She turned to the rows of bookshelves lining the vault. The massive volumes of dragon records held truths known only to the Guardians, facts believed to be fantasy by the rest of the world. The oldest of these writings came from the original Guardian, the sorceress Kareth, written in an ancient language that didn't even exist anymore. All Guardian trainees were taught Illian along with their native language, allowing for a secret worldwide communication system. It was something Tiernan hadn't yet mastered. Languages were just not her thing. Battle, that was her thing, and even though there was no practical use for those skills, all Guardians were trained.

Those were some of Tiernan's favorite classes.

The records were so old the volumes had to be kept in airtight wrappings to keep them from turning to dust. Kareth's writings made up the core studies for all the Guardian children—even those not in a direct lineage to become Guardians themselves. They were as much a part of growing up as learning the alphabet and primary colors were for "regular" kids.

Behind the Codex section stood rows of bound books and binders that comprised the Daily Logs. Tiernan was working on digitizing these records. The project, started by Coreen's predecessor in the 1960s, wouldn't be complete for generations despite the fact that Tiernan spent hours each day creating digital snapshot out of old microfiche then converting those into a searchable format. How it would ever be finished, Tiernan couldn't imagine. So far, the project had barely scratched the surface of more than fifteen hundred years of dragon records.

The monotonous purgatory contained in those files was mind numbing. Reams and reams and reams of sameness. Day after day. In nearly every case, absolute nothing under the heading of "unusual occurrences."

Except for once.

That deviation happened right here in Tiernan's Cheyenne Mountain den. She'd read the records from October of 1865. That was the only time in the entire Guardian's history when something other than normal occurred. It had become known as The Hanna Vorman Incident. It happened during a decade when one of the Amulets was on premises.

Why Hanna Vorman stole the Pfife and Amulet nobody was sure. The Incident was a dark mark in the Guardian history, one that spawned whispered legends over the years. Some said Vorman wanted to find the legendary Dragon Treasure, but most Guardians doubted the existence of the Treasure at all. The Elders didn't even officially acknowledge it was real. It wasn't mentioned in any of the Codex.

Tiernan sat at the computer in the back of the vault and logged into the database. None of her searches hit on anything and she found no record of a temperature anomaly like what was happening in Drynfyre's den, at least, not for the time period from 500 A.D. to 800 A.D., which was all that had been digitized so far.

Twisting her thick hair back from her face, Tiernan threaded a pencil through it and stared at the computer screen, chewing on a fingernail. This was going to require digging through hard copies. And that would take time. Time she wasn't sure she had.

Man, she could use a pop.

She was in the kitchen pouring Coke over crushed ice when a high-pitched hum pulsed through the den.

What the heck was that? Tiernan had never heard a sound like it before. Abandoning the Coke on the counter, she raced out into the hallway, trying to pinpoint the source of the sound.

Oh no.

Tiernan's heartbeat accelerated with the rush of panic. She ran for the conference room, hands itching for her crossbow. Easing into the room, she circled the large black conference table cautiously, making her way back toward the open vault, drawn to the hum like a siren's slave. As she reached the threshold, she froze, gaze locking on the Amulet box.

It sat on the shelf, exactly where she'd left it minutes before. Except now the black box shook and vibrated.

Like something inside was trying to get out.

CHAPTER 5

EXPLORING THE CANTON HOTEL was like every Christmas and birthday rolled up into one gigantic ball of awesome; like Willow had been allowed behind the scenes of a top-secret museum.

Everything that wasn't sheet-draped was coated with thick dust and cobwebs. Arrows of dusty sunlight pierced the open air of the tall lobby atrium as she dashed from room to room, the floors protesting under the unaccustomed pounding of adventurous feet. Each gallery revealed another fantastic discovery. A perfect tea set laid out on the coffee table. An enormous gilded mirror leaning against the wall of a bathroom, miraculously unbroken. And in the library off the lobby, ceiling-to-floor shelves packed with thousands of books.

Willow's imagination wiped away the dust and age, bringing the old hotel back to life. She saw a tall woman in a flowing Titanic-style gown standing at the top of the wide, wooden staircase. A man in a tuxedo strode toward her across the black and white tiled lobby, a glass of champagne raised in his hand. A huge vase of flowers sat atop the round lobby table on a sheet of silk. A line of people waited to check in at the reception desk against the wall to the right of the staircase.

The desk was carved from wood so dark it was nearly black, and topped with a creamy marble counter. Willow ran her fingertips along the smooth surface, giving the rusty old service bell a tap. It managed the feeblest of pings.

Willow's dad stood in the front doorway, hands on his hips, surveying the scene. "Well, it's certainly seen better days, huh?" he said, his nose wrinkling. "And what is that horrible smell?"

"Why, *Father*," Willow said, using in her best British accent so that it sounded like Fatha. "That is the scent of treasure, of course!"

Her dad raised one eyebrow. "My little pirate." The tone of pride beneath the surface of his words stirred up an odd mix of happy and sad in Willow's heart. He was standing right there but all of a sudden she was hit with an empty longing, like she missed him terribly.

Oblivious, as usual, her dad moved to the reception desk and peeked over the high counter. "Any sign of a ledger?"

"Yep, right there." Willow answered, pushing her feelings away. He grabbed the thick book and placed it on the counter. Ben and Willow went up on their tiptoes as he carefully turned the flimsy pages.

"The handwriting is impossible to read," Willow complained, sinking to flat foot. Ben followed her to the other side of the desk where they found rows of empty cubbies.

Willow pouted. "No treasure here."

Her dad pulled an old black telephone from one of the larger cubbies. "Check this out." Willow lifted the receiver and put it to her ear even though she knew she'd only hear silence. "It's a rotary," her dad explained as she stuck her finger in the hole next to the "0" and turned the plastic circle as far as it would go. The dial slowly spun back to its starting place in a series of sullen clicks. "I know," she said, trying not to sound snippy. "I see these at estate sales all the time." She turned and looked up the staircase. "Can we go see what's upstairs?"

Her dad hadn't even answered when she grabbed Ben's hand and dragged him away.

"Hold it!" Her dad hollered so loud it stopped her in her tracks. "This place is condemned. First floor only. No going upstairs, do you understand?" After they nodded in agreement, he pulled his cell from his pocket. "I need to get someone out here to make sure it's safe before we shoot."

"Dad! These floors are solid!" To prove her point, she jumped up and down a few times, the flat soles of her purple Chucks slapping against the tile. "Besides, there's probably a basement level, which would mean that these floors aren't any safer than the ones upstairs." Willow froze, hoping she hadn't just blown their entire adventure with her stupid comment.

"Yeah, that's true," her father said, holding the phone to his ear. "You know, maybe — "

Willow didn't let him finish. "C'mon Ben!" She grabbed his hand again, pulling him past the staircase and into a long hall that wound toward the back of the building. There was a large kitchen, an expansive dining room, and what must have been some kind of a nightclub, complete with a small stage draped by a dark velvet curtain. A dilapidated grand piano stood in a corner, dejected and forgotten, its black sheen long since faded.

They poked around for a few minutes and, finding nothing of interest, made their way to the end of the hallway. There was a door. "The basement," said Willow, grabbing the knob.

"So says the sign." Ben grinned, nodding at the plaque on the wall that read *Basement*. Willow rolled her eyes at him and pushed the door open.

Ben's smile dissolved as he gazed down the wooden steps into complete darkness. "Umm, maybe this isn't such a good idea."

Willow ignored his concern. "If only we had some flashlights. You know there's a ton of cool stuff stashed down there. Course, if we can't see any of it …"

"Not to mention we could fall down the stairs and break our necks," Ben murmured.

Willow looked around the hallway; thinking maybe there was some kind of lantern or something they could use. "Hey, look!" The door directly across the hall from them also had a sign, identical to the basement's. This one read: *Attic*. She opened the door to reveal another dark stairway similar to the one leading down into the depths of darkness. Except this one led up. And it wasn't quite as dark up there.

"Excellent," she breathed.

Ben still sounded nervous. "We won't be able to see if any of the steps have rotted away." Willow sighed. And here she'd thought maybe Ben would be kind of fun. Willow moved into the stairwell and craned her neck. She could just make out the landing at the top of the first flight of steps.

"Willow? Ben?" Her dad's voice echoed down the hallway. "Where'd you go? You all right?"

"We're fine, Dad!" Willow called.

"Come here! I found something!"

There was an intriguing note of excitement in her father's voice that was enough to make Willow run and race back to the lobby.

"Hey, wait up!" Ben yelled, running down the hallway behind her. They burst into the lobby to find her dad holding a large leather-bound book that looked like an old photo album.

"I found the desk ledger and you won't believe who's in here. It just can't be coincidence!"

"Who?" Willow snatched the book from her father's hands and peered down at it. He leaned over her shoulder, pointing to a name on the page.

"She stayed at the Canton Hotel back in 1943," he said, running his finger beneath the elegant script.

Willow tried to make out the name. "I can't read that … Ma …"

"Matilda Billingsly!" her dad burst out. "Can you believe it?"

"Who's Matilda Billingsly?" Ben asked.

"Yeah, who's that?" Willow looked up at him.

"Willow!" Her dad was flabbergasted. "What was mom's last name before she married me?" He trailed off waiting for an answer.

"Oh my gosh. Of course! That's Aunt Matilda?"

"Must have been before she got married," her dad mused.

"We have to ask her about it! Can we take this with us?" Willow asked.

"Mmm, I don't think so. We haven't finalized the deal to use this place yet and I don't want to jeopardize anything." He looked around, hands on his hips. "It's perfect for the zombie lair."

CHAPTER 6

TIERNAN STARED AT the black box. Could the Amulet be making it do that? She had no idea. It sure hadn't ever happened before.

Maybe she should call Coreen. No, Guardian protocol stated contacting the den's Elder. That was one of the elder cousins, Faylene.

But Tiernan had to know what was happening first, right? So instead of immediately returning to the monitoring station for the comm unit that would link her to Dragon Elder headquarters, Tiernan opened the black velvet box again.

The Amulet's dark surface now glowed like its core was on fire, the light pulsing in time with the hum's slow beat. She slammed the lid shut. What the heck was happening?

Box in hand, Tiernan ran back to the monitoring station and slipped a comm unit into her ear. She keyed in the phone number with trembling fingers and waited.

"Winged Victory Insurance, may I help you?" said the receptionist, using the name of the front company that allowed the Dragon Guardians to operate in secret.

"Guardian 111 reporting a code 425 deviation," Tiernan said, her tone all business. "Connect me to Faylene immediately, please."

"Right away," said the receptionist without skipping a beat, like Tiernan called in a 425 every day and she was totally expecting it. Of course, there was no way the receptionist had ever heard that code reported before. Maybe she didn't know what it stood for; she seemed awful calm. Or maybe she thought it was a drill, whichever, Faylene came on the line almost immediately. "Tiernan? Report."

"Well," Tiernan's voice trembled. She eyed the temperature gauge in the den, which had crept up another degree. "I have temperature deviations. We've reached 105 degrees and... um, well... the Dragon Amulet is ... uh, doing something strange."

"Repeat that?" Faylene's voice was stern. Tiernan pictured the older woman; her thin pale lips pressed together, her severe eyebrows arched over her deep-set brown eyes.

"We are up three degrees. And the Dragon Amulet is glowing. And humming." That pretty much summed it up.

"Humming?" Faylene scoffed.

Seriously? Why would Tiernan lie about something like this?

"Explain what you mean. What kind of hum?"

Instead of answering, Tiernan opened the box. The humming echoed off the monitoring room walls for about five seconds. And then it stopped.

Tiernan looked at it. "Hey! It stopped! Did you hear it before it stopped?" She wiped the back of her arm across her forehead, glancing at the thermostat. The temperature in the den was down a degree. "Whoa, wait. Now the temperature is going back down! I don't know what is going on here."

"Tiernan, go to visual."

With the tap of a button on the console panel, a hologram of Faylene's face appeared in the air over the console. Faylene wasn't ugly exactly, but compared to Tiernan's grandmother, Faylene's cousin, she hadn't aged nearly as well. The whole hologram thing didn't help. Faylene's shoulder-length hair looked stringy and even more grey than usual and, since she never wore makeup, her face appeared much older than her sixty-five years.

Plus Faylene was kind of a crab. Crabby people were never attractive, in Tiernan's opinion. She'd always kind of wondered if Faylene was jealous of their side of the family. Maybe that was why she was so hard on them.

"What exactly is going on?" Faylene snapped.

Tiernan swallowed hard and used her most respectful tone of voice. "I'm not sure. There was a three-degree temp variance and, shortly after I discovered it, the Amulet started making this freaky humming sound. And it … glowed." Tiernan looked at the temperature gauges again. "But now the sound has stopped, the gem is dark again, and the temperature in the den is almost down to normal." Tiernan paused. "Could Drynfyre be waking?"

Faylene paused briefly before answering. "I don't see how, it's not like she can decide to do that on her own. I'm sure it was some technical malfunction. I will advise the Council of the situation and get back to you about next steps. In the meantime, keep the Amulet with you at all times."

"Yes ma'am." Tiernan took the gem from its box and slipped the silken cord over her head. The weight of the stone felt comforting, resting against her chest. "Coreen will be back shortly."

"Don't worry, I'm sure it's nothing …" Faylene's voice trailed off and then continued as if she wasn't really speaking to Tiernan but to herself. "Or … it could mean something rather interesting indeed."

CHAPTER 7

WHEN WILLOW SET her mind to something, it was pretty much impossible to change it. In the brief time Ben had shared a home with his cousin, he had learned the truth of this statement. So when it came to the old hotel, there was no talking Willow out of exploring its riches. On the third morning of camp, a way to return to the old place finally presented itself, and it happened because Ben stood up for Willow.

Deep Forest Music Camp held Sunday morning worship services in a large clearing a half-mile walk from the mess hall. This was about the only time when the campers weren't required to bring their instruments to a gathering. Sunday was free day with no scheduled group practice (although individual rehearsal time was highly encouraged, but few kids did.)

The campers chatted and laughed as they hiked single file down the narrow trail toward the clearing. The morning was bright and fresh, and the sounds of the forest enveloped them in birdsong. Camp had turned out to be better than Ben had anticipated. Not great but it not terrible either. Willow had been pretty cool, hadn't abandoned him or anything, and he'd made a couple of new friends. Now, walking through the crisp morning, nature mixed with cheerful laughter, it made him think maybe the rest of his life didn't have to completely suck after all.

And then Alex Macklin decided to snap Willow's bra.

Alex was one grade older. He played the tuba and Ben had pegged him as a bully from the first second he walked into the gathering room. Counselors constantly reprimanded him, and Ben had heard that the camp director had already called his parents, possibly more than once. So, as Alex stepped between Ben and Willow on the narrow path, it was obvious he had something devious in mind.

Grinning his past-due-for-braces grin, he snatched the back of Willow's shirt. In an instant, it was over. The pull and release. The elastic thwack. The wicked sting. Willow yelped, as surprised as she was hurt. As she whirled on Alex, Ben's stomach took the express elevator to the basement.

"Why would you do something like that?" Willow demanded, all up in Alex's face. They were almost the same height.

"Why'd you wear something like that?" Alex shot back, with an accompanying laugh that sounded something like a demented circus clown. "Ya sure don't need it!"

Before his brain had the chance to warn him off of the stupid idea, Ben threw himself on top of Alex. He tackled him all the way down to the pine-needled dirt, a feat almost as stunning as the attempt itself. "Take it back!" Ben snarled. What was he doing? Too late to back down now, he'd committed to this insanity. Ben was short, but solid, and he was able to straddle the older boy's chest, yanking Alex's hands over his head. "Take it back or …"

"Or what?" Alex barked, clearly not intimidated, but unable to get free. Ben worked his mouth, gathering saliva. Marcus had done this to him once and, in hindsight, Ben had found it quite effective. He'd given up, completely grossed out, but basically unharmed.

His mouth full of spit, Ben glanced at Willow. He saw not a warning look, or even disgust, but an expression of such awe and admiration that he nearly lost his balance when Alex jerked side to side, trying to buck him off. Pride welled up in his chest, and Ben shoved Alex back down, letting out a thin line of spit until it dangled over Alex's wide eyeball.

Their campmates gathered in a circle, some cheering for Alex, some encouraging Ben to let the spit drop. Alex swore revenge, trying to free his wrists. The next moment, a counselor was pulling Ben off Alex. He quickly sucked the spit back into his mouth.

"Hey! What's going on? No fighting during processional, dudes." The second counselor, he was named Michael, helped Alex to his feet and shot Ben a look that was part warning, part "good for you."

Josh, the one who pulled Ben off, scolded them. "This is done, are we clear? Alex, this is your last warning." Alex and Ben nodded as the crowd of kids reformed their line down the path. "Alex," Josh growled. "You'll sit by me where I can keep an eye on you." Alex followed him, but turned back to Ben and drew a finger silently across his throat with a sneer. He wasn't going to forget about this. Michael shook his head, watching him go.

"That guy is trouble. You two need to stay away from him," he said.

Ben brushed off the dirt and pine needles embedded in his knees. "Yeah, well …" he muttered.

"Alex is a jerk." Willow folded her arms over her chest. "He did something completely inappropriate to me that I won't mention because it's totally embarrassing but my cousin here was simply defending my honor. He should get no punishment whatsoever, in fact, quite the opposite." Willow sucked in a huge breath and nodded her head once to emphasize her point.

Michael studied them. "Just see it doesn't happen again, Ben. Alex gives you trouble, you come to me or one of the other counselors. Don't take the law into your own hands, got it?" Michael jogged down the trail.

They walked in silence for a while, until the path opened wide enough for Willow to walk right next to him. "Who'd have thought you'd turn out to be my hero." She elbowed him in the ribs, apparently her version of thanks.

Ben tramped along, thinking about what had just happened. That was stupid, drawing attention to himself like that. Completely unlike him. He swallowed hard and tried to calm his galloping heartbeat, his rising sense of paranoia. Everyone was probably talking about him now. He focused on the hypnotic crunch of everyone's sneakers on pine needles and dirt. Birdsong passed from tree to tree; a melody chirped nearby was taken up by its fellows farther down the trail. He inhaled a deep breath of warm wildflower-and-pine-scented air. Okay, he told himself, just relax. Relaaaaax.

Willow froze, pulling him to a stop. She pointed off into the woods at a warped, wooden sign made from broken slats and nailed to a tree.

Canton Hotel … 1½ miles.

Carved below the well-worn words, a red arrow pointed to the right. Ben let his gaze shift in that direction, finding another path, one that led into the woods. It was even narrower than the one they'd walked, and definitely more overgrown. It looked unused, but it was, unquestionably, a trail.

"Look," Willow's stage whispered. "That path leads to the hotel!"

"Shhhh, someone will hear you," Ben growled, continuing down the path. Willow jogged to catch up.

"We should totally go."

"Are you kidding? A mile and a half is not exactly a short hike. Plus that trail looks like nobody's been on it for a looooong time."

"A mile and a half isn't that far. We'll need flashlights and probably a compass, just to be safe."

"Why flashlights?"

"Because it'll be dark in the middle of the night. Duh."

Ben shook his head. "Nope. No way. I am not hiking a mile and a half on a creepy trail in the middle of a creepy night to explore a super creepy old hotel."

"What are you so worried about?" Willow said, exasperated.

"For one, something could happen to us and nobody would know," Ben hissed.

"What could happen?"

"We could get lost. We could fall through a rotten floorboard in that attic. Drug addicts and criminals could hide out in there at night and murder us when we show up. There are a million possibilities! Trust me, bad things happen. Usually when you least expect them." Ben's voice cracked on the last word.

Willow's eyes softened. She got what he meant. "Aw Ben ... c'mon. It'll be fine. What if we go after lunch instead? While it's still light?"

Ben didn't respond. They'd reached the fire pit, the same one from last night's bonfire and marshmallow roasting. Six-foot sections of tree trunks circled the pit for seating. As the other kids claimed their spots, Willow grabbed Ben's arm and pulled him down onto a trunk next to her, claiming their exact spot from the night before. "Please?"

Ben looked around, eyeing his fellow campers. "Willow, c'mon. Do you really think it's a good idea to be poking around that old place?"

She looked Ben straight in the eyes as she answered. "Yes, Ben, I do. I absolutely do."

A FEW HOURS LATER, Willow stepped onto the overgrown path that led to the hotel. She glanced back at Ben to make sure he was keeping up. "I really am glad we decided to do this," she said. She meant it to be nice, to try to make up for talking him into something he didn't want to do, but it seemed to make him madder.

"It wasn't exactly a 'we' decision," he muttered. "I sure hope this isn't all for nothing."

"An adventure is never for nothing! Look, the trail is marked much better than I expected. I packed plenty of water, bug spray, a compass and I even have my emergency cell phone. Just in case."

They walked in silence for a while. Ben pulled a water bottle out of his own pack and took a swig. "So..." he said in that way that told her he was filling the silence, "you pretty much, like, blow everyone else in the orchestra away."

"What? Oh. Um. Well," Willow said, her insides suddenly squirming. Now who was embarrassing easily? "Nah. Music just kind of comes naturally to me, I guess. I took piano lessons for a while but once I tried the violin, I knew that's what I wanted to play."

Willow marched on and silence fell again. "Sometimes when you play," Ben continued, "you seem ... different. Like you're somewhere else."

He wasn't the first person to tell her this. "Yeah, it feels like I'm somewhere else sometimes. I've seen videos of me playing and it's pretty wacky — the swaying back and forth and those strange faces I make and all. But that's just what happens when I play. I can't help it. Playing is very intense."

They walked without speaking for a while, the forest singing with some kind of insect call. Willow wondered if Ben was thinking about how he didn't feel that way when he played the tympani. Or maybe he did feel that way but he just didn't want to tell her.

Ben tapped a rhythm on his thighs as they walked. The wind whistled through the tops of the tall evergreens, a high note accompanying their steady, crunch crunch crunch across the leaves and pine needles. Willow added in another layer of music, whistling the melody of a piece the orchestra was practicing for Wednesday's parent performance. As she reached the end, Ben gave his thighs a dramatic drum roll, just as he did on the tympani. They grinned at each other and, in that moment, everything was forgiven.

They walked and walked. The trail veered right here and left there, weaving a path through the forest. Finally, it led up a short slope and emerged onto the back lawn of the hotel. Willow slapped her hands together, triumphant. "YES!"

"Yahoo." Ben's tone dripped with sarcasm, but Willow was determined not to let him spoil this for her. She sprinted along the side of the hotel toward the front door.

"Last one to the attic is a LO-SER!"

Ben tried to keep up but she'd had more than a head start and easily beat him to the front porch. "You totally cheated!" he yelled as Willow launched herself up the stairs and smacked the front door in victory. She did a little happy dance to rub it in, then grabbed the door handle. Her excitement dissolved with a gasp.

"No!" she moaned.

"What?" Ben asked, joining her on the porch.

"It's locked!" She gave the handle a ferocious jiggle.

"Oh, well. That's too bad," Ben said, checking his watch. "If we head back now, we'll be back in time for the volleyball game."

"Why would we come all this way just to head back at the first sign of trouble?"

Ben sighed. "Oh, I don't know Willow, because the door is locked? Because when we were here three days ago, we left it open and that it is now locked means someone has obviously been here?"

Willow growled in frustration. "Maybe we accidentally locked it when we left. Have you ever thought about that?"

"Willow ..."

"We might have!" she protested hotly. "It's fine. We'll just have to find another way in." She leapt down the steps and raced around the side of the building, calling over her shoulder. "I think I saw a door over here!"

There was a side door but it was locked as well. Willow gave the door a kick. "Arggg! What's the deal with this place?"

"Maybe your dad stopped by on his way home and made sure it was locked up because he knew you'd try to come back and snoop around."

Willow's head snapped toward Ben. "OMG. You're right! That's totally what he did!" she bellowed. "How could he? It's not fair! We walked all the way here! I am NOT going back to that camp without getting into this hotel. I'm just not."

"Hey, relax." Ben put his hands up in surrender, but Willow was too worked up now. Her mind spun trying to solve the problem.

"We could break a window—"

"Nobody is breaking anything!" Ben heaved a sigh. "This is a big place. Let's walk all the way around and see if there's another door."

Willow looked at him, considering. "Okay, for now." She ran for the back of the hotel and fist pumped the air when she found a small porch. She steeled herself for disappointment and tried the door.

Unlatched.

"Yes," she hissed. "We're in!" She pushed through the door. Ben followed her down the hallway, which took them right to the attic entrance. She pulled a flashlight from her pack and shined the beam up the stairwell.

"Those stairs don't look very solid, Willow," he said, shaking his head. "That one has a big hole in it!"

Willow whipped another flashlight from her pack and handed it to Ben. "We'd better be careful then." She picked her way up the staircase, careful to avoid precarious spots. A mouse scrabbled across one step but Willow didn't even notice.

She could almost feel the slump of Ben's shoulders as he followed her up the stairs. Luckily, the handrail ran unbroken all the way to the top to a landing. There, more steps lead to the second and then third floors. By time they reached the top, they didn't even need their flashlights.

Willow's breath caught as, finally, the attic opened up before her. "Whoa…" The expansive space stretched the length of the entire building; a sea of dressers, bed frames, tables, chairs, and boxes. Lots of boxes. Storage boxes, jewelry boxes, hat boxes. Dappled afternoon sunlight streamed through the shutter slats on the dormered windows along the left wall. An ancient wooden rocking horse stood next to a pair of tall, thick candlesticks. Half-a-dozen racks of hanging clothes lined the back wall. Larger items were draped in sheets making it impossible to tell what hid underneath.

An aisle zigzagged down the middle of the attic like a river carving its way through rock. Willow moved down it reverently, as if she were walking into a church. An old rusted toolbox caught Ben's eye and he squatted down to rummage through it as Willow slid her fingertips along the delicate pink fabric draped over a tailor's dummy. A wide-brimmed hat sat on the head, a large orange flower woven onto the brim.

"This is so cool!" she murmured.

Abandoning the toolbox, Ben followed her down the aisle, turning and staring all around the room as if trying to take it all in. As he passed her, Willow's gaze dropped to the floor behind him.

"Stop!" she yelled, grabbing a fistful of his shirt. Ben froze, mid-step. "Put your foot down in front of you. Don't step back …"

Turning around, not looking where he was going, Ben had nearly backed onto a patch of floorboard so fragile Willow doubted it would have held a mouse. Heart pounding, she imagined him crashing through the ceiling to the floor below.

She released both her grip on his shirt and her breath as Ben eased forward, his face pale as the sheets draping the furniture around them. "That was too close for comfort," he gasped.

"I thought you were supposed to be the careful one," Willow said, looking at the dangerous section of floor. "Hey, what's that?"

Ben looked over his shoulder. "A footlocker. Check out that massive lock. No way we'll get inside that thing. Don't even bother."

"Don't be so negative. Look how rusty it is," Willow said. She crossed her arms over her chest and studied it with a tilt of her head. "I bet if we smashed it with something it would break."

"We can't do that if we can't get to it," Ben countered.

Willow's determination flared like lighter fluid sprayed on hot coals. She slipped the pack from her back, setting it safely aside. "Imagine all the things that could be in that trunk …"

Ben sighed. "Okay, if we drag those chairs into the aisle, we might be able to get to the trunk from the other side and turn it around."

Willow raised her eyebrows. "Not bad, Cosgrove." Willow grabbed hold of the red, wingback chair and scooted it into an empty space in the main aisle. Ben tugged the other one free and pushed it next to its twin. After careful examination of the floorboards in the space they'd cleared, they decided the floor was strong enough. But when they tried to turn the footlocker, it wouldn't budge.

"This isn't going to work, Willow."

"Maybe you're right," Willow conceded. "Okay, new plan."

Ben looked at her. "You have one?"

"No, we need one." Willow scanned the attic. "Ah ha!" She trotted down the aisle toward the far end of the attic.

Ben followed her. "Looks like an old door or something."

The large piece of wood leaned against the wall. "Bet we could put it over that bad section of the floor," Willow said. She tilted the board, walking her hands up the sides until she got a good grip. Ben took the opposite side and they lifted it together. "Man," Ben grunted. "Why are old things so heavy?"

They scooched back down the aisle and set the door down. Then they sat on the floor and put their feet against the edge of the board and pushed. It slid over the rotten floorboards, covering the hole completely.

"Yes!" Willow crowed. "We rock! Now, to take care of that lock."

Ben raised a finger, silently indicating he had an idea. He returned to the red toolbox and retrieved a hammer.

The lock shattered on the third blow. Willow and Ben exchanged expectant looks, then, they shoved open the lid.

CHAPTER 8

FAYLENE SLAMMED HER hand down on the large, round conference table. Why did the Elders always have to make things so difficult? "Belinda, please. Surely you see that we must prepare for the possibility?"

"Please drop the dramatics, Faylene. There's simply no proof," her cousin sighed, looking around the room as if she was sure the other ten Elders completely agreed with her. "Everything has returned to normal. Whatever happened is over and done with."

As leader of the Cheyenne Mountain Elder Council, Belinda was the one to ultimately choose whether or not the group would take action. Faylene had anticipated such an apathetic response.

"But what else, cousin," Faylene hissed, "could possibly cause those deviations, if not the dragon's Pfife?"

"For the last time, cousin," Belinda's tone bit deep, "Drynfyre slept peacefully near that Pfife for hundreds of years before Vorman stole it. And every other den keeps a Pfife within their walls without issue."

"This Pfife has been missing for over a hundred and fifty years! If the connection between a dragon and her Pfife is eternal, could a long separation not have such an effect?"

"That is an assumption. It's not that I don't understand your concern, it's just that I don't agree with it." Belinda ran her fingers tightly along the collar of her white blouse, reinforcing its crease. Her gray eyes, perfectly shadowed and mascara-ed, showed nary a wrinkle. Oh, how Faylene despised her cousins, particularly Belinda, who was older than Faylene by only eighteen months. If not for that simple year and a half, Faylene would have been council leader. Clenching her hands into fists, she forced her emotions back as the other five members of the council waited for her to respond. She kept quiet just to spite them.

Belinda sighed. "It is very likely Vorman destroyed the Pfife and the music."

"Now who's making assumptions?" Faylene couldn't resist the retort.

Belinda ignored her. "Stay on high alert if you wish and, should the situation develop further, THEN we can discuss next steps. Now, can we get back to our Sunday afternoon? Please?" Belinda waved a hand at Faylene. "Next time, please ask first before assembling an emergency meeting. Especially on a weekend."

"Perhaps next time, I'll simply deal with the problem myself," Faylene snapped. Without waiting for a response, she spun on her heel and marched from the conference room.

Teeth clenched so tight her jaw throbbed; Faylene stomped down the hall toward the elevators. Fine. The council didn't find the rise in Drynfyre's temperature cause for alarm. Or interest. They were content just going about their business. But Faylene took it as a sign. Of course, the council didn't know all the things Faylene did. None of the other Guardians in this generation did. And she had no plans to let them in on her secret.

As the elevator doors closed, she dropped her act—one she'd played rather well, actually. A slight smile turned her lips. Those women were a pack of fools. Complacent idiots.

The elevator reached the first floor and Faylene walked briskly from the building. She allowed the sound of traffic to drown out the memory of Belinda's condescending tone replaying in her mind. Faylene felt her blood pressure drop a couple of notches. This Denver summer was hotter than last year. Global warming. Ha! Maybe that was why the dragons were stirring.

Except none of the others were. Only Drynfyre. It had to be the Pfife. Faylene was positive Drynfyre sensed its presence. Had Vorman passed the secret down through her family? Was one of them planning to finish what Hanna began all those years ago?

Her phone chirped an alert. Faylene glanced down at the screen and stopped walking. The text read 9-1-1. D.

The code was an automated text to alert her to an alarm at Drynfyre's den. After a split second's hesitation, (she'd allow herself no more than that) Faylene tapped the ENTER button below the text, which immediately connected her to the den in question.

Coreen didn't pick up on the first ring, which irritated Faylene. When the line connected, she heard an unsteady voice. "Yes ma'am?"

"It appears the temperature in Drynfyre's den has reached 110 degrees," Faylene said, her voice clipped and harsh. She needed to get back upstairs to her office, but the cell signal would be lost in the elevator so she'd have to complete this call first or run up two dozen flights of stairs, which was not appealing in the least. With a sigh, she looked up at the late afternoon sky. Puffy clouds floated like cotton balls above Brown Tower, taunting her with their peacefulness. Faylene felt chaos inching ever closer, soon to fill that peaceful blue sky with storm clouds. If she couldn't tame that chaos, it would destroy her. She must be the one in control.

"The gauges read 110," Coreen confirmed. "There doesn't seem to be any other physical changes, though. Drynfyre's REM state remains stable. As is the flame rhythm."

Faylene sighed, putting one hand to her forehead. "Well, the Council doesn't believe there's anything to worry about, so we will just have to deal with this ourselves. Key in override code 1175 and let me know immediately if anything else changes. You are officially on lockdown."

Silence from the other end. Faylene pictured the disbelief that must be on Coreen's face as that moment. They'd never put a den on lockdown before.

"Are you sure—"

"Do it." Faylene spat, ending the call and spinning on her heel.

Back inside the Brown Tower, she punched the elevator call button, a thrill of anticipation stirring in her chest. This was proof. Drynfyre was waking up. The Council had missed their chance to do the right thing. She was the one with the power now. Which was appropriate, since she was the one with the secret Codex.

CHAPTER 9

WILLOW SQUEALED, THEN squealed again as the trunk revealed its treasures. Six lacy tablecloths. Four boxes of silverware. Lots of musty clothing. Two round hatboxes packed with linen handkerchiefs and delicate lace gloves. Willow slid one over her fingers, and decided she was glad to live in a time when such ridiculous clothing wasn't required.

The next item out of the trunk was a hooded cloak. "Wow," Ben marveled and flung the dark wrap around his shoulders. "This is so LOTR."

"LOTR?" Willow raised an eyebrow.

Ben blushed madly. "You know, Lord of the Rings." He swallowed hard and shrugged off the heavy garment. "Except I'd bet a Ring Wraith doesn't stink like old socks! Ew, disgusting!"

Willow waved her hand in front of her nose in agreement and turned back to the trunk. "I guess that's it. Bummer. Kind of boring ...."

Ben tilted his head and gave the trunk a curious look. Then he peeked inside. "Huh. That's strange. Inside, it doesn't seem as deep as it looks from the outside …" He put one hand against the inside wall of the now empty trunk and the other on the outside, sliding them down to demonstrate how the inside hand stopped before the outside one did. He looked at Willow, questioning. "See?"

"A false bottom!" Willow grinned. "There must be a release latch or something." They ran their hands all over the trunk, hoping to spring the secret compartment, but found nothing. Willow sat back, considering. She studied the curlicues and fancy markings on the trunk's exterior. Could any of those hide a secret switch? She slid her hand along the curlicues, feeling for something that poked out, anything that felt different.

A raised spot just beneath the left hinge on the backside released the false bottom when Willow pushed it.

Ben grinned. "Excellent."

Inside the compartment they found three things: an old hat, a black leather case, and a thin velvet jewelry box that looked about the right size to hold one of those fancy fountain pens. Ben grabbed the leather case and untied its black string. Notebook-sized pages of loose parchment slithered out from between the covers.

Willow helped Ben gather them up. "Look at that weird writing. I can't read that, can you?"

"No. The paper feels really old," Ben said. "See how the edges are disintegrating?"

Willow scowled. "Those markings are funky." There was something vaguely familiar about them but she wasn't sure what.

"Is it Greek? They used lots of glyphs and stuff, right?" Ben said, studying the inky slashes.

"I don't know, I don't read Greek. It just looks like a bunch of lines to me." Willow slipped the pages back inside and Ben held the case together so that she could re-tie the string.

Willow then studied the hat. "This thing is UG-lee," she commented, handing it to him. It was thick and woolen, fitted along the back with a double brim out front.

"Looks like something an old-timey golfer would wear," he said, putting it on his head and tugging it down over his brow.

Willow grinned. "It probably has bugs in it."

He snatched it off, grimacing and looked inside. "I don't see any."

Willow jabbed him with her elbow. "I was joking, ding dong! So, got a guess about what's in the box?"

Ben tossed the cap back into the trunk. "Let's find out." He handed her the box and she opened the top. There was something wrapped in a dark red cloth inside holding a thin, white ... something.

"It looks like some sort of whistle," Ben said. He was right. The smooth, polished bone was tapered at one end, with a silk cord strung through two holes in the other. The cord was held together with a marble-sized pearl. A row of tiny black symbols was carved into the whistle's underside. Willow ran her finger over them, feeling the ridges.

"Give it a shot," Ben urged.

Willow put the tapered end to her lips and blew, but the only sound was rushing air. She frowned.

"Could it be a dog whistle?" Ben said. "Only dogs can hear those, right?"

Willow covered one of the tiny holes along the top of the whistle, like playing a recorder, and blew again. Still nothing. "Oh well," she said, wrapping it in the red cloth and putting it back in the box. "Maybe it is a dog whistle. But I'm gonna keep it anyway," she said.

Ben hesitated, tensing up. "I didn't think we were going to take anything. Isn't that ... stealing?"

Willow was afraid of this. Ben was far too goody goody for his own good. "Ben, look around. No one has been in this attic for decades. This stuff is as good as thrown away. If anyone cared they wouldn't have left it up here to rot in a run-down old hotel."

Ben shrugged. "It just feels ... wrong," he mumbled.

"You'd feel different if you'd found a first edition of *Lord of the Rings* up here or something."

Ben's eyes lit up. "You think we might find some old books up here? I didn't think about that, maybe I should take another look around." He wandered down the aisle, peeking in boxes and under sheets.

"Ben, Ben, Ben," Willow shook her head. She looked down at the white box in her hands. So what if the whistle didn't work. There was something about it that made her stomach feel full of butterflies—a good kind of nervous. She slipped the box into her backpack and, after considering for a moment, rolled-up the leather folder and stuck it in there as well. Then she returned all the stuff to the trunk and slammed the lid.

At that exact moment, a car door slammed shut outside.

Ben turned and looked at her, like he wasn't sure if the sound was her shutting the trunk or something else.

WHAM. Wham. More car doors slammed outside.

"Oh no," Willow breathed.

Ben's eyes went wide. "We are so dead."

Willow ran to the window and peeked out. Sure enough, she could see the tail end of a red car parked in front of the building. Whoever had gotten out of it was nowhere to be seen.

"Come on!" Willow grabbed Ben's arm and dragged him toward the staircase, snatching up her pack as they passed.

"Watch out!" Ben warned as she swung it onto her shoulder.

It was too late. Her pack knocked into the tailor's dummy, which toppled and smashed into a table, sending stacks of plates crashing to the floor.

"Oops," Willow said, swallowing a terrified giggle.

They flew down the stairs, moving so quickly they barely touched the steps at all, although Willow's foot did crack a section on the next-to-the-last step. Before the sound of the splitting wood even registered in her ears, however, the two of them were down the hallway and nearly at the back door.

"Hey! Hey you! Kids!"

Neither of them recognized the man's voice and they didn't turn to find out if they knew the face, either.

They burst out the door and were into the woods in a heartbeat. Legs pumping, lungs heaving, they didn't stop running until Willow tripped over a tree root and face planted onto the path.

"Oh my gosh, are you okay?" Ben helped her to her feet and brushed the dirt from her shoulders.

"Yeth, blech, pffft. I'm fine." She spit dirt from her mouth. Her scraped palms stung something fierce, but there was no blood.

They froze as something rustled in the distance behind them. Ben pulled Willow behind a boulder. Footsteps crunched as someone ran past, down the path. The running slowed, then stopped. Ben put a finger to his lips and widened his eyes at Willow. "Don't move," he mouthed. She nodded to show she understood, terrified her pounding heart would reveal their hiding place. But after a few tense moments, their pursuer turned and headed back up the path toward the house.

Willow finally allowed herself to breathe, nearly collapsing with lightheadedness. Ben peeked over the boulder, then dropped back down, satisfied the guy was gone. "Okay, let's get out of here!" he hissed. "Oh, and by the way? I told you so."

CHAPTER 10

IT WAS ONE of the longest weekends of Tiernan's life.

Since turning sixteen, weekends had taken on a whole new meaning for her. Those 48 hours away from the den had become the highlight of her week: her time at home, away from dragons and temperature readings and, especially, tedious transfer of uneventful data. It was her time to do normal things like go to the movies or out to eat with her friends. To sleep in. To live without a schedule.

For the last twenty years, Aunt Coreen had served as Primary. Until Tiernan turned twenty-one, Coreen would continue to live in the den with her, just as Grandma Sadie had with Coreen. How lucky Coreen had been that Faylene had been elected to the Elder Council, or she'd have had to live with the grumpy old woman instead of Grandma Sadie, who had taken her place. Grandma was a much more pleasant a roommate than Faylene ever would have been, that was for sure. Grandma had served ten years without a secondary waiting for the first girl of the next generation to come of age, and that happened to have been Coreen. Tiernan was the firstborn of her own generation.

Such had been the way for Guardian families for thousands of years. Ever since the dragon hibernation, or as it was called in Illian: *Dormitus*.

Those first months in the den were rough for Tiernan. With its white walls and endless stainless steel, the space made her claustrophobic. The lack of freedom was just as confining. The droning monotony, exhausting. While real-life dragons were super cool, watching one hibernate just wasn't that thrilling.

When she was younger, Tiernan loved the whole Guardian thing. Her first time in the den, she'd amused Aunt Coreen with her bubbly, ten-year-old excitement; her genuine awe of Drynfyre's immense size and beautiful scales, so surreally iridescent and hard as iron. Even in hibernation her curved, sharp claws exuded terrifying power.

On the day of her sixteenth birthday, Tiernan blew out her candles in the den's tiny kitchen with her parents and little brother proudly watching. Later, after they'd all left, she and Aunt Coreen stood watching Drynfyre sleep. "I know I don't have to remind you that this job comes with many … challenges," her aunt murmured. "By far, the biggest one is boredom."

Tiernan straightened her back. "I know it won't be any big adventure or anything. But it's a great honor."

Aunt Coreen smiled. "Of course it is. But the truth is, this day is the beginning of years of watching over something that never moves or changes or does anything. Ever. Hour after hour, day after day, year after year. A huge responsibility, yes. But tedious doesn't even begin to describe it."

Tiernan's face must have shown her disappointment because Coreen chuckled. "Don't worry. It's not all doom and gloom," she said, wrapping her arm around Tiernan's shoulder. "Generations of Dragon Guardians have passed down extensive knowledge about these sleeping beasts, reams of learning. Plus," Aunt Coreen added, her expression serious. "I have a little secret that makes time move faster."

"Really?" Tiernan said, hopeful.

Aunt Coreen raised a wicked eyebrow. "Follow me."

Ushering Tiernan to the two tall filing cabinets standing side by side in the back corner of the conference room, Coreen revealed her secret: the lowest drawers were packed with dozens of video games, everything from karaoke to Super Smash Brothers and the latest Wii Fit and Dance Dance Revolution games.

"These games," Coreen said, voice deep with dramatic suspense, "and those that came before them, unquestionably saved my sanity. There are also board games and cards in the other drawers but most of those you can't play alone. There was an actual Atari here when I took over, but it went belly up years ago. No biggie. Trust me, you can only play so much Pong."

Tiernan took in the hoard. "This is amazing! Hey, is that what I think it is?"

Coreen picked up the case and handed it to Tiernan. "Yep, the Japanese Guardian has a friend who works at Nintendo, so we get beta copies sometimes. They never released this one to the public. I had a feeling you'd appreciate this one."

"Zelda is my favorite," Tiernan murmured.

"Word of warning: no more than an hour of playing at a time or Faylene will have your head. She's cool with these, but she gets cranky if you start binging."

In the weeks since that conversation, Tiernan had certainly put those games to good use, but after last week's events, their distraction wouldn't be necessary.

Anxious to see if anything had developed with Drynfyre over the weekend, Tiernan returned to the den a few hours before her 7:00 pm deadline on Sunday. "Completely quiet?" Tiernan said when Coreen told her the news, or lack of it. Dropping her overnight bag on the floor, she collapsed on the bed in Coreen's apartment. It was hard not to be disappointed. "I swear I didn't just imagine it."

"Nobody thinks you did," her aunt smiled in that way people do when they're telling a white lie. Great. So some did think she was making it up. "Faylene believes you. It's been over 150 years since Drynfyre's Pfife was stolen and we don't know what the long-term impact of that could be. The Pfifes were created as part of the hibernation spell. It makes sense that Drynfyre might have adjusted to its absence in all that time, but if the Pfife is nearby again, and active … who knows?"

Tiernan sat up, crisscrossing her legs beneath her. "So, do you think that's what is happening? That someone nearby has the Pfife? Could someone be trying to wake her?"

Coreen shrugged. "Hanna Vorman took the Pfife to keep The Awakening from ever happening. She wouldn't want it to be used, so odds are she destroyed it along with the music."

Tiernan sighed. The Dragon Songs were powerful, so much so that even copying them by hand reduced their effectiveness. So when Hanna stole them, there were no other copies. Each set of Songs was particular to each dragon's Pfife, and therefore, each particular dragon. "But, theoretically, if someone had the Pfife and music, and played the Awakening Song …"

Coreen raised a wary eyebrow at her niece. "If someone was playing that Song, that dragon would be awake, and trust me, there'd be no question about it. Remember book four of the Codex? Where Kareth described what would happen if The Awakening happened too soon?"

Tiernan did remember the scene Kareth described—complete chaos. The way she wrote it, and she would know since she was the one who created the spell, dragon Songs had instantaneous effect, not this gradual stuff that was going on with Drynfyre now. Maybe Coreen was right. But Tiernan's gut instinct wasn't convinced.

"The Elders will never vote for The Awakening, will they?" she asked Coreen, not for the first time.

Coreen gave her the look she always did. Beyond skeptical. Tiernan wasn't sure if that made her feel safe … or sad.

An alarm shrieked, making them both jump. The red light above the bedroom door flashed on and off in time with the bleating squawks. "Are you kidding me?" Coreen barked, a sharp edge to her voice as they bolted for the monitoring station.

Coreen ran her hands over the temperature gauges like she thought by touching them they would read something other than the unfathomable truth they showed.

"Um, Coreen?" Tiernan's voice squeaked. "That's not good, is it?"

Coreen swallowed hard, enough of a response for Tiernan to take it as affirmation. "This just can't be." The phone on the desk buzzed, loud and accusing. Coreen took a deep breath. They both knew who was calling. Neither wanted to answer.

Finally, Coreen snatched up the handset. "Yes, ma'am."

As her aunt listened to Faylene's orders, Tiernan pushed through the door to the Inner Den. She stared at the reading. It was just as shocking in here as it was in the monitoring station.

110 degrees.

Tiernan quickly examined the dragon. Drynfyre didn't look any different. No movement. No color change. Tiernan extended her hand, easing toward the sleeping dragon. Then, Coreen was right beside her, jerking her back. "Don't touch her!" she snapped, her voice filled with an unfamiliar intensity. "Everything's changed. Faylene just locked down the den."

CHAPTER 11

ONCE THEY'D MADE it back to camp unnoticed, Ben went to the volleyball game and Willow went back to her empty cabin. She wasn't in the mood for fun at the moment. She flopped across the bottom bunk, listening to the far-away sounds of kids shouting and laughing through their free afternoon.

Willow couldn't stop thinking about the men who chased them out of the hotel. She'd been chased away from tons of dumpsters and trash cans in her treasure hunting adventures, but nobody had ever chased her with such intent to catch her. It left her feeling rather shaken.

She glanced over at her backpack where it sat on the floor next to her bunk. After moving the rolled up case of parchment into her music bag, she opened the lid of the jewelry box and unwrapped the red cloth. The bone-like surface of the instrument felt captivatingly smooth. She turned it in her fingers, studying the markings on its underside. They looked like hieroglyphics or something. That's what Ben had thought about the writing on the parchment, that they were glyphs. Were these markings the same thing?

Willow strung the whistle around her neck, letting it rest against her chest. A strange sort of calm settled over her. She took a deep breath and relaxed back on the bed. Everything was going to be fine. The man on the trail hadn't caught them. He might have seen them, but he didn't know who they were … there was nothing to worry about.

Threads of a tune bubbled to life in her ears, like the memory of a soothing lullaby. Willow couldn't place the melody. The memory was too thin, barely even there. It perched on the tip of her mind like a word just out of reach …

The dinner bell clanged, pulling her out of her thoughts. Willow tucked the whistle into the neck of her t-shirt and ran for the mess hall.

ALL THROUGH THE REST of the night—during dinner, evening rehearsal, a game of charades and even the nightly campfire sing-a-long—Willow kept thinking about that tune. She slept fitfully and woke early from a dream where she was playing the melody on that whistle she'd found. That could never happen, of course, since the whistle didn't work that way. It was a dog whistle and made no noise. But somehow, Willow didn't believe that was true.

If only she could remember where she'd heard that tune before. Every time she pulled it close enough to identify, the memory slipped away like a balloon in the breeze.

At breakfast, the Camp Director made an announcement. "Please remember, no one goes into the woods without supervision." Willow cut her eyes at Ben who had turned fourteen different shades of purple. He sunk down in his chair, oatmeal forgotten. That was all that was said about it, but Willow couldn't help worrying. Had the men from the hotel known they were from the camp? Had they come looking for them? At morning rehearsal, Willow was so lost in thought she missed her cue. The rap of a baton on her stand startled her back to the present and she looked up to see Mr. Hooten, as well as the entire orchestra, staring at her.

"Miss McLain," Mr. Hooten asked, mock concern on his face. "Is the first chair part not challenging enough to hold your interest? Perhaps you would prefer a transfer to the wind section?"

Willow looked down. Her violin and bow sat across her lap, abandoned. Her fingers curled around the whistle, as if ready for her to play. She gulped, a hot blush seeping across her face. "Umm, no … sir. I didn't …"

"Well, until you're sure, I would appreciate it if you played the part to which you were assigned. And I believe the rest of the violin section might appreciate that as well."

A few kids sniggered. Her stand partner, Alecia, scowled. What was she so mad about? Willow was the one in trouble.

"Sorry," Willow muttered, tucking the whistle back inside her shirt and the violin under her chin. Embarrassed sweat beaded her forehead. What had happened? She didn't remember putting her violin down, much less taking the whistle out of her shirt.

As Willow awaited her cue again, that tune trickled back into her mind. It could be a whistle playing, couldn't it? A flute, or maybe … a piccolo? She shook off the unfocused thoughts, concentrating on the music. This time, Willow came in right on cue, and played the stanza perfectly.

Fifteen minutes and what felt like a million repetitions of the stanza later, Mr. Hooten gave them a break. Willow and Ben waited in line at the concession stand but by time they made it to the counter break was nearly over and Willow still had to go to the bathroom. She set her granola bar and water bottle on the floor next to her chair and ran to the restrooms at the far end of the rehearsal hall.

She only had a few minutes before Mr. Hooten would ring the cowbell to end break so she had to move fast. Latching the door behind her in the first stall, she hurriedly situated herself on the toilet. Ah, sweet relief.

That was when she heard the buzzing.

An enormous bug hovered in the corner above her, where the ceiling met the wall. It flitted about, looking for escape. Panic zapped through Willow's veins like a bolt of lightning. She reached carefully for the toilet paper, careful not to make any sudden moves that might attract its attention. As she eased her shorts back up over her hips, the insect flew down and hovered a few feet above her head before landing on the latch of the stall door.

Willow's stomach turned to ice. She was trapped. Scrambling backwards, she pressed herself against the wall. How was she going to get out of here? The EpiPen was in her backpack, under her chair in the other room. Of course, that was for bee stings and this didn't look like any bee she'd ever seen. This was some skinny, nasty flying thing with yellow and black stripes and big ole nasty black eyes. A hornet maybe, or a wasp.

"Shoo! Go away!" she yelled as if the bug could understand her. Keeping an eye on it, she leaned over and yanked some toilet paper from the roll. She wadded it up and threw it toward the door. It missed by a foot, fluttering to the ground. The insect didn't move.

There was only one thing left to do.

Loosening the laces on her left shoe, she slid the red Converse sneaker from her foot, holding it out in front of her like a weapon. She just needed one good thwap and the mean old thing would be mush. Then she could get back to her chair before Mr. Hooten freaked out that she was delaying rehearsal again.

The hornet sat on the latch, unaware of its impending doom. Willow slowly raised the shoe, her throat so tight with fear it was like just the thought of anaphylactic shock was bringing it on.

Willow's right hand brought the shoe down quickly, but the bug dodged out of the way. Right toward her. Landing on her left hand.

Without thinking, she brought the shoe down on her own hand, smashing the hornet against her skin.

She felt the stinger's jab like a piercing needle.

Oh no no no...

Heart-racing, head-spinning panic soaked her in horror. What had she done? Her throat tightened. She couldn't swallow. She couldn't breathe. Fumbling with the door latch, she burst from the stall, stumbling, catching herself on a sink before she hit the floor.

The EpiPen was all she could think about. She had to get to her backpack.

Ben turned as she crawled out of the bathroom. Standing in the back of the orchestra by the tympani, he was closest of anyone. "Oh my God!" He dropped his drumsticks and bolted for her, eyes wide, face pale. "Mr. Hooten!" he screamed. "Help! Something's wrong with Willow!"

Rolling onto her back, Willow reached out to Ben with her stung hand, her other hand clutched at her throat. He needed to see the sting, then he would understand. He would know what to do. Her mom had sat him down that first week after they'd moved in, and explained about her allergy. About the EpiPen. How it could save her life.

Willow's fingers clawed at her neck as if she could loosen the paralysis. Her fingers found the whistle's cord instead. She pulled it out of her shirt. Holding it made her feel better, calmer. Everything would be okay.

She turned her head so her cheek pressed against the cool tile floor and saw Ben and Mr. Hooten digging through her backpack, searching for the EpiPen. She wanted to tell them not to worry about it, she was fine, but Willow still couldn't move. It was strange, the way she wasn't afraid anymore. She just needed to hold on to the whistle. As long as she did that, she'd be fine. Her fingers stroked its smooth surface.

Willow sat up. Swallowed. Gasped, sucking in a deep breath.

Ben, already headed back toward her with something clutched in his hand, skidded to a stop. "Wha—?"

"It's okay," Willow croaked. "I'm feeling better. Just thirsty."

"But ..." Ben's brow unfurrowed. "I mean ... wow! Oh my gosh, Willow! You scared me to death!"

Mr. Hooten squatted next to her, looking at her eyes, examining her face. "Did you have an EpiPen with you?" he asked, confused.

Willow shook her head. "No, I just—" She stopped, sensing it would not make sense to mention the whistle because that would be illogical, right? It didn't have anything to do with this. The reaction just wasn't as bad she expected. "I think I just panicked. I'm so sorry. It wasn't a bee; it was a hornet or a wasp or something. I guess I'm not as allergic to them and I got over it faster." She smiled, hoping it would make everyone go back to normal because right now they were all staring at her like she'd just grown another set of arms.

"Hmmm. All right, then." Mr. Hooten helped Willow to her feet. "But I'm keeping a close eye on you, Miss McLain. I want you to rest on that couch over there for a bit. Ben, how about some water?"

"Huh? Oh! Right." Ben fetched the bottle by Willow's chair as she settled on the couch. Everyone returned to their seats, their eyes still on her. Willow studied the sting, expecting to see a big red welt but there was just a small bump. Her heart lurched in disbelief. She wasn't sure which to feel: relief or confusion. She leaned back against the back of the couch and slipped the whistle out of her shirt again. She swore she hadn't imagined it. The insect had stung her. But how could it just disappear like that?

Hornet or wasp, even if she wasn't as allergic to it as she was a bee sting, she should still have a swollen mark on her hand.

She knew what had happened, even if she didn't want to believe it. The whistle had saved her.

PREPARATIONS FOR THE FINAL concert didn't give Willow time to discuss her miraculous recovery with Ben, which was fine by her. She skipped the bonfire that night and went straight to bed, mostly to avoid him, but also because she needed some time to think without everyone asking if she was okay and hovering over her.

Did the whistle have some magical powers? Had it actually healed her? And if it did, what did that mean?

Mr. Hooten had called her parents to let them know what had happened, that Willow seemed fine, and that the camp nurse was keeping an extra close eye on her. Willow was shocked her mother hadn't flipped out and insisted she come home immediately.

The concert went well, especially her solo during the finale. Somehow, this piece that she'd played so many times felt electric and alive and new. She stroked the bow perfectly across the strings, her fingers flying up and down the violin's neck, each note precise. As she bowed the final note, she looked into the audience and saw her parents' beaming faces. Her family jumped to their feet with enthusiastic applause. Willow couldn't stop grinning, even if it did take her dad longer to stand up than everyone else. She went back to her chair knowing she'd just given a top-notch performance, quite possibly her best yet.

Willow tracked down her family when the concert was over. Her mother glowed with pride. "Honey, that was spectacular!" She kissed Willow hard on the forehead then whispered in her ear. "Are you feeling all right? Oh, baby girl if anything ever happened to you …"

Willow hugged her tight before pulling away. "Mom, I'm fine! I promise!"

Her mom nodded, eyes brimming with tears.

"I guess you outgrew your allergy," her dad said, all matter-of-fact as if he knew about such things from many years of medical education. Her mom's jaw clenched in frustration.

Ben appeared, a tympani mallet in each hand. "Hey, guess what? Mr. Hooten says I did such a good job, I can take these home with me!"

Clapping Ben on the shoulder, Marcus agreed. "That was some wicked drumming, little dude."

Ben's cheeks flushed but his smile stretched wide. "You think?"

"Sure!" Marcus squeezed Ben's shoulder. "I'm not really an expert on orchestra music, but it sounded pretty good for a bunch of kids." Then his eyes turned to Willow. "And you! How did I not know you could play the violin like that?"

"Clearly she's not practicing very much at home, then." Her dad acted like it was a joke, but Willow's mom raised an eyebrow at her. Willow's practice schedule was a sore subject. Luckily, Marcus kept talking.

"How about I treat you both to a Coke before we head back?" Marcus offered, jabbing a thumb toward the snack shack.

"Cool," Willow said. "But we'd better hurry. It's only open for another five minutes. And I still have to pack for home."

CHAPTER 12

THE SUN HAD NEARLY set when Faylene arrived at the Cheyenne Mountain guard booth in her blue Acura. Traffic between Denver and the Springs was horrible lately, and it put her in a foul mood. She flashed her credentials and the uniformed guard gave a bored nod, waving her through. She stomped her foot on the gas pedal, kicking up gravel as she sped down the winding road to the den entrance.

If only those gate guards knew what her credentials actually meant. If only they knew she was in charge of a beast capable of destroying their world. If they knew, maybe they'd show her a little more respect. But of course it wasn't possible for them to know. The United States Government supplied them. That was part of the arrangement. And what they were guarding, along with the precise location of the den's entrance, was classified, known to only a handful of people—the Guardians themselves, the Elder Council, and a few high-ranking members of the government. Even the Guardian's family members didn't know how to get in to the den.

Limiting this knowledge to the President, the Secretary of Defense, and the Air Force's Chief of Staff helped ensure security of the two American dens. Even the Vice President wasn't aware that two dragons hibernated on U.S. soil, or that there were five other dragons doing the same on other parts of the planet.

As Faylene pulled into the parking lot, she wondered how far the Elders would allow this little disruption to go before notifying the President. It would be a last resort, of course, because they knew his response would be a swift and quick annihilation of the two American dens followed by calls to the leaders of each of the countries in which the other dens were located. The current President's predecessor had made it pretty clear, from the moment surveillance teams discovered the true nature of the huge red blob on their sophisticated infrared radar screens, that he would not hesitate if he felt Americans were at risk. He was less than thrilled to learn the Guardians existed in the first place, much less that they'd kept such a secret for years. But he understood the historic significance of their mission, and certainly didn't want to be labeled as the world leader who extinguished the last dragon.

In most countries, the agreement with leadership was quite diplomatic. In America, however, the accord was tenuous at best, and the hint of an awakening dragon might be all it took to shatter it.

Especially since the Guardians hadn't revealed the part about the missing Pfife and Amulet. If the President found out he'd protected a dragon that could not be controlled if awakened, he would not be a happy camper.

Since the beginning of the 21ˢᵗ century, American tax dollars had funded fortification of the dens—using Guardian family construction and engineering teams, of course—rendering the dens technologically invisible, in case a terrorist organization had the wild idea of using dragons as weapons of mass destruction.

While the other parts of Cheyenne Mountain housed a small zoo, various tourist attractions, and even what used to be the NORAD military facility, there was one large and remote section that remained privately owned, and had since way before Major Stephen Long became the area's first official explorer, and long before the area became known as the Garden of the Gods.

Faylene parked her car in front of the one-story brick building. From the outside it looked like any other national park building, about the size of a small gas station, backed up to the mountainside and tucked between two thick patches of evergreens. She punched her code into the keypad, unlocking the front door. The interior of the building was dressed out like a small office, real enough to fool anyone who came poking around. A grey metal desk stood near the north wall. On it was a black rotary phone. A large blotter spread across the desk, all its days X'd out as if someone had marked time until the end of the month, and left when that date arrived.

Faylene picked up the phone and dialed 0. Slowly and distinctly, she said the words "Kareth's Secret" into the phone. The voice recognition software was finicky, requiring careful pronunciation. She waited until she heard the sigh of hydraulics behind the door on the wall to her right before she replaced the handset.

In the elevator car, Faylene punched the only button on the panel. It read DOWN but once the doors closed, the car actually moved horizontally backward, deeper into the mountain before pausing for the gears to change direction. Then, it shot upwards. When the doors slid open again, Faylene found Coreen and Tiernan waiting for her. She paused, curious. Why in the world, with all that was going on, were these two grinning like complete idiots?

"What?" she demanded.

Tiernan's words bubbled with excitement. "We found something."

Faylene's heartbeat sped up but she was careful not to expose a smidgen of emotion. "Show me." She followed them to the conference room where Tiernan took a chair at the table behind an open laptop. Coreen slid a yellowed file folder across the table. Faylene eyed it, nervousness swelling in her chest.

Tiernan rubbed her hands together. "We dug into the database, cross referencing anything that had to do with the Amulet, and we found something curious."

"There's a gap," Coreen added.

"A gap?" Faylene managed to keep her voice flat and steady. This was impossible. "What do you mean?"

"There is a two-month time frame missing from the earliest journals. Kareth's Codex."

"We double checked it against the microfilm. There's a gap there as well."

"A gap." Faylene raised her eyebrows as if she didn't understand what all this meant, when of course she knew exactly what it meant. She knew the reason for the gap. And the information inside the gap.

Tiernan continued. "There's a big chunk of data that's just ... missing. So we checked the original documents to see if they'd somehow missed those pages when they were captured on microfilm. Inadvertently, of course." Tiernan's cheeks colored. She'd realized she was calling Faylene out for an error during the first transcription, which, of course, took place back in the 1960s. Under Faylene's watch. "But there was no mistake," Tiernan said quickly, as if wanting to be sure to clear Faylene of any blame. "The gap is there, too. In the original documents."

"What is the gap? Exactly?" Faylene felt the sweat all along her back. She prayed it didn't show on her face.

"An entire journal," Coreen said. "The title page of the 11th volume indicates 1 of 2. But the second volume is nowhere to be found." Kareth's Codex set forth the reason for the dragons' hibernation, explained how to care for them, called for the formation of the Council and set up the rules by which the dragons could be awakened. Written in Illian, a language now virtually extinct, the journals contained the backstory of the Guardians' very existence.

"It would have been easy to miss during the original microfilm transfer," Tiernan affirmed. "None of the other journals have an additional volume. It's just that the digital format makes the gap easy to see, but only if the search terms are just right." The new digital scans translated the text and made it searchable, compared to the microfilm, which had to be read (and translated) just like a hard copy on a screen. Stupid technology, Faylene thought, her nervousness turning into anger. This is exactly why I didn't want the microfiche digitized.

60

But Belinda had. Belinda had insisted.

Faylene's knees wobbled a bit as she sunk into one of the conference room chairs. "Now, let's not jump to conclusions. Perhaps Kareth intended there to be two volumes, but never wrote the second."

"We considered that," Tiernan nodded, holding up a finger in an ah-ha gesture. "But we actually found some loose pages from the missing journal. They were in the same bag as the first volume."

The only thing keeping Faylene from giving into her rising panic was that clearly neither Coreen nor Tiernan had any idea about what they had actually uncovered. Could she have really left pages behind? How could she have been that careless? She looked at the yellow folder. "Are these the pages?"

Like so many of Kareth's original volumes and documents, certain sections required a delicate touch to prevent their destruction. Coreen handed Faylene padded tweezers so she could examine the backs of the pages. "I took digital images to preserve them before we messed with them too much. We've added them to the database as well," said Coreen. Faylene silently cursed Coreen's thoroughness. "There's no doubt. The handwriting is Kareth's."

"No doubt," Faylene snapped, finding it more and more difficult to hide her growing anger. The girl was simply to have digitized the microfilm. That was all. Not dig around. Not analyze and pick it apart.

"So, you have a translation, then?" Faylene asked, already knowing the answer.

Tiernan and Coreen glanced at each other, grins wide on both their faces. "This seems to be part of what is obviously a longer section, but it does contain one vital piece of information."

Faylene waited, heart hammering. There was nothing she could do but let this play out however it would.

"It says that the Amulets can be used to track the Pfifes," Tiernan blurted. "Can you believe that?"

Faylene stared at her, honestly shocked. "What?"

"It's true!" Tiernan said. "So if someone is using the Pfife, and that is what's causing the temperature fluxuations, then we should be able to use the Amulet to find them."

"Hold on, we're not positive that's what it means. The translation is difficult because the last sentence is incomplete. It goes onto the next page, which we don't have," Coreen said quickly, moving her finger on the computer's touch screen to zoom in on one section of the text. "But it does mention following the Pfife. And there's one sentence just at the end of the page, that mentions Treasure." She looked hard at Faylene. "I thought we'd always been told the Codices don't mention anything about a Treasure?"

Tiernan almost squealed. "Isn't it amazing? Everyone thinks it's some fairy tale passed down through the generations, because there was never anything written about it in any of Kareth's journals. But if this translation is right, it just might be real!"

"Let's not get ahead of ourselves." It was becoming more and more difficult for Faylene to remain calm.

"We can't worry about that now, we need to find the Pfife," Coreen put a calming hand on Tiernan's arm. "The Amulet humming and glowing did coincide with Drynfyre's temperature jump. "

"It did. And now look." Tiernan pulled the Amulet out from her collar, lifting the silken cord over her head. The dark gem pulsed with a soft light and hummed softly, so low Faylene hadn't heard it before. "If we've translated the Illian properly, it seems the speed of the pulse has to do with proximity."

"The Amulets traveled from den to den," Coreen went on, thinking out loud. "Since the beginning, they were always with one Pfife or another. Maybe this Pfife, being separated from its dragon and away from an Amulet for so long, maybe it triggered this reaction from the Amulet. It's acting like a homing beacon or something."

Tiernan pushed her chair back from the table and nodded at the Amulet, still dangling from its cord in Faylene's hand. "Let me drive the Amulet around town. Maybe it'll lead me somewhere, maybe not. If not, no big deal, but what if it does?"

Faylene glanced at Coreen, who shrugged. "If someone does have the Pfife nearby, we need to know who. I honestly don't know another way to find them." Faylene lifted the gem up and stared into its ebony depths. It hummed back at her, continuous and persistent, urging her to do something.

"Fine. Give it a try." Faylene conceded, handing the Amulet back to Tiernan. She was going to have to go along with this for now, at least until she could figure out how to make this work in her favor. Besides, she did need to find that Pfife. And if this theory proved true, it might actually accelerate her plans. "But let's keep this between the three of us, shall we? If it works, we'll be heroes. If it doesn't … well, I don't want anyone knowing I authorized such an attempt. Is that clear?"

Tiernan grinned. "Crystal."

CHAPTER 13

BEN SCOOPED UP A last spoonful of Honey Nut Cheerios as Willow plopped down in the chair next to him and drummed her fingers on the kitchen table. This morning she wore athletic shorts, a black Colorado Rockies t-shirt with the sleeves rolled to her shoulders and a beat up pair of Chuck Taylor high tops the same shade of purple as the Rockies insignia on her shirt. Her hair was loose and Ben realized how long it truly was—a reddish blonde wave reaching halfway down her back.

Willow dressed like an athlete, even though she wasn't on any teams, as far as he could tell. Ben preferred shorts and sandals. Back in Texas it was warm enough most of the year that he never had to wear closed-toe shoes except for school. He knew when summer was over here in Colorado, he'd need something warmer but, at least for now, he could get away with his usual attire—khaki shorts, brown leather flip flops and some kind of t-shirt. Today's was a dark blue polo type from Old Navy. Ben dreaded the coming winter. He hated the cold.

"Hey, did you ask your dad about my book?" he asked, before she could say a word. He'd accidentally left *Widershins and the Angel* in the back of Uncle Grant's car on the way to camp and hadn't read it in a week.

"Yup. We can ride our bikes over to his office and pick it up, if you want." Willow slipped a hair band from her wrist and pulled her hair into its usual high ponytail.

Ben dropped his spoon in the empty bowl and leaned back in his chair. "Cool. Maybe we could go to the pool later?" Willow's mom had mentioned a neighborhood pool and Ben kind of wanted to check it out, if it got warm enough.

"Maybe. Not sure if it's open on Sunday." Willow pulled the whistle from inside her shirt and twirled it between her fingers absently. "What's Marcus doing?"

"Working. Busy day at Game Stop getting ready for the release day for World of Warcraft part four million and two."

Willow snorted, amused. Ben was glad that things still seemed good between them. He'd been worried that once they got back from camp, she'd go back to acting like she hated living in the same house with him. But she hadn't. Which was nice.

Aunt Matilda shuffled into the room, her long white-grey hair a mess from sleep, her dark blue eyes unfocused. The edge of her pale pink robe revealed her slippered feet as she scooted across the floor.

"Hey," Willow leaned toward Ben and whispered conspiratorially. "We should ask Aunt Matilda about the hotel."

Ben was kind of hoping Willow had forgotten about that. Silly idea. He sighed.

"Good morning!" Willow called to Aunt Matilda. Ben shot her a look that said she has Alzheimer's, she's not deaf! Willow grimaced and mouthed "sorry."

Aunt Matilda looked at Willow, expression vacant. "Who are you? What are you doing in my house?" she asked in a monotone voice.

Willow's smile melted and she cut her eyes at Ben. Maybe Sunday wasn't a good day to try to have this conversation. The nurse didn't come on weekends and he hadn't seen Willow's mom yet. It was early, so she was probably still in bed. Ben got up and approached Matilda slowly.

"Aunt Matilda, I'm Ben and this is Willow. We live here, too. Can I make you some breakfast?"

Ben could tell that even though she didn't remember him, she realized she should. "Children? There are children in this house?" she said, talking to herself. Then her face lit up. "Of course! The children! Oh, good morning, Ben! Did you sleep well?"

Willow gently took Aunt Matilda's other arm and led her to the Lazy-Boy in the den. Together, they eased her into the chair and Willow shook out a blanket to smooth over her lap. Ben patted her arm. "Now how about that breakfast?"

"Just a piece of toast, if it's not too much trouble."

"None at all," Ben said, Willow following him back into the kitchen. Sudden changes like that weren't unusual for Aunt Matilda, but they were still kind of unnerving. Willow gave him a half smile. "What?"

"Nothing," she said with a shrug. "She seems better around you, that's all."

Ben didn't know what to say to that. If that was better, he couldn't imagine what was worse.

Willow popped some bread in the toaster as Aunt Matilda clicked the remote, turning on the TV. The local news blared from the flat screen. Ben microwaved a cup of water and added a chamomile tea bag to steep. Aunt Matilda's favorite.

He set her breakfast on the side table as Willow settled on the floor at her feet. As Aunt Matilda picked up a triangle of toast, Willow switched off the TV. Her voice casual, she asked, "Hey, Aunt Matilda, have you ever heard of a hotel called The Canton?"

Aunt Matilda nibbled the corner of toast like a mouse sneaking cheese off a trap that might spring at any moment. She didn't answer at first; just chewed silently like she hadn't even heard the question. Willow's foot wiggled with anticipation and she gave Ben a pointed look. He patted her arm and she gazed up at him with a brilliant smile. "Hello, Ben! Thank you for the breakfast."

Resisting the urge to glance at Willow, Ben kept his gaze locked with Matilda's. "You're welcome. Would you mind if I asked you a question?"

"Anything at all," she said, sounding completely normal.

"Have you ever heard of The Canton Hotel?"

"Of course I have heard of The Canton Hotel," she said. "My father was the desk manager there for twenty years."

Ben's heart did a somersault. He looked at Willow and she shook her head slightly, placing her hand over the bump in her shirt. Ben nodded to say he understood. She didn't want him to mention the whistle. At least, not yet. "Really?" he continued to Aunt Matilda. "That's amazing! Can you tell us what the hotel was like back then?"

Ben sat down on the edge of the couch as Aunt Matilda swallowed the last bite of toast. She closed her eyes and leaned her head back in her chair. "We used to live there ... at the hotel. When I was a little girl."

"You actually lived in the hotel?" Willow asked.

"Yes, in a small room, back by the kitchen."

Ben realized they must have walked right past their living quarters when they explored the hotel the other day. The thought made goosebumps pop up in his scalp.

"How old were you?" asked Ben.

"I was ten. We lived there for five years, until Father passed away."

"Oh," Ben swallowed hard, exchanging a look with Willow. He didn't want to make Matilda upset but he thought it must be a good thing for her to be able to remember stuff like this. "I'm so sorry," he said, but Aunt Matilda went on as if she hadn't heard, lost in the memories.

"Mother and I would go back as guests sometimes. The staff was like family to us, and Morgenstern allowed us to stay. He never made us pay. He felt badly, you see," Aunt Matilda opened her eyes and gave Willow a small smile, tears pooling in her eyes. Willow's fingers absently pulled the whistle from the neck of her shirt and she ran the cord back and forth through the hole in the top, drawing Aunt Matilda's attention. Her wrinkled hand went to her neck, mirroring Willow.

Matilda's eyes widened to the point Ben could see all the white around her irises. "How? No! That can't be ..." Matilda whispered furiously.

"Aunt Matilda?" Her wrinkled skin had gone totally pale, alarming Ben.

"No ... NO!" Loud and insistent, Matilda reached for the whistle, then quickly pulled back her hand like it might burn her fingers. Clapping her hands over her ears she started screaming. "NO! NO! NO!" She squished her eyes shut and rocked madly back and forth. "Impossible! Impossible!"

Willow and Ben scrambled to their feet as Willow's mother stumbled into the room, eyes puffy with sleep, wearing an oversized, grey Colorado State University t-shirt that nearly reached her knees. "Wha— what's going on?" she demanded.

"I don't know!" Willow grabbed the plate of toast before Matilda knocked it to the floor. "She just started yelling."

Willow's mom kneeled next to the easy chair, putting a hand on the woman's frail shoulders. "Calm down, now. Everything is okay."

"No, no, no," Aunt Matilda shook her head. "Not okay. Not!"

"Children, go upstairs please," Willow's mom ordered, voice stern and sharp.

"Mom," Willow protested, but her mother interrupted.

"Willow, please. Let me handle this."

Willow grabbed Ben by the hand and pulled him out of the room. But instead of going upstairs like her mother asked, she paused halfway down the hallway, in front of the room that her mom used as a home office. She gave Ben a sly look. "There are other ways of finding out about that old hotel."

Fetching a folding chair from the closet for Ben, Willow rolled the high-back office chair up to the shabby brown desk where her mother's computer sat. "Canton ... Hotel ..." she said aloud as she typed the words into the search bar. She clicked through the results, finding a couple of posts that mentioned the hotel briefly, mostly in historical references to the area, but no great detail.

She sighed, disappointed. "Maybe it's been too long since it closed down." Willow held the whistle, her thumb rubbing the markings etched on the bottom. It gave Ben an idea.

"Let's try this." Ben slid the mouse closer, clicking to clear the search bar. He typed in "whistle." That brought up 30 million results, the top hits showing little pictures of the kind of whistle a coach or referee might use.

He pointed to the whistle. "How would you describe those carvings?"

Willow studied the whistle. "I've always thought they kind of look like a dragon."

Ben nodded. "Yeah, I can see that. Let's add dragon to the search and see what comes up."

Willow typed, then took the mouse back and scrolled down. "Wait ... what's this? Dragonography.com?"

"Click on it," Ben urged.

"It's all about dragons. Look, there's a search box for the site." Willow typed in the words "whistle" and "Colorado." The site repopulated with articles featuring those words. "Look, there's one about Cheyenne Mountain."

"Well, click on it!"

They both silently read the article.

According to ancient Ute legend, there is a place in Colorado where a dragon is trapped beneath the earth. Thousands of years ago, people were anxious to leave their earthly existence behind and asked the gods if they could go to Heaven. It made the gods angry that people didn't appreciate the wondrous gifts they had been given. So the gods sent a great flood that covered everything, almost to the mountaintops. Only one man and one woman survived this flood, swimming through the flood waters for days on end until they found a giant cornstalk that helped them stay afloat as the waters rose over the mountain peaks. The survival of this man and woman pleased the gods who decided these two would begin a new family of people on the earth.

"Sounds like a strange version of Adam and Eve," Ben frowned.

Willow picked up from that point, reading aloud. "The gods sent down from the Heavens a very thirsty dragon to drink up the floodwaters. He drank and drank and slowly the waters receded. But the dragon's body swelled as he drank. Worried that the dragon might drink all the water on earth, the gods turned the dragon to stone. He became Cheyenne Mountain."

They looked at each other. "That is so cool!" Willow said.

Ben nodded, reading on to the end of the article. "You can see the dragon if you look closely at the peak: his horns, his flat head, his water-logged body, and even his spines."

"Nothing about a whistle, though. Let's go back to Google and see what else we can find," Willow said. When the images of referee whistles returned to the screen, Ben grabbed Willow's hand to stop her from clicking further.

"Wait, look at that." He took the mouse and double clicked on the picture, zooming in. "Do you see what's inside the whistle?"

She studied the image on the screen. Then she nodded. "There's something inside the hole."

"A whistle like that needs that little ball thing to work. I wonder if that's what the pearl on the string is for?" Willow took the whistle from around her neck and they studied the pea-sized sphere connecting the silken cord.

"Could be," Willow said.

"Try putting the pearl on the cord into that hole on the top of the whistle," Ben urged. Willow dropped the pearl into the opening on top of the whistle. It fit, with enough room for it to move a bit.

They looked at each other and grinned.

Willow put the whistle to her lips and blew gently. What came out was the most pure and beautiful sound either of them had ever heard, a single note shimmering in the air like something solid and real. It rang on and on, even after Willow stopped blowing.

Willow stared at him in rapt silence.

In the den, Matilda screamed.

CHAPTER 14

TIERNAN HAD ONLY BEEN gone fifteen minutes when they saw the smoke. Faylene stared at Drynfyre through the Plexiglas. The dragon's temperature was now so consistently over 110 they'd had to cut power to the alarm system to keep it from going off. Drynfyre still hadn't twitched a scale but now tiny tendrils of smoke snaked from her nostrils.

"Room temperature?" Faylene barked, even though the display on the console right in front of her flashed 115.

"115," Coreen confirmed, as if Faylene had no other way of knowing. "Correction. 116."

"It's actually happening," Faylene breathed. She tapped on her cell phone, raising it to her ear without ever taking her eyes from the dragon. "Any luck?" she asked when Tiernan answered.

"The pulse has quickened as I've moved farther east. What's happening there?"

"Temp is 116 and there is smoke seeping from Drynfyre's nostrils."

After a pause, Tiernan responded. "Whoa. I just can't believe it …"

Without acknowledging the fear she heard in the young Guardian's voice, Faylene snapped, "Focus on your task. We need to find that Pfife."

WILLOW'S MOTHER WAVED them away but Willow and Ben stood transfixed as Aunt Matilda thrashed in the chair. Willow had no idea the elderly woman could move that way. It was almost comical, but so horrifying that it killed any laughter.

She pulled Ben into the hallway. "Oh my gosh, Ben! It was the whistle! That's why she's freaking out! I bet that's why she freaked out earlier, too." Willow pulled the string loose from the collar of her tee shirt. "She saw it."

"I'm sure it's just a coincidence," Ben said, following her toward the stairs.

"I don't believe in coincidences. Think about it, Ben! We found that whistle in the same hotel where her father worked. She freaked out when she saw me wearing it and now, when we finally figure out how to play it, she completely loses it?" Willow points down the hall toward the kitchen and stopped. "Too big a coincidence to be a coincidence, in my opinion."

Silence fell in the other room. Ben sighed. "Your mom must have calmed her down."

Willow headed up the stairs. "C'mon. I want to take a closer look at that case of papers we found with the whistle. I have a theory."

Ben followed Willow to her bedroom, standing in the doorway as removed the folded leather case from her backpack. She spread it flat on her bed and untied the string, fanning out the yellowed pages. "I think this is music." Willow traced her fingers along the three horizontal lines. "See? These lines are connected on the left side, just like a staff."

Moving to stand beside her, Ben considered what she'd said. "I don't know. Maybe."

"Well, there are only three lines instead of five, so it doesn't look exactly like a regular staff. But what if these lines here are notes?" Willow pointed to the series of vertical marks slashed across the horizontal lines. "I mean, there aren't any note heads, just stems, but still ... they could be notes."

"No flags either, how would you count the rhythm?" Ben mused. "Wait a minute. Look at the bottom of the stems. They rest on different lines. This one on the first line and this one on the third? And this one stops on the space between. Maybe that's the note? It might just be random, or —"

"Or it could be the note."

Willow dug in her backpack for a short, stubby pencil and lightly sketched small ovals at the bottom ends of the lines. "There," she said. "That's better. It really does look like music."

"That has to be what it is," Ben agreed.

"There are no measures, either." Willow scratched her cheek with the eraser end of the pencil. "Let's say it's 4/4 time, so you'd played each note as a beat." Willow patted on the bed to demonstrate, humming along. Ben moved closer to sit on the bed, his finger following across the music, touching each note as she hummed it.

"That's totally it," he said as Willow reached the end of the page. "Can you play it on the whistle?"

The challenge bubbled nervous excitement in her belly. "I don't know, maybe. Woodwinds aren't really my thing, but I have played the flute a couple of times. My best friend Emma plays the flute in orchestra, and we've swapped instruments a couple of times. Of course, this whistle is more like a recorder. But I don't know which fingering matches which notes on the page. Or even which notes are which." She looked back down at the music again wishing everything she just said wasn't true.

70

"Willow, you have perfect pitch. If you play a note, you'll know what it is."

"I can tell by the sound, but with only three lines on this staff, I can't connect the sound to what's written down."

Ben thought about this. "We need a tuner. Hey, I bet there's an app for that."

"Good thinking!"

As they waited for it to download onto Ben's phone, they studied the music some more. "What if this staff is just the top three lines of a normal staff?"

Willow shrugged. "Good place to start." When the app was downloaded, Ben tapped a few buttons until the phone produced a pitch.

"That's middle C," he said.

Willow closed her eyes, as Ben played the note a few more times. "Okay," she said. "Got it."

She placed the pearl inside the whistle. "Okay, so let's see which fingering plays middle C." She positioned her fingers over all three of the holes along the whistle's length and blew gently, making a high, sweet sound. Willow frowned. "Nope, I think that's F." A tap on the tuner app confirmed she was right.

"Try leaving the middle hole open," Ben suggested. Willow did, but that wasn't right either. The tuner told them the note was A.

"Okay," Willow sighed. This time, she covered only the first hole, leaving the second and third open. She played the note a little louder than she had the first two, but gave a little cheer as soon as she heard the pitch. "Yes! That's C!"

"Okay," Ben figured, "if this staff is the top three lines of a regular staff, and that first note is C, then you can play the tune as long as we figure out the fingering for each note, right?"

"I think so ..." Willow grinned. It was like the most excellent puzzle code ever; one she was determined to crack. "If those were the top three lines, then that first note would be a C. The next note is F." She covered all three holes with her fingers again and blew. "Yep. That's F."

They both sat quietly for a moment, deciphering the music. "If that's a C and this one is F, that means the next note should be E. Since it's a half-step down from F, maybe the fingering ..."

She covered the first hole again, but only half of the second one. A tentative blow proved her theory correct. "Okay, I think I'm getting this."

Using this same procedure, Willow figured out the next few notes until she had the first line completely deciphered. "I think I can put it all together now," Willow grinned, lifting the whistle to her lips.

"No!" The voice screeched so loud it made Willow drop the whistle and clap her hands over her ears. "Stop playing! STOP!"

Aunt Matilda stood in the bedroom doorway, that same expression of wide-eyed horror on her face. She pointed a skinny accusing finger at Willow. "You must not! YOU MUST NOT!" she screeched before collapsing.

TIERNAN SPUN THE WHEEL to the right and drove down another street, glancing at the Amulet hanging from the rearview mirror. The pulse remained steady, so after a few blocks Tiernan braked and made a U-Turn.

Three hours of driving around Colorado Springs and she'd gone through almost an entire tank of gas—Pfife hunting sure wasn't doing anything to curb global warming. She was about to stop and fill up the tank, when there was a quickening in the Amulet's beat.

The Pfife had to be close! It was only a matter of time until she found it. But would it be soon enough?

CHAPTER 15

BEN MOVED OUT OF the way so that the tall, dark-skinned paramedic could shut the ambulance doors. Seeing Aunt Matilda lying on the stretcher with the oxygen mask on her face as the paramedics loaded her into the ambulance made him want to throw up.

"You'll need to ride your bikes to dad's office," Aunt Amanda instructed Willow, her voice amazingly calm. "Marcus can't give you a ride, he's stuck at the store. Uncle Josh will meet me at the hospital. I'll call your cell as soon as we know something." She put her hands on Willow's cheeks. "Promise me, you'll ride straight to dad's office?" she asked.

Willow blinked back tears. "I promise." Her mom pulled her into a hug and kissed the top of her head. "I love you, sugar."

Ben's stomach twisted harder and he suddenly missed his mom so much it was ridiculous.

They watched Aunt Amanda drive away, her car following the ambulance. "She's going to be fine," said Willow softly.

"Yeah, of course she will." The words felt like a lie, but he knew it was the right thing to say. "I can't believe that just happened.

"I still don't see how she got up the stairs. Mom says she just stepped into the bathroom for a minute." Willow looked at Ben, dropping her voice. "You heard what she said, right? Before she fainted?"

"Yeah," Ben sighed. "I heard. But I can't believe that whistle has anything to do with this. Don't you think it's probably the Alzheimer's?"

Willow ran her fingers along the whistle's cord, hanging around her neck. "I don't know. It's all so strange."

"I feel so bad. I hope she'll be okay." Ben swallowed hard. It was getting tough to keep the tears from coming. He squeezed his eyes shut, but then he saw his mom in his mind, smiling at him, and that made him want to cry even more. Willow slipped her hand in his and squeezed.

Ben didn't know what to say, so he didn't say anything. Willow had never done anything like that before. He squeezed back. Things had definitely changed between them since camp, and especially since they found the whistle.

"We should get to dad's office. Mom will worry if I take too long to let her know we're there."

"I need to use the bathroom first," Ben said.

"I'll get the bikes."

Ben ran up the stairs to the bathroom. After doing what he needed to do, he grabbed his backpack out of his room and paused at Willow's bedroom door. The sheets of music were still spread all over the bed, forgotten in the chaos of Aunt Matilda. He gathered the pages, secured them in the leather case, and slipped it into his backpack.

They coasted their bikes out of the driveway, gliding downhill to turn left at the intersection. The morning was sunny but not too warm; the perfect kind of summer day for a ride if only the dark cloud of what had happened with Aunt Matilda wasn't hanging over them. After the morning's events, it felt strange to be doing something so ordinary.

Ten minutes later, they arrived at Uncle Grant's "office." Cheyenne Mountain Productions, where he worked as a producer, operated out of a restored Victorian mansion formerly owned by a wealthy Denver widow back in the early 20th century. As they pulled up out front, Willow dismounted her bike next to the short white picket fence that ran along the lawn's perimeter.

"Cool place, right?" Willow said. "Dad says years ago there used to be an amazing view of the foothills, until they built those apartments across the street." She glared at the four-story building like it had no right to be there. "These days, only place around here with a good view of the mountains is up at the park."

They leaned their bikes against the fence and clomped up the squeaky stairs to the big wrap-around porch. The house was quite impressive, although Ben imagined it was pretty creepy at night. Willow opened the front door, and Ben discovered the inside was just as well preserved as the exterior. "Each room is a different edit suite," Willow explained. "They make commercials and movies here, but mostly commercials. This new zombie movie is kind of a big deal. Dad's office is upstairs, c'mon."

Ben followed her up the big wooden staircase. "Hey guys," Uncle Grant said, a sympathetic smile on his face. "Gosh, sure sorry to hear what happened to Matilda. I bet you're pretty shaken up, huh?" Ben shrugged and nodded, not sure what to say. "Hope you don't mind hanging out while I finish up some work," Uncle Grant went on. "I dug up a deck of cards … or there's the Xbox, if you prefer." Didn't have to ask Ben twice. He plopped down in the chair and grabbed the remote. He didn't want to think about Matilda anymore and some 2K would be a perfect escape.

A soft fragrant breeze drifted in through the tall-framed double windows, ruffling Ben's hair. Willow sat in the other black chair, turning it in lazy circles with the toes of her Chucks while Ben set up his virtual basketball team.

The desk phone shrilled and Uncle Grant kept his eyes on the computer screen as he answered. "Grant McLain," he said, tucking the receiver against his shoulder so he could use both hands to type. Then he stopped typing. "What's that? Now? Oh, right. No, no it's fine. Three minutes." He hung up and stood, digging in his pocket for a wad of money. He motioned toward Willow. "Sorry, guys. Need to have an emergency meeting in here. Here, run down to the corner shop and get a smoothie why don't ya?"

WILLOW SUGGESTED THEY TAKE their smoothie up to Broadmoor Crest Park. "We could try and see the dragon in Cheyenne Mountain, like in that article we read online?"

After leaving Smoothie Lu's, they walked their bikes up the steep hill to the small neighborhood park. Wheeling their bikes with one hand wasn't easy, but the park was worth the trouble. Its thick grass was in need of a mow, still heavy with dew even though the sun had climbed to mid-morning. Tall evergreens stood sentry along the edges, separating the park from the neighboring houses. A small playground nestled between the single basket half-court and the street. When they reached the fork in the sidewalk, Willow went left into the park. Right led to the last house at the top of the hill. They made their way to the western edge where three picnic tables perched near a scenic overlook, a picture-perfect view of the southwestern part of the city and mountains beyond.

Willow pointed out the sights. At the view's far left was The Broadmoor Hotel, its green patches of golf course stretching farther south along the foothills. Straight ahead was the massive northern face of Cheyenne Mountain. Then Willow pointed toward the base of the mountain. "Right over there is a tunnel to an underground military base."

"NORAD?" Ben guessed.

"How'd you know?"

"I saw War Games," he said, surprised when she looked at him blankly.

"Really?" He was shocked. "Your dad is in the film business and you've never seen War Games? It's a classic. Never mind. Anyway, I thought the army closed it down," Ben said.

"Nah, it's not closed, but it's just not the big deal is used to be, I guess. Like back whenever that movie War Games was made."

"It's pretty good, we should watch it sometime."

They dropped their bikes on the grass and sat on top of a picnic table, talking more about their favorite movies. During a lull in the conversation, Willow studied the mountain. "I totally see it," Willow said.

Ben slurped loudly. "Not me."

"Seriously? It's right there!" Willow said, tossing her empty cup into a recycle bin a few feet away. "Okay, the angle is kind of funky from here, but you can kind of see the dragon shape." She pointed. "Start way over there on the left—that's the nose. The mountain ridge is his spine. Then down more toward us, there's the tail."

Ben stared, squinting, then shook his head again, frustrated. "I still don't see it."

"You have no imagination," Willow rolled her eyes.

"Hey, don't let me forget to get my book when we go back to your dad's office," Ben reminded her. "I keep forgetting."

"Okay."

Willow fished the whistle out of her shirt.

"I brought the music with me," Ben said, reaching for his backpack.

"I don't think I need it …" Willow murmured, putting the whistle to her lips. Ben found his heartbeat picking up at the thought of hearing Willow play the whistle, which he found strange. From the first note, he felt himself relax. The pure, sweet sound of the melody floated out over the park, drifting through the evergreen branches, mingling with the bird song. There was a comforting quality to it, like hearing something you remember being sung to you from babyhood.

"Keep playing," Ben said when Willow paused, the sense of awe making him tingly. "It's amazing."

Willow lifted the whistle to her lips again, but before she could play the first note, someone screamed, "Stop!" The voice was rabid with panic. "STOP!"

Whirling toward the street, Ben saw a girl who looked about high school age leap out of an open-topped red Jeep. She raced across the grass toward them. The girl was tall, lean and tan, with long curly dark hair that streamed behind her as she ran. Her clothing was like cosplay, or something out of *Widershins and the Angel*—a light brown belted tunic, slim black pants and leather boots that looked way too hot for the summer day.

"STOP!" she screamed again.

"Ben?" Willow grabbed his arm. Ben stood up, the urge to run vibrating through him.

And then some kind of explosion ripped open the side of Cheyenne Mountain.

Across the valley, debris tumbled down the side of the mountain, raining like shrapnel as a winged creature took to the sky with a triumphant roar. Ben's eyes tried to confirm what he saw, but his brain refused to accept the assignment. Willow screamed, putting a word to his fear.

"DRAGON! It's a dragon!"

Yes, it was. It was a dragon. A magnificent, enormous dragon circled over the valley, sunlight glimmering off its silver scales. It roared, belching fire into the sky.

This is what it means to be paralyzed by fear, Ben thought. He didn't even realize the girl who had screamed STOP was standing beside him until she spoke.

"No," she moaned. "I'm too late! No, no, no, this can't be happening!" The girl whirled on Willow. "This is all your fault!"

Willow visibly jumped. "Me? What'd I do?"

Ignoring Willow's question, the girl grabbed her arm. "You did this. And you have to fix it."

"Get your hands off me!" Willow squawked, yanking her arm out of the girl's grasp.

"Leave Willow alone!" Ben demanded, a surge of protectiveness welling up inside of him. His eyes dropped to the whistle in Willow's hands and he realized those dark markings on its underside were now glowing a deep, burning red. He glanced up at the girl to see her eyes follow his gaze to the whistle in Willow's hand.

"You have no idea what you're talking about." She grabbed Willow by the shoulders and spun her so she was facing the dragon as it soared over the valley. "That dragon is awake because you woke her. Which means Willow here is the only one who can put her back to sleep." The girl heaved a sigh, her expression suddenly more sad than angry. "Congratulations, Willow. You're a Dragon Whistler."

"A what??" Willow gulped.

"Who ARE you, anyway?" Ben demanded, stepping between the girl and Willow.

The girl pushed past them toward the fence at the edge of the overlook. The dragon soared in lazy circles, long neck craned toward the ground. "Oh that's just great. She's spotted the zoo. This is not good. So. Not. Good."

Willow and Ben couldn't help but join her at the fence. This had to be some kind of stunt, like a robotic dragon or something. Maybe they were shooting a movie. Certainly Willow's dad would have known about something of this magnitude.

"We've got to go. Now!" The girl reached for the whistle but Willow back-stepped quickly.

"Keep away!" she barked.

Ben couldn't believe what he did next. It was like someone else had stepped into his body and took over. He swung his backpack at the girl, making her stumble, then dragged Willow toward the bikes. "Run!" he screamed. By time they were pedaling down the path, the girl had recovered and was racing after them. "Wait, please you've gotta stop! I'm not going to hurt you! I need your help, please!"

Furiously pumping the pedals, leg muscles screaming with the effort, Ben focused on the sidewalk before him, riding as close to Willow's back tire as he dared. If they went much faster he would lose control and end up in a heap of blood and bones. The downward slope of the hill made them go even faster. Ben allowed himself a peek over his shoulder, wishing he had gone ahead and worn his bike helmet. The girl was back in her Jeep. She'd catch up fast.

"Don't stop until we get to Dad's office!" Willow yelled.

They barely slowed to turn at the base of the hill. Thankfully, the sidewalk was clear. They were in view of the old house now. Almost there.

A roar echoed in the sky above them.

She'd said it was Willow's fault. How could it be Willow's fault?

His brain kept asking the question and he kept ignoring it, focused on pedaling. And what was a Dragon Whistler, anyway? Could this actually be about the whistle from the hotel?

They skidded to a stop in front of Cheyenne Mountain Productions and dumped their bikes before racing through the front door and up the stairs to the second floor. Uncle Grant was on the phone, but at least there weren't a bunch of movie executives in his office.

"What—!" he admonished as they burst through his office door.

Willow and Ben both started talking at once, breathless but frantic with adrenaline. Uncle Grant stared at them. "WHOA! I can't understand a single word you're saying!" They both clammed up, looking at each other. Willow's eyes filled with tears. Her whole body trembled and Ben felt his knees doing the same. Uncle Grant spoke into the phone again. "Kate, let me call you back. Something's going on over here."

"Dad! Oh, Dad, there's a …" Willow bent over, trying to catch her breath so she could talk. "You won't believe it," she gasped.

"Try me," he demanded.

"There's a dragon flying over the zoo, hunting for lunch," Ben blurted. Well … he'd asked.

For a split second, it was as if someone had paused the scene. Then Uncle Grant burst out laughing. "You kids are hilarious. Such imaginations. You almost had me there."

"Daaaa-aaaaad," Willow panted, taking hold of his arm and pulling him closer. "I promise you. This is not a joke."

Uncle Grant sighed heavily, his smile evaporating.

"Willow …" Now he sounded exasperated. "I was on an important call—"

A flurry of activity in the hallway made him pause. Amid loud exclamations of protest, the girl from the park appeared in the office doorway. A tall, leggy woman with long, straight blonde hair teetered in after her, barely staying upright on her platform pumps. "Mr. McLain," she squeaked, smoothing her red skirt and white blouse. "I'm so sorry! I tried to stop her, but she said it had to do with the children …"

"It's okay, Vicky." Uncle Grant stood up and moved toward the girl. "Can I help you?"

The girl ignored him, speaking to Willow. "I know you are probably really scared right now, but you have to understand, you are the only person who can stop this."

"Uh, excuse me," Uncle Grant waved a hand in front of the girl's face. "Who exactly are you?"

"She thinks Willow let the dragon out," Ben explained, his voice rising in pitch as his panic resurfaced.

"Okay, that's enough of the dragon stuff," Uncle Grant growled. "I want to know what's going on, and I want to know right now."

The girl glared at Uncle Grant, her expression every bit as serious as his. She marched over to the television in the corner. "You want to know what's going on?" She switched on the TV and crossed her arms as Uncle Grant's jaw hit the floor.

CHAPTER 16

BREAKING NEWS TRACKED across the bottom of TV screen in all caps. That was never good.

Willow swallowed hard as the news announcer told them an "enormous unidentified bird" was seen flying over the Cheyenne Mountain Zoo, that there were reports of an attack.

Willow had been trying to convince herself this was all some horrible dream, but there it was, on the news, so it must be real. An honest-to-goodness dragon flew through in the skies above them at this moment and, somehow, she was to blame. She didn't know how, but this girl thought she had something to do with it.

"That's absurd. It must be a stunt!" Her dad grabbed the remote and thumbed the mute button. A cacophony of shouting, screaming, car doors slamming and car brakes squealing flowed in through the open window— and were suddenly eclipsed by a deep, throaty roar.

Her dad looked at the girl, then Ben. Then Willow.

"I saw it, Dad," Willow nodded. "It really is a dragon."

He turned back to Ben. "It's no bird, that's for sure," he said.

The girl put a hand over her mouth and her eyes filled with tears. "I can't believe this is happening," she moaned. "If only I'd found you one minute sooner. Just one minute!"

The girl had called her a Dragon Whistler. A Whistler.

The whistle.

Willow had forgotten all about it after their mad escape from the park. She'd shoved it into her pocket. Now she dangled it by the cord. "Is this why you called me a Dragon Whistler?"

The girl ignored her question. "Where did you get the Pfife?" She stepped toward Willow, hand out. Willow backed toward the window, looping the cord over her head, tucking the whistle safely back inside her shirt.

"All right, hold up here," her dad said, before she could answer. "So you're saying that thing flying over the Springs is a … dragon? A dragon. Like in fairytales?"

The girl nodded, serious.

"Nah, that just can't be right." Willow's dad chuckled, but the laugh was false and a little bit mental. He looked at the TV again, where the unmistakable image of a dragon moved in and out of focus as a camera lens tracked its flight. "That … can't …" His conviction deteriorated with each word. "Be."

"Listen," the girl said, taking another step toward Willow. "We really don't have time to argue about whether or not you believe your eyes. We need to get that dragon back into her den and back into hibernation. Unfortunately, Willow is the only one who can do that."

Willow's dad whirled back to her. "What does Willow have to do with all this?" Then he whirled on Willow. "And where did you get that thing around your neck?"

Willow grabbed her dad's arm again, more gently. If he found out she and Ben had snuck back into that hotel, she'd be in so much trouble.

The girl took a deep breath. "My name is Tiernan Kettleman. I'm a Dragon Guardian. I wish there was more time to explain, but time is one thing we really don't have right now. I get it, you have no reason to trust me, but it's extremely important that you come with me. You and the Pfife can fix everything."

Willow's brain fired, suddenly connecting the dots. "OMG! It all makes sense!" She grabbed Ben's arm. "It's the Cheyenne Mountain dragon! Just like in the legend."

"Oh, girl," Tiernan said, weary. "You have no idea."

BEN AND WILLOW LOOKED at each other as they buckled their seatbelts in the back seat of Tiernan's red Jeep. What was that sound? The hum wasn't any louder than the chaos erupting throughout the neighborhood but, somehow, it could simply be heard above the yelling and screaming.

People streamed into the streets, some of them ran up the hill toward the park. Willow wished they weren't so eager to see the dragon for themselves. Personally, she wished she could un-see it.

Well, that wasn't exactly true. As terrifying as all this was, and even though everything in her demanded she run away from the creature, there was a part of her that thought going after it was a fantastic idea, in fact, maybe the most awesome thing ever done in the history of the world.

Good thing, because that's exactly what they were doing.

Tiernan turned the key, pausing to touch a polished black rock hanging around her rearview mirror. The stone pulsed in time with the humming sound. Willow was entranced. What was that?

Tiernan grabbed a cell phone from the console between the seats and slipped the earphone into her ear. Lurching into traffic, she carefully maneuvered through the crowded streets. "I have the Pfife," she shouted to the person on the phone. "The Whistler is with me ... I know ... I understand, but ... Faylene, the Whistler, she's—" Tiernan glanced in the rearview mirror, meeting Willow's eyes. "She's a kid," she finished, her voice breaking despite her outwardly calm appearance. "I'll be there in ten minutes, maybe less."

"Okay, I want an explanation now," Willow's dad barked as Tiernan turned a little too quickly onto Cheyenne Mountain Boulevard, swerving to avoid the crowds of gawking pedestrians staring upwards.

Tiernan gripped the wheel tight. "Okay, this is all classified, secret stuff, but if you're going to help us, I suppose you have a right to know."

"You bet we do," Willow's dad growled.

"Okay, well, here's the quick version since we're kind of in a hurry. Fifteen hundred years ago, dragons were hunted nearly to extinction. A powerful sorceress named Kareth stepped in to protect them." Tiernan steered around two cars stopped in the middle of the street. Another roar ripped through the air as they zoomed past the Shop N' Sell. Mr. Botana stood in the parking lot, staring up at the sky. Willow watched him until she couldn't see him anymore. He never moved.

"So, dragons have always been real?" Ben asked.

"Yes, at one time, there were thousands, scattered around the world," Tiernan answered. "When there started to be more people around, there started to be problems between them and the dragons. People became afraid of the dragons, and you know what happens when human beings are afraid of something."

They were outside of town now, the only buildings some new neighborhoods still under construction. Soon, they'd left even those behind.

Tiernan went on, talking about as fast as she drove. "Well, Kareth believed a time would come when dragons and humans could co-exist again, like they had before. And since dragons hibernated during the warm season, she thought if she could convince them it was in their best interest to hibernate for an extended period of time, she could then awaken them when people stopped being so ridiculous and afraid. Kareth was able to connect with the dragons, using two magic Amulets," Tiernan touched the gem hanging from the rearview mirror again. "This is one of them. Part of what we do is to protect these Amulets, but its twin disappeared about a hundred and fifty years ago, along with that Pfife you have around your neck, Willow."

Tiernan suddenly whirled toward Willow. "You don't have the other Amulet, do you?"

"Watch where you're driving!" Willow's dad barked, grabbing for the steering wheel. Tiernan faced forward again, making a tight turn onto a dirt road. As she fought for control, the Jeep fishtailed, tires kicking up gravel and dust. Willow and Ben screamed. Her dad grabbed the metal bar mounted on the dashboard, like he was riding a rollercoaster.

"I've got it!" Tiernan yelled. "Don't worry!"

The Jeep zoomed into the foothills, slowing only for switchbacks as they headed toward the northernmost part of the mountain.

"What is that sound?" Willow's dad asked, sounding like he was on the edge of panic.

"That's the Amulet. It's how I found you," Tiernan continued. "Like I said, the Amulets have a magical link to the Pfifes, and each Pfife is then magically linked to a dragon."

"Magic. Right." Willow's dad laughed that high-pitched laugh again. "This is not happening." He still held onto the bar, his fingers turning white he held it so tightly. "Where are you taking us?" he demanded, looking around. "Old Stage Road doesn't go anywhere!"

"Exactly," Tiernan answered as the road curved to the left. The dragon appeared over the trees before them, flying low and close.

"There it is!" her dad yelled, as if they all couldn't see it. As if he hadn't quite believed it before. "Oh my God, it's real."

Tiernan steered through into another switchback as the dragon zoomed past overhead. The open-top Jeep allowed a perfect view of its underbelly, scales glistening like they'd been oiled. The fibrous silver wings stretched wide and, even from the ground, Willow could see the thick talons curling from the dragon's feet.

It was like getting buzzed at some kind of medieval airshow.

The dragon had to be over a hundred feet in the air above them, but it seemed much closer. Its serpentine head tilted and looked down at them, enormous nostrils trailing smoke. Willow wondered what the dragon thought about cars. After all, nothing like them had existed before the dragon went into hibernation. Did it see them as a threat? Or, God forbid, a snack to be roasted and eaten?

The dragon banked right and disappeared around a hillside of thick trees.

"Holy wow!" Ben crowed. "That was incredibly terrifying but also SO COOL!" Willow was shocked that Ben could get beyond what was scary to what was amazing. The two of them exchanged a stunned grin.

Tiernan threw Ben a look that made Willow think she felt the same way. "She's amazing, isn't she?"

Willow's dad wasn't as impressed with the whole situation. He started in on the interrogation again. "How is it possible we didn't know about this?" he barked, not bothering to hide the accusation in his voice.

"Keeping the dragons hidden was kind of the point, and we've got centuries of practice doing it," Tiernan answered, her voice filled with pride. "Kareth charged us to watch over the sleeping dragons until they could be reawakened. In hibernation, they were vulnerable. That's when most of them were killed off before. She knew there were people who'd try to take advantage of their dormancy to kill them off for good. The first Guardians were warriors. They physically protected the dragons when anyone found the den. As years went by, the locations of the dens weren't as known, and people forgot. Eventually, people stopped believing they ever existed in the first place."

As they continued to twist and turn up the mountain, alternately snaking through sections of forest so thick the pines blocked the sky, and fields barren of anything but brush, Ben and Willow continued to pepper Tiernan with excited questions. She told them about the seven dragon dens, guarded by Kareth's descendants. How Kareth flew all over the globe on her dragon partner Mysendrake to convince the dragons this hibernation was their saving grace. She explained about the Council of Elders who was in charge of deciding when the dragon Awakening would happen.

"It would be awesome if the world had dragons again," Ben said.

Tiernan raised an eyebrow. "You think today's world could live in peace with seven giant fire-breathing beasts? We can't even live in peace with ourselves."

Ben frowned like this made him sad. The thought sure made Willow sad. "The government would want to use them as a weapon," her dad said, and for the first time, Willow sensed he was coming to terms with what was happening and why.

Tiernan shifted gears as the road flattened out, picking up speed on a flat section of road that moved out of the trees. "Tell me about the whistle," Willow said.

"We call them Pfifes. Each instrument has Songs that only work when played on that particular Pfife. Those Songs control the dragon."

Driving into a hillside tunnel, they plunged into darkness for a moment. "So I guess you have the music, since you played the Awakening Song and all."

"There was a case of papers with the Pfife," Ben said carefully, exchanging a look with Willow that silently asked how much Willow wanted to reveal. "I have it in my backpack," Ben said.

"How in the world did you know how to play it?" Tiernan marveled.

"Willow figured it out," Ben said. "She has perfect pitch."

Willow felt her cheeks grow warm as she met Tiernan's eyes in the rearview mirror and saw admiration there. "No kidding? Impressive."

They approached a guard post at the top of the hill, but Tiernan didn't ease off the gas. The guard seemed to be waiting for her, and waved them through with frantic encouragement. Tiernan finally brought the

Jeep to a jerking stop in a parking lot next to a small building. There were a few cars and pick up trucks parked there already.

"Listen, I wish I could use the Pfife and Songs and Amulet to fix all this without having to involve you. But since Willow is the one who woke Drynfyre, she is her Whistler now. Nobody else can make the magic work."

Willow's dad shook his head, his tone of disbelief returning. "You keep talking about magic, but c'mon! There's no such thing."

Tiernan slipped the Amulet from the rearview mirror, and put it around her neck, giving him a pointed look. "I'll bet you thought the same thing about dragons before today, too."

CHAPTER 17

BEN WATCHED TIERNAN tap a series of numbers into a keypad outside the small brick building, unlocking the outer door. Inside, she picked up a black rotary phone, dialed a single number, paused, then said: "Kareth's secret."

On the far wall, a set of elevator doors opened.

This was all so unreal and strange, but also extremely cool. Clandestine, even. That was the perfect word, clandestine. It was a vocab word last year, a synonym for "secret." If this all wasn't so completely terrifying, he might have felt slightly spy-licious.

Tiernan ushered them quickly into the elevator. "Grab something and hold on," Tiernan warned. "I'm not kidding." It was a good thing they listened and held onto the rail because seconds later the car lurched horizontally backwards, then slowed, paused and shot upward. But the unusual elevator ride was nothing compared to what they saw when the elevator doors slid open.

The area was in complete shambles. It appeared to be the remnants of a lab—one where some kind of experiment had gone horribly, explosively, wrong. The main room was the size of a school gym, but half its roof was missing. Sunshine and blue sky peeked through the gaping hole. Huge clumps of dirt and rock littered the floor. To the left, a glass-enclosed room stood miraculously unharmed, and it was from there that the older woman emerged.

Her face was as dirty as her dark green blouse and black pants. She picked her way through the debris in low-heeled pumps, another woman entering from the hallway to their right. This one had similar features to Tiernan, but with blonde hair cut super short and spikey.

"Aunt Coreen!" Tiernan rushed over to embrace the blonde woman. "Are you okay?"

"It all happened so fast," she answered, a deep tremor in her voice. "Thank God the Plexi held or who knows what would have happened. She seemed so angry ..."

"Coreen," the older woman barked, her tone a warning. She walked over to Willow, running her hands over her long, salt-and pepper hair, picking bits of debris from its ragged tendrils. Her expression was serious, eyes suspicious and narrow. She extended her hand, palm up. "The Pfife, if you don't mind," she demanded.

Ben looked at Tiernan. Who was this old lady?

The woman never took her eyes off Willow's face. "Do not make me repeat myself. Give me the Pfife. Now."

"Faylene," Tiernan said, moving to stand by Willow. "She didn't know what she was doing." Tiernan was defending her. That was surprising.

"There is no time for discussion now. We'll get the details of how and why this happened later." The woman, Faylene, held out her hand to Willow, snapping her fingers impatiently.

Willow pulled the Pfife from around her neck. She let it dangle it from its silken cord. Faylene snatched the Pfife. "The music as well."

Ben unzipped in his backpack and removed the leather case. Faylene took it, nodding curtly, her lips pressed into a tight line. She untied the leather strap, glanced inside, and quickly strode out of the room.

"I thought you said I was the only one who could use it?" Willow said.

"You are. She's … I don't know what she's doing."

Coreen introduced herself to them, shaking Willow's dad's hand as they followed Faylene down a short hallway to a conference room. She spread the music out over a long table. Faylene focused on Willow again, her words sharp. "How did you know how to read the music? Or play the Pfife for that matter? Who taught you?"

"Nobody taught me," Willow said. "I … I just figured it out."

The flat line of Faylene's mouth twitched angrily.

"Willow has perfect pitch," her dad explained, and Willow dropped her head to her chest. Why did everyone obsess over that?

Ben stepped closer to Willow, feeling protective. "I don't get it," he said. "Willow played the whistle—sorry, Pfife, miles away from here. Are you sure—"

"The Pfife has a wide magical radius," Faylene said, cutting him off. Ben's heart lurched like it always did when someone was rude to him. "The Whistler needs to command the dragon when it is in the air, miles above her sometimes. If you figured out how to play the Awakening Song, then you should be able to read this as well." Faylene slid a sheet of parchment across the table toward Willow.

"This is the Sleeping Song. When you play it, Drynfyre will return to her hibernation. It was crafted with a safety mechanism, to ensure a Whistler could not accidentally put a dragon into hibernation during flight. For it to take effect, the Whistler must have direct eye contact."

Willow swayed, like she might pass out. "Eye contact? With who?" she squeaked.

Faylene cocked her head, as if the answer was obvious. "With Drynfyre, of course."

CHAPTER 18

TIERNAN STEPPED UP behind Willow, putting a steadying hand on her shoulder. The poor kid looked like she might pass out. Her dad, however, looked furious. "No way, no how. I am not letting my daughter stand next to a ten-ton fire-breathing monster. Absolutely not."

"Closer to fifty tons, actually, and if you don't allow it, that monster will die," Faylene snapped at Willow's dad.

"Good!" he barked. "Then this nightmare will be over!"

"No!" Willow gasped. Tiernan's heart clutched. Faylene knew the idea would horrify Willow. No Whistler could stand by and let her dragon die.

"Faylene—" Tiernan began but the Elder cut her off.

"I just spent fifteen minutes on the phone convincing General Sorenson to unscramble the bombers he'd already scrambled to shoot Drynfyre down. Never mind that the firepower it would require to accomplish such a thing would destroy all of Colorado Springs. He agreed to begin evacuation procedures instead, but if we don't get that dragon back in this den in—" Faylene checked her watch, "—sixteen and a half minutes, the good General will wait no longer." She let those words sink in for a beat before continuing. "So there really is no time to argue about whether or not this child will do what must be done." Faylene held out the Pfife and two sheets of music to Willow. "Play this one first, it will draw her back to us," she said, putting one sheet on top of the other. "When she's here, you can play the second. Remember to look her in the eye." She turned to Tiernan. "Fetch your bow. If we succeed, the only thing that will be shot at that dragon will be the Amulet."

WILLOW COULD BARELY stand her legs shook so. Was this really happening? Was she responsible for waking Drynfyre? It seemed like it was true, and now everyone was counting on her to fix the situation. Her heart slammed against her ribcage so hard it made her entire chest cavity ache. She wasn't one to scare easily, but this was a whole new level of fear. But she had to help, whether she was scared or not. Whether her father wanted her to help or not. Hearing that Drynfyre would be blown out of the sky by some military bomb if she didn't … well, there was no way Willow could let that happen.

She was a Dragon Whistler. For the first time, Willow believed it. Back in her room, when they'd figured out the music, the words at the top of the page were undecipherable runes, but now, somehow, she could read them. She should tell someone this, but there was no time. Faylene dragged her out of the room, ignoring her dad's protests as Coreen tried to reassure him. "Theoretically, the Whistler is actually the safest person around the dragon. Since Willow is connected to Drynfyre now, she just has to play the songs and Drynfyre will respond."

"Theoretically doesn't make me feel any better," her dad growled.

But Coreen's words slowed Willow's heartbeat a bit. They felt true. She studied the notes of the two Songs as they returned to the large main room—the fingering seemed so simple and natural to her now. There was no deciphering needed. In fact, it seemed unbelievable that it was such a struggle to figure it out before.

Faylene took them into the main room, placing Willow right in the middle of the rubble near a huge pile of straw and dirt. It was stiflingly hot in here, smelling like scorched, musty campfires mingled with a distinctly animal scent that Willow guessed must be eau de dragon.

"Drynfyre did all this?" Ben asked, looking up at the hole in the roof.

"She made quite the exit," Faylene snapped, changing her mind and repositioning Willow near a door to some kind of glass-enclosed computer station filled with equipment. "That's better. Are you ready?" she asked.

"I think—" Willow began, but once again, Faylene didn't let her finish. Willow suspected she didn't really care whether Willow was ready or not.

"Tiernan get into position!" This was all happening all too fast, and Willow didn't know what else to do but what she was told. "The Summoning Song will call Drynfyre to you." Faylene indicated the top sheet of music. "Once she lands, Tiernan will shoot the Amulet at her and when it is in place, and ONLY when it is in place, get close enough to look Drynfyre straight in the eye when you play the Sleeping Song. That's this one," Faylene tugged on the corner of a second sheet. "That is the only way it will work."

Willow's throat was so tight it only allowed her to squeak out a single word. "Okay." How did they know this would work? It wasn't like any of them had ever tried it before.

Tiernan returned holding a polished, black crossbow. Faylene showed her how to fasten the Amulet at the front of the bow's firing mechanism. "Just a flip of this switch here …" she said, fingering some triggers on the sides that seemed to secrete a white web-like substance. "The Amulet will stick to her scales. Remember, aim for the infinity mark."

Faylene took a deep, resolute breath. "All right, young lady. Time for the performance of your life. The rest of you," she snapped her fingers at Ben, Willow's dad and Coreen, "I suggest a safer distance."

As they retreated behind the glass of the computer room, Tiernan crouched near the elevators behind a pile of rubble. Willow met Ben's eyes. He gave her an encouraging nod. She couldn't hold the music and play at the same time, so she sat on the floor, placing the Summoning Song to the left and the Sleeping Song to her right. She hoped she had memorized them both correctly, especially the Sleeping Song since she had to look the dragon in the eye while she was playing it. She was used to a bit more practice time than this.

With Tiernan ready, Willow popped the pearl into the Pfife and put her fingers into position. She took one last look at the music and began to play.

The melody's sweet sound echoed off the cavernous walls, the notes ringing through the air in a way that seemed like they were dripping with magic. Settling into the rhythm, Willow played the melody over and over, the Song flooding her senses. She closed her eyes; her mind whirling away to a beautiful place as the music took hold with a thunderous jolt.

I am here.

The voice in Willow's head zapped her back to reality. Her eyes popped open and then so did her mouth, abruptly cutting off the Song.

The silver dragon had landed. Right in front of her.

THE PFIFE MUSIC stirred those same awe-struck feelings in Ben that had come over him in the park. The mystical sound swept around him like a warm, fuzzy blanket, soothing his panic. As he and Uncle Grant crouched in the control room with the two Guardians listening to Willow play, someone's cell phone rang. Uncle Grant half-stood to dig the phone out of his pocket.

"Hello?" he loud-whispered into the phone. Wild-eyed and tense, he never took his eyes off his daughter. "Yeah, yeah, don't worry. He's right here with me." Uncle Grant cut his eyes at Ben, then immediately returned his gaze to Willow. Handing the phone to Ben, Uncle Grant said, "It's your dad."

Ben felt a stab of guilt. With everything going on his Dad would be so worried. Ben should have called him to let him know he was okay, but he hadn't had a moment to think much less think about that.

Reluctantly, Ben put the phone to his ear. What should he say? Hey, I really can't talk because that dragon you're watching on the news is headed this way? Something told him that was not a good idea.

"Hi, Dad."

"Ben!" His father's voice burst with so much relief the bubble of guilt in Ben's chest grew to a balloon. "Are you okay?"

Keeping his voice low, Ben said, "Yeah, Dad, I'm fine. Don't worry; we're with Uncle Grant. How's Aunt Matilda?"

"Uh, okay, good. Matilda is stable. She's sleeping now. Actually, she was doing much better except we had the stupid TV on in the room and she saw that dragon on the news. Doctor gave her something; she was so upset. It knocked her out." He paused. "This is so weird, like finding out the Loch Ness Monster is real except, you know, it can fly and breathe fire."

"Yeah," Ben sighed.

"So, Ben, you should know that before the nurses were able to sedate her ... Aunt Matilda was asking for you."

"Me?" Ben said, surprised. "She actually asked for me?"

"Yes. When she was all upset. She kept screaming your name."

Ben's heartbeat kicked up a couple of notches. What did that mean? "We'll try to get to the hospital as soon as we can, but we have to ... uh, do something ... first."

A deep whomp-whomp-whomp filled the room, the sound of giant wings pushing air downward to slow the decent of the dragon landing through the gaping hole in the mountain. For such an enormous creature, Drynfyre touched down with remarkable lightness.

"Ben? What was that?" his dad asked.

"Gotta go now, see you soon!" Ben ended the call. Normally, he would never hang up on his dad, but there was nothing normal about this moment. Not one single thing.

"Sweet mother of God," said Uncle Grant, his words leaking from him like the last air from a withered lung.

Ben wasn't so much paralyzed with fear for himself, but for Willow. She must not have realized the dragon had landed because she kept playing the Song, repeating the two stanzas in a never-ending loop.

Uncle Grant moaned, clasping his hands on top of his head as if trying to keep the panic from shooting right out the top. "Oh Lord, you people better be right about this. If anything happens to her ..." He couldn't even finish the sentence.

The two women beside them said nothing. Ben glanced over and was unnerved at Faylene's strange expression. Her eyes glowed with a determination and a fire that, had Ben known her better, might have concerned him.

CHAPTER 19

WILLOW OPENED HER eyes. She's talking in my head, she thought.

The voice came again. *You hear me? You understand my words?*

Willow stood up, staring into the dark purple eyes of the enormous silver dragon. Yes, I can hear you.

The Song you play on that little instrument. It draws me to you. Her eyes darkened to almost black. *I cannot resist. I do not like it that I cannot resist.*

I'm sorry, thought Willow. The Songs are Kareth's. I—

You know the Sorceress?

No ... I don't know her. She lived a long time ago—

Willow stopped, sensing the dragon's surprise.

How long have I slept? Drynfyre asked.

Willow tried to remember what Tiernan had told her. Quite a long time. Over a thousand years, I think.

Drynfyre's roar shook the room, causing chunks of dirt to skitter down the walls.

Willow felt Tiernan creeping up behind her and tried not to think about her in case Drynfyre might pick up on the plan. She pulled her gaze away from the dragon's mesmerizing eyes to find the infinity mark over Drynfyre's heart where Tiernan would shoot the Amulet. When Willow looked back at Drynfyre, she could tell the dragon had spotted Tiernan.

Tell the Guardian I will not harm you.

Willow swallowed hard. Had her thoughts given Tiernan away? Man, it was hard NOT to think of things. Like thinking about the crossbow Tiernan held, and how it wasn't to protect Willow, but to shoot the Amulet at Drynfyre. To put her back to sleep.

NO!

Drynfyre shook her head in protest, expelling fireballs from her nostrils that exploded against the glass of the monitoring station. One narrowly missed Tiernan, and only because she ducked.

I refuse to go back into that dreamless nothing of a world. I want to FLY!

But those people out there in the world will try to kill you! Willow thought. It's why Kareth hid you all away, remember? You are big and scary and people ... well, they always want to get rid of what scares them. Willow felt tears prick her eyes. It's all my fault you're awake in the first place. I'm so sorry, I didn't mean it. And I couldn't stand it if you got hurt because of I accidentally woke you up. Willow looked up into those purple eyes. They sparked with defiance.

Let them try to kill me! Drynfyre's words bellowed in her head so loud Willow startled, dropping the Pfife. It clinked to the floor and she scrambled to get it. Doing so, she gave Tiernan a clear shot.

Tiernan fired. The Amulet flew, striking the mark. The webbing fingered out, clinging to the scales, holding the gem tight to the spot. The dragon reared up in surprise. Drynfyre's outrage coursed through Willow, hijacking her emotions. She whirled on Tiernan.

"Stop it! You're hurting her!" she wailed.

"Play the Song!" Tiernan screamed.

Drynfyre bent and twisted, trying to reach the sticky arrow with her teeth, her tail whipshotting in every direction. Willow scrambled backward, clutching the Pfife and the music, nearly becoming a dragon tennis ball.

She had no choice. If Drynfyre managed to get away, those military people would shoot her down. Willow couldn't let that happen. Saving Drynfyre was the most important thing.

Willow glanced at the second sheet of music for a quick reminder of the simple melody, and then her fingers went to work on the Pfife. Her breath pushed the soft, sweet lullaby from the instrument, instantly drawing Drynfyre's attention away from the Amulet. Her eyes locked with Willows and suddenly the dragon calmed, slumping, her tail falling to the floor of the cave with sullen resolution.

Willow wasn't sure whether there was actual expression on Drynfyre's face or if she simply sensed the sorrow in her heart.

Please. Don't.

One massive leg buckled and then another until, with an earth-quaking rumble, Drynfyre collapsed.

CHAPTER 20

BEN RELEASED THE breath he hadn't even realized he was holding.

Was it over? The group stood silently staring at the fallen dragon. A trickle of rubble skittered down the wall. A shard of broken glass tinkled to the floor. A hawk's cry echoed through the cavernous opening in the roof. Ben heaved a sigh.

Willow had collapsed as well, hands over her face, shoulders quaking and breath hitching. The crossbow clattered to the ground as Tiernan rushed to her.

"Hey!" Tiernan pulled Willow into a hug. "You're okay! It's all fine now. You did awesome!"

"No! It's not!" Willow snarled, yanking herself away from Tiernan's hug and bursting into sobs. "She didn't want to go back to sleep! She begged me not to play the Song … but I didn't want her to get hurt …" She buried her face in her hands.

Tiernan's eyes widened. Out of the corner of his eye, Ben saw Faylene take a step forward, her hand against her chest.

"You could communicate with her?"

Willow nodded, wiping at her wet cheeks. "I could hear her voice in my head."

"Wow," Tiernan breathed.

Faylene strode to Drynfyre and worked at the sticky webbing holding the Amulet in place over the infinity mark. Uncle Grant rushed to Willow's side, folding her into his arms as Faylene snapped the last of the webbing free. She lifted the Amulet above her head, victorious. It caught the light and the dark stone shimmered and glowed. Ben felt the edges of a memory uncurling. He grabbed at its wisps, pulling it forward …

Aunt Matilda in her easy chair watching television, nervous fingers fiddling with a silvery cord, a glint of purple against her chest …

It couldn't be. Could it? How had he not made the connection before?

Ben looked down at Uncle Grant's cell phone, still clutched in his hand. He thought about Aunt Matilda's name on the hotel ledger. About her father working at the hotel. About her reaction to the Pfife. His heart pounded hard. He sucked in air, and when he finally found his voice he turned to Tiernan. "Can you help me?" Ben squeaked.

She looked at him. "What's the matter?"

"Could you take me to the hospital?"

THE CLEAN UP AT the den would be unfathomable, but as Tiernan drove back down the mountain, she saw the city hadn't sustained as much damage as she'd expected. Scorched sections of trees smoldered but, according to the radio reports, no one had actually been injured. While Drynfyre had made lots of noise and flamed some trees, her escape left behind a bunch of scared people (who now knew dragons were real) and one dead goat. The radio announcer explained that the deceased was a resident of the Cheyenne Mountain Zoo, a billy goat snatched during a tightly performed dive that was, unfortunately, captured on video by a zoo visitor and witnessed firsthand by a group of kindergarteners on a field trip. None of the children were physically harmed, but just listening to the audio of their encounter was disturbing. That scene was sure to play in those kids' nightmares for years.

Luckily, they'd had lots of rain this year, so the fires didn't spread before the fire department was able to put them out. If this had happened the year before, when wildfires were a big problem, the aftermath would have been even worse.

As Tiernan drove Ben, Willow and Willow's dad to St. Francis hospital, Willow explained what had happened with their great aunt earlier that day. When they reached the parking lot, Ben asked Tiernan to come inside with them. She barely knew Willow and Ben, and they'd sure been the source of quite a bit of trouble for her, but for some reason she felt protective of them. Especially Willow. She felt flattered that they wanted her to join them. "Okay, sure. If you want. That mess at the den isn't going anywhere."

Inside, they asked for directions to the great aunt's room and filed into the elevator. On the fourth floor, they met a pretty golden-haired woman and a man who looked like an older Ben coming out of the room. Tiernan had been surprised to find out Willow and Ben were cousins. They didn't look much like each other, but you could certainly tell their parents were related.

The woman clutched her daughter in a long, relieved hug. "I was so worried about you! Are you okay?"

"Mom! I can't breathe!" Willow gasped.

She released her, but didn't let go, smoothing strands of Willow's loose hair behind her ears, wiping at the dirt and grime on her cheeks. The woman turned to Willow's dad, suddenly furious. "Why didn't you call me? I had no idea where you were and that … THING was flying around—"

"Mom, don't blame Dad. It's a long story and I'll tell you everything, but Ben needs to see Aunt Matilda first."

"Okay, but just one at a time," said Ben's father, his arm around Ben's shoulders. "The doctor doesn't want a big crowd in there. She's had a tough day."

Ben and Willow exchanged a look. "You're the one she asked for," Willow said. He nodded and followed his dad down the hall.

Tiernan shifted awkwardly as Willow and her parents moved over to a small waiting room. "Y'know, I should probably just—" She jerked her thumb toward the elevators.

"No, don't go!" Willow cried. "Not yet, okay?"

Tiernan shrugged. "Yeah, sure. Okay." She wasn't sure what to do in this situation. She should get back to her post, but she really didn't want to deal with Faylene right now. Willow gave her a good excuse. She sat down on one of the hard plastic chairs. Willow took the one next to her.

Willow's mom whispered something to her dad and he scowled, glancing at Willow. "Uh, listen, we're going to go find some coffee. You want anything?"

Willow shook her head. "I know I should be hungry, I haven't eaten a thing since the smoothie this morning, but my stomach is still in knots."

Her mom touched her head in that way moms do before she and Willow's dad headed down the hall. Before they were out of earshot, the argument began.

Willow sighed. "She's totally furious at him, I knew she would be." She glanced at Tiernan with a half smile. "They're divorced, can you tell?"

"I'm sorry. That must be hard."

"I don't know. Yeah. Sometimes. She's better now with my uncle around."

Tiernan raised an eyebrow. "They live with you?"

Willow shrugged. "Yeah, just since last month. They used to live in Texas but Ben's mom died."

Tiernan sucked in a breath. "Man, that's horrible."

"Yeah. Car accident. Drunk driver."

A sad ache settled in Tiernan's chest. She didn't know what to say. She shifted in her chair, turning toward Willow. "Maybe this would be a good time for us to talk about the Pfife."

"Yeah … about that." Willow paused, glancing in the direction her parents had gone. "It wasn't really stealing. I mean that old hotel closed down over fifty years ago, at least, that's what my dad said."

Tiernan looked at her, blankly. "What old hotel?"

"It's near our music camp. My dad's company is gonna shoot a zombie movie there. He showed it to us, but we didn't really get a chance to properly explore. So we went back. And that's when we found the trunk in the attic."

"A trunk? Like a footlocker?"

Willow nodded. "We found the Pfife and that case of music hidden under a false bottom. We didn't think it belonged to anyone, I mean, there's a ton of stuff up there. Super old stuff."

"So, you figured it was all right to just ... take it."

Willow squirmed. "Abandoned treasure is fair game, everybody knows that." Her cheeks pinkened. "I'm really sorry I caused all this trouble."

"Hey, how could you have known what would happen?" Tiernan got up and walked to the tall windows at the edge of the waiting room. She looked out over the southwestern part of the city. A cleaning woman mopped the hallway near the elevators, working her way towards them. Willow joined Tiernan at the window.

"That trunk must have belonged to Hanna Vorman," Tiernan muttered. "Or someone she passed the Pfife on to. I guess someone could have found it after she died, and without knowing what it was, packed it away like it was nothing special."

"Who's Hanna Vorman?" Willow asked.

Tiernan looked at her, considering. She supposed it didn't hurt to tell her the story now; the secret was pretty much out. "Hanna Vorman was a Guardian around the time of the Civil War. She stole Drynfyre's Pfife, music and one of the Amulets. And just disappeared." Tiernan paused, looking out over the city. She could see Cheyenne Mountain from here, but tall evergreens blocked the view of the den. She was glad. She had no desire to see the gaping wound in the side of that mountain.

"Maybe she didn't want anyone to wake Drynfyre," Willow said.

"That's what some believe," Tiernan agreed. "Most people consider her a traitor. Guess it doesn't matter anymore. The Pfife and music are back. I wonder whatever happened to the Amulet. You didn't see it in that trunk?"

Willow shook her head. "I think I would have noticed a big ole black diamond looking thing."

Tiernan nodded. "Yeah, probably would." They stared out the window without speaking for a moment before Willow spoke again.

"It seems weird that I just met you this morning."

Tiernan turned to look at her, a strange pang tripping in her heart.

Ben burst into the waiting room, slipping on the freshly mopped floor. "Whoa!" He nearly fell but steadied himself at the last moment.

"¡*Tenga cuidado! Esto es un hospital!*" the cleaning woman cried, grabbing Ben's arm to steady him before his feet went completely out from underneath him. "¿*Qué tiene de malo?*"

Willow ran over and grabbed Ben's other arm, scowling at the woman. "You don't have to be so mean. There's nothing wrong with him!"

The woman's expression froze. She looked from Willow to Ben, then Tiernan. "*Lo siento. Yo no sabía que hablaba español.*" She looked sheepish as she put her mop in its bucket and wheeled it away. Tiernan gave Willow an impressed look, but before she could comment on the fact that Willow apparently understood Spanish, Ben grabbed both of their hands and dragged them down the hallway. "C'mon!" he yelled. "You're not going to believe this!"

CHAPTER 21

AS THEY REACHED Matilda's hospital room, and the familiar thrumming sound reached their ears, Ben looked at Tiernan and Willow, anxious to see their reactions.

Tiernan froze, eyes wide. "What is that?" she asked.

"You'll see," Ben grinned, opening the door. They stepped into the room and the sound grew louder.

"No way," said Willow, her voice high and thin with disbelief.

Ben's dad met them at the door. "It started right after you all arrived." Aunt Amanda had somehow made it back to the room, but Uncle Grant was missing.

"I think I know," Ben said, pulling Willow and Tiernan toward the bed. "I wanted them to be here when I showed you." The thrumming quickened, and his grin grew wider.

Matilda's long white hair spread over the pillow. One hand clutched at the throat of her hospital gown, a thin white sheet covering her frail body from the waist down. Her eyes were open and her deep blue gaze was bright and sharp. "Aunt Matilda?" he asked, gently. "Could you show us your necklace again?"

Her fingers worked at her throat, a small smile on her lips. "You need it," she croaked, her voice raw as if she'd been screaming for hours. "For the dragon."

Ben put his hand over hers. "Ben," his father warned with a glance to the monitors that beeped quietly beside the bed.

"It's okay." Ben kept his voice soft and soothing. Aunt Matilda's gaze moved from Ben to Willow. Then she looked at Tiernan and her eyes widened. She moved her fingers to reveal a smooth, black gem. Its soft glow pulsed against the hollow of her neck, keeping rhythm with the throbbing hum.

Tiernan gasped. "It's true."

"When I saw the Amulet hanging from your rear view mirror this morning, I kept thinking it seemed familiar," Ben said. "At the den, I remembered Great Aunt Matilda's necklace but I wanted to be sure before I said anything."

"She's worn this ever since I was a little girl," Amanda said. She leaned over and unclasped the necklace, holding it by the cord. Matilda smiled.

"Hold on," Willow said, putting up a hand. "The Pfife is back at the den. If the Amulet only does this when it's close to a Pfife, then how is this happening?"

"I'm not sure, but I think the Amulet is reacting to you, Willow," Tiernan said, her voice thick with amazement. "Like it senses a Whistler nearby."

Willow scowled, not seeming to like that answer much.

"Matilda," Tiernan moved closer to the bed. "Could you tell me where you got this necklace?"

Aunt Matilda looked back at her for a moment, then her gaze shifted to the ceiling and her expression grew blank and dull. Aunt Amanda sighed. "She drifts in and out of lucidity, it's been this way ever since this morning."

Tiernan briefly explained to the kids' parents about the Guardian history, the missing Pfife, music and Amulets. "Nobody knows what happened to the artifacts after Hanna Vorman disappeared."

Willow explained about going to the hotel with her dad on the way to camp, and how they'd hiked back later and found the Pfife and music in the trunk.

A funny feeling settled in Ben's stomach. "Aunt Matilda's father worked at that hotel," he said.

"Right, Aunt Matilda told us that," Willow added. "We found her signature on the ledger."

"You need it …"

They whirled to see Aunt Matilda's eyes sparking with brightness again. She reached a hand toward Willow. "You need it," she croaked again.

Ben frowned. If the necklace was for Willow, why had Matilda been asking for him?

"I need it?" Willow asked, glancing at the necklace in her mother's hand.

"Hold on," Tiernan said. "The Amulet belongs to the Guardians. When Faylene finds out about this, she's going to freak."

Willow looked at Ben, her meaning clear. He nodded in agreement. "Of course," he said, "the necklace belongs to the Guardians."

"I'm really sorry the secret about Drynfyre is out," Willow said. "But at least the Pfife, the music and the Amulet will be back where they should be."

Aunt Amanda handed the necklace to Tiernan and she slipped it around her neck.

Ben wasn't sure how this all made him feel. He'd been so excited about finding the Amulet, knowing the Guardians would be thrilled, but now that it was leaving—

The piercing scream of an alarm interrupted the moment, drawing every eye in the room to the monitor's next to Matilda's bed. The screen displayed a flat white line.

"Oh no," Willow breathed.

Matilda was gone.

PART TWO

CHAPTER 22

THE DEN'S ELEVATOR doors slid open to the sound of whirring drills and clanging metal, controlled chaos infused with purposeful energy. The air tasted metallic and sharp. Faylene had wasted no time assembling a team of Guardian workers to begin repairing the damage the day had left. They had installed a barrier around and over the sleeping Drynfyre to protect her from falling debris as they assembled steel scaffolding around the gaping hole in the mountain's side.

Tiernan pulled Coreen into the conference room. "I have to tell you something. At the hospital. The kids' great aunt … had this." Tiernan pulled the Amulet out from inside her tunic collar.

Coreen's jaw dropped, so stunned by the news, her mouth just worked without a sound.

"Can you believe it? The old lady was wearing it, and apparently had for decades! Willow's mom remembered her wearing it back when she was a child."

"I … I don't even know what to say."

"There's more. It hummed when Willow got close to it. I think it reacts to a Dragon Whistler just like the Amulet reacts when it's near the Pfife."

Coreen sank into one of the conference room chairs. "It makes sense. But who is this woman? How did she come to have it?"

"No idea. Maybe she's a descendent of Hanna Vorman?"

"It's possible." Coreen shook her head. "I just can't believe it."

"That would be the most logical answer, given how long she's had it. Faylene is going to lose her mind when she finds out we've got the Amulet back! Maybe it'll make up for everything else." Tiernan sighed heavily.

"None of this was your fault," Coreen insisted.

"If I'd reached the park thirty seconds earlier, I could have stopped her. Drynfyre wouldn't have been in danger. And the world would still be blissfully ignorant of her existence."

Coreen couldn't argue that.

"I wanted to tell you first, but I can't wait to tell Faylene. Where is she?" Tiernan headed for the door.

"She's meeting at NORAD with the FBI and the military folks ever since you left for the hospital. She should stop by before heading back to Denver, but I have no idea when that will be." Coreen smiled. "You must be exhausted. Why don't you get some sleep? You can tell her everything in the morning."

Curling up between crisp, cool sheets did sound appealing. "Okay, but promise you'll let me be the one to tell her?"

"I promise. Just put that thing in the vault before something happens to it."

Tiernan wondered what the other Amulet would do, together with its twin, but the other gem welcomed it back with a disappointing lack of fanfare. Tiernan placed the lost Amulet in the black velvet and watched for a minute, expecting … what? A two-toned hum of satisfaction? A magical hiss of relief? Nothing. Just two necklaces sharing a box.

After locking the vault, Tiernan tore off her clothes, leaving them on the floor where they fell, something she would never have done on an ordinary day. Without showering or even brushing her teeth, she climbed into bed and was asleep in moments.

A METALLIC CRASH jolted Tiernan out of a dream. Bleary-eyed, she squinted at her cell phone. Midnight. It felt like she'd only slept moments, but it had been over six hours.

She pulled on some yoga pants and a t-shirt, then sprinted down the hall to see what had made the noise. She found Coreen in the monitoring station. Her aunt had deep purple circles under her puffy eyes.

"Sorry about that. These guys aren't exactly quiet." Coreen jabbed a thumb at the crew working in the den. As with all Guardian projects, the crew was made up of in-laws, cousins and extended Dragon Guardian family members who knew the importance of secrecy. The young man apparently responsible for the loud crash was collecting tools scattered across the concrete floor, putting them back in a red toolbox.

"Faylene has crews coming in shifts, working 24/7. You good to take over supervising?" Coreen yawned. "I'm ready for bed."

"Sure, just let me go change. Any word from Faylene?"

"Oh, yeah, about that …." Coreen put an apologetic hand on Tiernan's shoulder. "She left for Chicago right after her meeting."

"Whaaat?" Tiernan said, her voice far more winey than she'd intended.

"The World Council called an emergency meeting to discuss … this." Coreen looked out at the den and squeezed Tiernan's shoulder. "She needs to know about the Amulet, because it will sure make that meeting easier, but I kept my promise to let you give her the good news. The plane lands in an hour, you can call her then. She'll be thrilled."

WILLOW LAY IN BED watching the headlights from passing cars arc across her dark ceiling. She counted the seconds of silence between each car, hoping it would help her fall back asleep. She always had trouble after a bad dream.

The digital clock on her bedside table read 12:30. She switched on her lamp, needing its warm, comforting light. It was so strange that less than 24 hours ago she thought dragons were just fairy tales? Now, she knew better. Her heart sped up at the thought of Drynfyre—her shimmering silver scales, her deep purple eyes, her massive wings. Now that the dragon was back in hibernation, Willow would probably never see her again. This made her feel hollow and wooden, like a lifeless puppet forgotten in some dusty old trunk. This made her think of the hotel attic, and that made her think of the Pfife and everything seemed to come back around to Drynfyre.

Drynfyre.

Willow rolled over and stared out the window. Today had changed her. It would change the whole world ... the way people saw things, what they believed. She still had a hard time computing that she'd been a part of it all. Not that anyone else knew about their involvement, of course. Willow understood why Faylene had insisted they keep that a secret. The military and the government didn't want the public knowing two kids managed to not only find, but wake, an enormous mythical beast that no one believed existed in the first place. Might not look too good to the rest of the world.

After dinner, they'd watched the news on TV. The President made a live address to let everyone know that yes, there was a real dragon, but not to worry, everything was under control. She was back in hibernation and no one had been hurt. Well, except that goat.

The President looked right into the camera lens and told the people of the entire world that Drynfyre was the last of her kind and hidden for her own protection. That she had hibernated for more than a thousand years without mishap and now she would hibernate again—no longer a threat. Only part of that was a lie.

Willow was probably the only person on the planet who knew, beyond a shadow of a doubt, that Drynfyre was never a real threat. She sensed Drynfyre's goodness with her entire being.

The memory of Drynfyre begging Willow not to play the Song brought on a fresh surge of guilt. She wished so much Drynfyre could have remained awake. She'd only had moments to enjoy and explore their connection. It wasn't fair!

Tears stung her eyes and she buried her face in her pillow. Then she heaved a sigh and sat up, pushed all her pillows behind her back, and wrapped her arms around her knees.

So many strange things happened yesterday, like how she couldn't read the words written on the music at first, and then when she got to the den, she could. She couldn't explain it. And Ben said that hospital cleaning lady was speaking Spanish, even though Willow swore she was speaking English. She didn't understand Spanish, so how was that possible? And what about how completely insane it was that Aunt Matilda had had the missing Amulet all these years?

Aunt Matilda. Willow's sadness deepened. She was gone. It wasn't like Willow had been close to her or anything, but she still felt sad about it. She'd sure never seen anyone die right in front of her before. It was horrible. Both she and Ben were shaken up by it.

Willow wished she'd known Matilda back before she got the Alzheimer's. They probably would have gotten along really well, certainly better than they had the whole time Matilda had lived with them.

A soft knock on her bedroom door pulled Willow out of her thoughts. She opened the door a crack to find Ben standing in the hallway.

"I couldn't sleep and saw your light go on … I thought you'd want to see this." Ben held a dark leather-bound book in his hand.

"What is it?" she asked.

"My dad found it in Aunt Matilda's dresser."

Willow opened her door wider and Ben slunk into the room. They perched side by side on the edge of the bed. "You were already asleep when he brought it in and showed me." He handed her the book. The dark cover was worn and cracked. "Look inside the front cover."

Willow carefully opened the book to the first page. A list of names, each in different handwriting, corresponded with a series of dates, beginning with Constance Goodman, 1725. Willow scanned the list and saw a familiar name. "Hanna Vorman!"

Ben nodded. "It's some sort of diary. Look at the last name on the list."

Just below Matilda's name, written in the same scrawling handwriting, was … Ben's name. Ben Cosgrove.

Willow's heart leapt to her throat. She and Ben stared at each other. "Whoa."

Willow's bedroom door creaked open and Willow's mom peeked in. "What are you kids doing up?" Willow lifted the book to show her.

"Ah," she said, joining them on the bed. "Josh showed me that earlier. Pretty interesting, huh?"

"Why do you think she wrote Ben's name on this list?" Willow asked, her emotions spinning in strange and confusing directions. Why wasn't her name on that list? She was the Dragon Whistler, after all.

"I don't know, honey," her mom answered. "I guess you'll have to read through this and see if there are any clues. But not tonight, okay? It's been a long day and the diary isn't going anywhere."

"But I'm not tired, Mom!" Willow protested. "Please?"

"Sorry, kiddo," her mom said, taking the diary from her. "I'll hang onto this and you guys can dig into it tomorrow."

"It's already tomorrow," Willow pleaded, then bit her lip at her mother's expression. "Well, technically ..." she muttered.

"To sleep. Now!" Her mom gave each of them a pointed look, and left, diary in hand.

Willow pouted. "Dang it."

Ben shrugged. "Sorry about that. It is almost one in the morning."

"Like I'm going to be able to sleep wondering what's written in that diary." She crossed her arms over her chest. Why did her mom always have to be so ... parental?

"So, you doing okay? Why are you awake, anyway?"

"Yeah, I'm fine. Just had a bad dream. Why aren't you asleep?"

"Can't seem to stop my brain." They both sat on the edge of the bed, staring at their feet, not talking.

"Well ... see ya at breakfast?" Ben headed for the door.

"Yep," Willow answered, sullen.

Ben shut the door behind him and Willow crawled back under the covers, curling up on her side. The pillow felt soft and cool against her cheek.

Could Matilda be Hanna Vorman's great-something granddaughter? If so, that would mean Hanna Vorman was their ancestor, too. And what did it mean that they were the ones the ones to find the Pfife. Seemed like less of a coincidence when you thought about all that.

There are no such things as coincidences.

Coincidence. Fate.

Destiny.

These were epic words and they tugged at Willow's mind, lulling her into a stupor. Finally, exhaustion won. Drynfyre flew through her dreams.

CHAPTER 23

TIERNAN ONLY ATE three bites of granola before she lost interest and dumped the bowl in the sink. Dang it! She had really wanted to see Faylene's face when she told her the Amulet was no longer missing. Pouting, she shuffled back to the monitoring station, giving Drynfyre's readings a cursory glance. The crew seemed to have made little progress in repairing the den and she didn't feel like watching them move at a snail's pace so she decided to put in some digital transcription time.

She'd just reached the conference room when a volley of shouting met her ears. Oh, what now? She sprinted back down the hallway, the argument intensifying as she rounded the corner.

"What is going on?" she demanded. The two arguers abruptly fell silent. One was the same boy who'd been picking up the scattered tools earlier. The other, Tiernan didn't recognize. They were both about her age and, she guessed, doing this as a summer job. Both boys tried to explain at once.

"He was supposed to—"

"There's a rule about moving those—"

"—he knocked over the shelter—"

"—But the dragon seems fine—"

It suddenly hit Tiernan that the mess of girders and piping scattered all over the floor was what used to be the makeshift shelter protecting Drynfyre. Only one side was standing, and it wobbled precariously.

"Please stop arguing and fix it before the rest of it falls on her!" Tiernan snapped. She was too tired and grumpy for this.

The young men hustled about silently gathering the pieces of the shelter as Tiernan moved closer to inspect Drynfyre. She seemed all right. It would take more than a few metal pipes to do any damage, but Tiernan didn't like the idea of anything falling on the dragon while she was in such a vulnerable state. Even if it didn't hurt her, it seemed ... disrespectful.

Tiernan's cell phone rang and she glanced at the screen. Faylene! Now was her chance!

She moved into the monitoring station, shutting the door to block out the loud clanging of metal on metal. "Hi Faylene! How's Chicago?"

"I'm in a cab," Faylene responded, with unsettling curtness. "Coreen left me a message. Said you were anxious to speak with me." Her tone was expectant but cool.

"Yes, I have some fantastic news," Tiernan said, eagerly. "I wish I'd had a chance to tell you last night but Coreen said you were in that meeting and—"

"Get to the point," Faylene interrupted.

Tiernan gulped. Why did she have to be so rude all the time? "Right, sorry. Well, I just wanted to be the one to tell you that yesterday, when I took Willow and Ben to the hospital to see their great aunt, I discovered that she was wearing the missing Amulet." Tiernan held her breath as she waited for the joy and appreciation to pour across the line.

She kept waiting. Faylene said nothing. In fact, the silence went on for so long, Tiernan thought the call must have dropped. "Faylene?" she said. "Are you there?"

"The missing Amulet?" Faylene asked, quietly yet maintaining her voice's trademark bossy quality.

Like there was another one? "Yes, I was just as shocked as you are! The kids' great aunt, a Matilda somebody, she'd had it for years, apparently. She was really old, like her 90s I think. Had Alzheimer's. She—"

"Tiernan, shut up for a second and let me think. Did this woman say how she came to have the Amulet?"

"No, I ... she passed away before I could really ask her much about it." Tiernan didn't understand. Faylene should be thrilled, but she sounded furious.

"Where is the Amulet now?"

"In the vault," Tiernan tried to keep from sounding wounded but knew she wasn't succeeding. "Faylene, what's wrong? I thought you would be happy!"

"I am!" Faylene snapped, then, more calmly. "I ... I'm sorry. I am happy. Very happy. Just ... surprised."

"Holy cow, me too!" Tiernan brightened. "Maybe all this craziness happened for a reason, so that we could find the Amulet."

"I think you're right, Tiernan." Faylene's tone was now so sweet her words almost dripped with sugar. "Maybe this did happen for a reason. You should be quite proud of yourself. Yesterday, you recovered two of the Guardian's most prized artifacts. You've made yourself a place in history. While yesterday was the day we were exposed to the world, it was also the day our full power was restored."

Tiernan couldn't decide if the Elder was being sarcastic or not. Faylene was never nice about anything, certainly not this nice. Tiernan hesitated, unsure. "Well, I guess it all worked out okay, then," she said, finally.

"Well done," Faylene said with an audible smile that, for some reason, sent a shiver of dread up Tiernan's spine. "Well done, indeed."

BEN WOKE UP realizing in all the chaos of yesterday, he forgot to get *Widershins and the Angel* back from his uncle again. But that could wait because this morning's reading was all about Matilda's diary. He leapt out of bed, forgoing his usual cargo shorts for a pair of dark gray basketball shorts and a Dallas Mavericks t-shirt Aunt Amanda had given him for his birthday. He'd never worn them before. He even put on an old pair of basketball shoes he'd inherited from Marcus.

Downstairs in the kitchen, his dad and Aunt Amanda sat at the kitchen table, fingers curled around thick white mugs. "Good morning!" they chorused. The room smelled of coffee and cinnamon and butter. Ben's stomach growled.

"Mmm, it smells like Cinnabon in here," he said.

"There are rolls warming in the oven," Aunt Amanda smiled at him. "Help yourself."

Ben pulled a small plate from the cupboard, glancing at the wall clock. "Dad, aren't you late for work?"

"Yes. Yes, I am," he said. "I figured, after yesterday, I would wait for you to wake up so I could say good morning." He pushed back from the table and hugged Ben. "I'm so glad you're okay," he said. "If anything had happened to you ..."

"Don't worry, Dad," said Ben. "I'm fine." He pulled out of the hug and shuffled to the pantry for a box of Life cereal. "It was a pretty amazing day, that's for sure."

"One to tell your grandkids about," said his dad, returning to his coffee.

"I'm still astounded you kids got all mixed up in that. It still hasn't sunk in," said Aunt Amanda.

"Same for me." Ben used an oven mitt to remove the pan from the oven, then forked one of the rolls onto his plate. The scrumptious scent made him ravenous despite their late night fast food taco dinner the night before.

"It's all over the news this morning. All the national channels are covering it," his dad said. "They're calling it 'The Day That Changed Fairy Tales'. CNN even had special theme music and graphics."

Ben looked at them. "They didn't say anything about Willow and me, though, right?"

"No, not at all. Fox News is trying to make it all some big governmental conspiracy, which," his dad laughed and scratched the back of his neck, "I guess it kind of is ... But those people spout off about everything, so I'm not surprised they're having a field day with this." Ben carried his plate to the table and popped a chunk of cinnamon roll into his mouth. His dad smoothed his hair, and then squeezed his shoulder. Dad did this a lot since Mom died, touched him all the time. Head rubs, shoulder squeezes, spontaneous hugging. It would probably happen even more often now.

"Marcus already left for work, but he made me promise I'd tell you he thought it was pretty cool that you saved the world and everything."

"I didn't save anything," Ben muttered, swallowing hard. A strange sick feeling gurgled in his stomach. Funny, the cinnamon roll didn't taste so good anymore. He noticed the leather diary next to the fruit bowl.

"Ready to see what's in there?" his dad asked.

"When Willow gets up," said Ben. "Did you look through it?"

His dad paused, exchanging a look with his sister. "We skimmed enough to confirm Matilda was definitely connected to the Dragon Guardians."

Ben stared at the diary, dying to know what was inside its pages. "I can't help but wonder, if we hadn't gone into that attic, if Willow hadn't found the Pfife, none of this would have happened." He paused. "Aunt Matilda would still be alive."

"Oh, Ben." Aunt Amanda put a hand on his arm. "What happened had nothing to do with you or Willow. Matilda was very old and very sick."

"Yeah, but I think she knew what was going on. She saw the Pfife yesterday morning. She was afraid we would wake the dragon. That's why she got so upset …" Ben's voice cracked and tears burned behind his eyes. "And why did she write my name at the bottom of that list? Why would she do that? She barely knew me!"

Willow appeared, dressed in a bright purple scoop-neck tee shirt and skinny denim shorts rolled up at her knee. Like most mornings, her hair hung loose but Ben noticed she was wearing a couple of purple ponytail holders around her wrist like bracelets. She slid onto the remaining empty chair at the table. "Morning," she said.

"Morning," they all answered together.

"Cinnamon rolls in the oven," said Aunt Amanda.

"I'm not hungry," Willow said, glancing at Ben. "I've been waiting all night for this."

"I hope you slept some," her mom raised an eyebrow.

"Some," Willow nodded.

Ben pulled the diary across the table and thumbed through the pages. Faded markings lined the bottom of each: a series of angular hash marks and X's. They sort of looked like rhythm patterns, like the music he followed when playing the tympani.

He turned to the first entry. The thin, angular cursive was difficult to read, but the date written at the top was clear. November, 1725. "Wow, almost 300 years ago," he said. His eyes scanned the sentences, but the writing was too small and tight to decipher. He flipped more pages, searching. He knew he'd find it eventually and then, there it was. A name at the top of one page.

Hanna Vorman.

CHAPTER 24

September 1885

This is the hardest decision I have ever had to make, but I know in my heart it is the right one. As I write this, just days after leaving the den, I imagine Maribel arriving to discover my absence. She will see the Amulet and Pfife are gone as well, and for a brief moment she may consider that something treacherous has befallen me. She will soon realize the suspicions she and Nanette have about me were well founded. I discovered their secret and did what was necessary to prevent their tyranny.

If I know my cousin, she and that horrid Nanette will ensure the name Hanna Vorman carries a mark as dark as Hawthorne's Scarlet Letter.

It breaks my heart that my beloved cousin fell in with that scheming girl, that they believed they could accomplish such trickery, but it pains me more to know they were not alone in their deceit. It seems my lot to be the one believed traitorous, but if by carrying this burden I can keep the Dragon Treasure safe, it is a burden I shall gladly shoulder.

Yet I know it is not just mine to bear. I must pass the burden like an heirloom to my daughters, and on to their daughters. Through them I will create new Guardians. Secret Guardians. We cannot allow the forces crouching behind dark curtains to carry out their reprehensible plans. The Dragon Treasure is sacred, bestowed upon our Order hundreds of lifetimes ago. It is a trust that must be upheld. I refuse to allow Nanette and her circle breach it. I do not know whether waking all seven dragons would accomplish what they believe, but I do know that such an attempt would carry disastrous consequences, regardless.

My only regret is that I was not able to take both Amulets. Only then could I be sure of stopping them. But then, I suppose that it why we are never to keep them together in the first place.

I must trust in the divine being who surely brought this to pass. Discovery of their plan could not be accidental. There are no coincidences. I was meant to intercept their communication. I was born and now doomed to live this secret existence for no other purpose than to prevent a tragedy. I believe this with all my heart. And I must instill that belief in my family. My beloved Harold believes it ... believes me ... and if our child is a daughter, I will teach her to believe it as well.

The Guardians were called to serve the Creator's plan. Nanette, Maribel and the others lost sight of that but I, Hanna Vorman, never will.

Ben sat beside Willow on the couch, silently reading along. Reaching the final words, they exchanged looks of dumbfounded amazement.

"Hanna Vorman wasn't a traitor at all," Willow breathed.

"No, but that Maribel chick sure was," Ben said, looking back down at the entry. "And Nanette, too. I guess nobody ever found out about her or whatever she was trying to do. What's a Dragon Treasure? I don't remember Tiernan saying anything about that."

"Me either," admitted Willow.

"Wait until she hears about this."

Ben's dad came in, holding a cup of coffee. He had changed into work clothes: khaki pants and a button down shirt. He settled in the easy chair across from the couch. "So what does Miss Hanna Vorman have to say?"

"Tiernan had said that Hanna Vorman was a traitor to the Guardians," Willow said. "That she stole the Pfife and that Amulet, but in her diary, Hanna Vorman says she did it to stop some other Guardians from getting something called the Dragon Treasure. I'm guessing since Hanna Vorman was willing to abandon her entire life to stop them, it must have been pretty important."

"You can tell she really believed she was doing the right thing," Ben pointed out a paragraph and handed the book to his father. "See? Look there." They waited while he read.

He nodded. "Interesting," he said, handing the diary back to Ben. "How does Matilda figure into this?"

Ben shrugged. "Dunno. Haven't read her entries yet."

"Well, I'll leave you to it, then. I'm off to the office," Ben's father said, heading out the garage door after kissing both of them on the head.

Ben thumbed to the next section, which was written by Hanna's daughter. He kept paging through until the handwriting changed again.

"I think this is Matilda's section."

Willow reached for the diary. "How about I read it out loud?"

"Okay," Ben agreed, leaning back into the couch cushions.

"May 20, 1932. Today was my sixteenth birthday and my entire life changed. We went for supper at the Canton, and they seated us in The Pike Room. How wonderful it was for father to be treated like a guest! Everyone made us feel so special. During the meal, the maître d' told us he heard that Amelia Earhart had taken off on her solo flight across the Atlantic Ocean. As amazing as that was, it could not compare with what happened when we arrived home. Mother shared with me a most amazing secret. It began with giving me this very diary I write in now."

It was like hearing a voice from the past as Willow read aloud. Ben closed his eyes. Willow read about Matilda finding out about Drynfyre and the Guardians, and the terrible, but brave, choice her grandmother was forced to make. About how Matilda's mother had kept those secrets, and charged her daughter with keeping them as well. About how Matilda wished she could see Drynfyre with her own eyes and how it broke her heart that she never would. Willow read it all to him. Matilda meeting her husband, a kind and gentle man who never knew his wife had a secret history. Matilda wishing and praying for a daughter but in the end unable to have children at all.

"There's only one more entry. May, 1991." Moments passed in silence. Ben's eyes popped open. "Hey! Stop reading in your head!" he accused.

"Sorry," Willow said, not sounding sorry at all. She sounded excited. "Listen to this. 'Last week's episode frightened me so. What if I forget where I am again? What if I forget everything mother told me? There is no other choice. I called Mr. Bugliosi's son. He says they are still fighting the demolition order but he doesn't think they can win. I told him what I wanted to do and he agreed. Last night he came to collect the trunk. He promised to lock it away in the attic. The hotel will be torn down and destroyed. The Pfife and music will never fall into the wrong hands.'"

He should have been thrilled to find this confirmation. To know that their Great Aunt had not only hidden the Pfife that they'd found, but that she was, no doubt, a Dragon Guardian descendent. But he just felt hollow and empty. And sad.

"She had no one to pass down the secret to, so it stopped with her." Willow said, slowly closing the diary.

"You understand what this means, right? We're part of that family. I think that's why we were the ones to find the Pfife. Since it was still out there, unguarded … it's like, it wanted us to find it." Ben glanced at Willow. Why did saying that make him feel so stupid?

But Willow nodded, agreeing. "It's like Hanna wrote, right there in the diary … there are no coincidences. I was thinking that same thing last night when I couldn't fall asleep. I mean, really, it'd be a pretty dang big coincidence that we are the ones who just happen to find that hotel and it just happens to be the one Matilda hid them in, right? Our great Aunt just happens to be the descendant of a Guardian? And it just happened not to get torn down after all?" She was getting excited now. It all made sense, in a nonsensical way. "Think about it! If my dad hadn't been scouting for that movie, we'd never have known the hotel was there. Everything happens for a reason. There are no coincidences." Willow paused, staring at him. "We've got to call Tiernan. The Guardians need to know Hanna didn't really betray them."

"But how are we going to do that? We don't have her phone number. And we can't exactly look up the den's phone number online."

Willow crumpled, dropping her forehead onto the arm of the couch.

"She said she would call us," Ben said, hopeful.

"Did you give her our phone number?" Willow jerked her head up.

Ben sighed. "No."

"I didn't either." Willow's face squinched up stubbornly. "I think I can find that back road to the den. Remember, dad said it was Old Stage Road. We can map it. Let's just go."

"Right, that's not a long bike ride or anything."

"We need someone to drive us. Mom's not here and your dad just left," Willow grumbled.

"Your dad?" Ben suggested.

"He's on a shoot today. Can't even call him," Willow sighed.

"Guess we'll have to ride our bikes."

"What about Marcus?"

Ben considered. "He's the only one at the store in the mornings, I don't think he'll leave."

"I bet he would if he got to see a real, live, hibernating dragon," Willow said, her smile confident.

Ben shrugged. "We can ask, but I'm telling you there is no way he's just going to leave the store unattended to drive us up there. Even Marcus isn't that stupid. He'd get fired for sure."

CHAPTER 25

"OKAY, LET'S BLAZE!" Marcus locked the front door of the video game shop behind him and grinned. Willow gave Ben a smug smile. He shook his head. He should have known Marcus would abandon his post.

"Marcus, aren't you worried about leaving the store?" he asked.

"Nah, Kenny should be here any minute, and I usually go to lunch early anyway." Ben was about to protest further, but Willow spun him around and shoved him toward the truck. Marcus lifted their bikes into the pickup's bed. "I'll text him, don't worry. It's cool. Not like we have any customers right now."

They climbed into the front seat of the dark blue F-150 pickup. Ben sat between them, his backpack on his lap, Aunt Matilda's diary inside.

Using the GPS on her phone, Willow directed Marcus through town to the city limits, and the turnoff onto Old Stage Road. They bumped up the twisting, turning mountain while Ben brought Marcus up-to-date on the previous day's events.

"Serious? That is messed up!" Marcus said, awe in his voice. "I watched it all online. When that dragon turned and flew into the hole in the mountain, you could hear the cheers from all over the city. Y'all are heroes!"

"Willow is the hero, I didn't really do anything," Ben muttered.

A surge of guilt sucked the energy out of Willow. "It was my fault it happened in the first place. And nobody knows it was us, so keep it quiet, Marcus."

"What? I can't brag on my little brother and cousin?"

"Sorry, it's classified," Ben smiled thinly.

"Good thing I didn't post it to Instagram or anything," Marcus muttered.

"Willow you have to admit, it was pretty cool getting to talk to a dragon, right?" Ben nudged her.

"What do you mean, talk to a dragon?" Marcus asked.

"Because I played the Pfife, I'm her Whistler now. We're like … bonded. We can communicate with our minds," Willow said. "I hear her in my head, and I can answer her just by thinking about it."

"Holy mind-meld." Marcus sounded impressed. "I want to be a Dragon Whistler."

"Only one per customer," Ben quipped.

As they drove, Ben told Marcus about Aunt Matilda, the hospital, and the family's connection to the Guardians. He even read him parts of a few entries.

When they reached the guard gate, it was abandoned, so they drove straight through. "Huh, there was a guard here last time," Willow said, directing Marcus to the same parking lot where they parked with Tiernan before.

"Hey, look at—" Ben said, still reading the diary.

"Lookout!" Willow yelled, and Marcus swerved, narrowly missing a blue sedan speeding out of the parking lot. It raced back down the dirt road the way they'd come, leaving behind a cloud of gravel dust.

"No worries, we're just driving here!" Marcus yelled after the blue sedan. "Some people are so rude!" He parked across from the door because the five construction trucks had taken all the spaces nearby.

Ben stuffed the journal back into his pack. "These trucks weren't here yesterday, either. The guards are gone but the trucks are here."

"There's Tiernan's Jeep," Willow pointed. "Well, at least she's here."

Marcus eyed the small brick building. "Guys, that sign says Authorized Personnel Only. Are you sure this is cool?"

"It's fine, we were just here yesterday."

Marcus didn't have a chance to continue his protest because the door opened and a tall, burly bald-headed man in orange overalls came out carrying two big buckets of something wet and oogie that had already sloshed all over his work boots. He would have been menacing looking, like someone you would definitely be afraid of, if not for his wide, friendly smile. "Hey, kids. Can I help you?" He glanced down at the empty guard station. "This is a restricted area."

"I'm sorry sir. There weren't any guards. We're here to see Tiernan," Willow explained. "We were here with her yesterday, when the dragon … uhh …"

The man eyed Willow, one brow arching. "Ohhh. You're the Whistler, eh?" he asked.

Willow and Ben exchanged a look. "Yeah, that's me," Willow nodded, smiling shyly, turning on the charm in hopes he'd let them in.

"Huh," the bald man eyed her. "Coreen said you were young, but you really are just a kid."

Ben grabbed Willow's arm to stifle the response he knew was about to pop out of her about how mature and responsible she was for her age. "Please," Ben said, "we really need to talk with Tiernan. Is she here?"

"Yeah, but … now that you mention it, I haven't seen her in a while."

"Can we go up and find her?" Willow asked. "We promise not to get in the way."

The big man considered, setting down the buckets and pulling a cell phone from one of the many pockets in his overalls. "Let me give her a call."

When there was no answer, he stuffed the phone back into his pocket. "Hmmm," he muttered. "She's supposed to keep that phone on her at all times. Well, I suppose you've already been up there. Not like it's a big secret anymore," he looked pointedly at them. Willow felt her cheeks redden. He motioned them inside and walked to the desk. Picking up the black, old-fashioned phone, he pointed at the outside door. "Make sure that's shut all the way, would you?" Then he dialed "0" and said the words "Kareth's secret." The elevator doors opened immediately.

"She answered that time?" Ben asked.

"No, it has voice recognition software," the man replied. "I'd better ride up there with you, just to be sure you find your way." He ushered them into the elevator, extending his hand to Marcus. "I'm Thomas, by the way, Tiernan's uncle."

"Nice to meet you. I'm Ben's brother, Marcus." Marcus took his hand with a smile, seeming more relaxed now that they had official permission to be there.

The elevator doors shushed closed and the car moved backwards into the mountain. The three startled and exchanged worried looks. "Yeah, ordinary elevators just go up and down. This is no ordinary elevator."

"Why do I feel like I just stepped into some strange version of Willy Wonka?" Marcus muttered.

They rode in silence for a moment before Thomas went on. "Normally, just the ladies work in the den, you know. That's the Guardian way. According to Kareth, men were the reason she had to put the dragons into hibernation in the first place. Guess she sure wasn't going to let us watch over 'em! Would like to think men today would be different." He paused, clearing his throat. "Except sometimes it seems not much has changed."

The elevator car slowed. "Get ready, we're going up now." He wasn't kidding. Once the car came to a stop, it rose quickly. Willow grinned, but Ben's stomach flipped over and he groaned.

Thomas just kept talking. He was a friendly sort, but didn't seem to like silence. "Most of us in the Guardian family have regular jobs down in the city, but I work up here more than the others, since I'm married to the former Primary. Gives me a bit more access than the other guys." He jingled a ring of keys on his belt and smirked. "Kind of like the den super."

Finally, they reached the top and the doors slid open. Workers hustled everywhere and construction sounds filled the air. They'd made an amazing amount of progress since the night before, Ben thought, taking in the scene. Thomas ushered them into the den area, searching for Tiernan. His expression darkened. "Where the heck is that girl?" He hollered at a couple of younger workers sweeping up by the monitoring station. "Yo, Jordan! Where's Tiernan?"

A good looking young guy about Marcus' age looked up from his work on some big metal pipe, pushing his plastic goggles up into his thick dark hair. "She went in the conference room with that Elder lady a while ago," he said. "Haven't seen her since."

Thomas growled in frustration, stomping down the hallway. "Elder lady? Clearly Jordan hasn't been studying his org chart." Following Thomas, Ben realized Marcus wasn't behind him anymore. He grabbed Willow and they backtracked to find him frozen, just outside the elevator, staring at Drynfyre with his mouth hanging open.

Willow took his arm. "It's okay Marcus. Just breathe!"

"That's ... a dragon," Marcus said. "A real dragon."

"Yes, Marcus," Ben couldn't help but laugh. "That's why we're here, remember?"

"But ... it's ... HUGE!" Marcus stammered, allowing them to pull him down the hallway after Thomas. He kept his eyes on Drynfyre until they rounded the corner.

"She is huge, that's true," Willow corrected with a giggle.

Thomas banged on the conference room door. "Tiernan! Open up!" he hollered.

"Is everything okay?" Willow asked.

He sounded quite concerned, actually. And he shook the door violently. "This door is never locked," Thomas said. "The vault inside, of course that's a different story. Only four of us can get into that, but this door ... never." He shook the handles again, but it didn't help at all. "Something's wrong. Something's definitely wrong." He put his hands on his hips, pacing back and forth for a second. Then he turned and kicked the double doors just above the handles. The doors shook but remained closed. He gave them another kick and the doors crashed open.

The conference room was empty. Thomas ran to the tall iron doors in the back of the room, placing his finger on a keypad scanner. Then he pushed down on the long metal handle below the pad and opened the vault door.

There she was. Gagged and tied to a chair between the shelves. She was conscious, but her eyes looked glassy and dazed.

"Holy—" Thomas swore, quickly removing the gag. "Let's get you outta there," he said, controlled panic in his voice. Thomas picked up the entire chair, with Tiernan still in it, and moved it into the conference room. Marcus helped him untied the ropes while Willow fetched a bottle of water from the conference room side table. Ben didn't know what to do. He just stood there, unable to move. Who would do this to Tiernan? And why?

Tiernan rubbed her wrists and gulped the water. After a long, deep drink, she gasped, "Wasn't much air ... left."

"Who did this?" Thomas demanded.

"I'm not sure. I opened the vault for Elsbeth ... next thing I knew ... I woke up in the dark ... could barely breathe," Tiernan panted. "Wasn't even sure where I was." Then her brain seemed to get enough oxygen to register what had really happened. "Oh no! Oh no oh no no no no no!"

She stumbled back into the vault, grabbing a black box off a shelf. When she snapped it open, she visibly relaxed. "Oh thank goodness," she murmured.

"What is it?" she asked. Willow craned her neck.

Tiernan held the open box out so they could see the Pfife, nestled against the black velvet. Willow smiled like she was seeing an old friend for the first time in a long time.

Tiernan returned the Pfife box to the shelf and took down another somewhat larger black box. She opened the lid. "No!" she blurted, the empty box clattering to the vault floor. "I can't believe this!" Tiernan whirled to face them, her face pale, eyes wide with panic. "They're gone! They're both gone!"

Thomas picked up the empty box. "But we just got the other one back ..." He seemed totally confused. "Why would Elsbeth take them?"

"I trusted her! I can't believe ..." Tiernan burst into tears.

Willow swallowed hard, dread forming a thick knot in her belly. "Who is Elsbeth?"

Through her sobs, Tiernan sucked in a breath and tried to speak. "Elsbeth is Faylene's sister. I can't believe this. It's Hanna Vorman all over again."

CHAPTER 26

FAYLENE ENDED THE call and smiled out the hotel window. The Chicago sunset blazed victoriously.

In two hours, Elsbeth and the Amulets would arrive in Baltimore on the chartered jet, which had taken off from the small Colorado Springs airport with no intervention. This was not one of the usual jets the Guardians used. Falcon Air was more discreet.

The whole thing had gone almost too smoothly. Faylene had certainly expected that little wildcat Tiernan to put up more of a fight, or at least show some suspicion when Elsbeth asked to go into the vault. Blind trust was not a quality Faylene admired, but Tiernan had believed Elsbeth when she said Faylene wanted her to check on the Amulets.

Stupid girl.

Elsbeth had left the Pfife, which wasn't ideal, but there really was no reason to take it, too. Its bond to the Whistler rendered it useless to Faylene as long as the Whistler was alive. And with both Amulets, Faylene didn't need it anyway. From what Faylene had gleaned from the hidden Codex, their magic would override the Pfife's.

Faylene carried the ancient pages with her everywhere, never letting them out of her sight. Like the other volumes of Kareth's Codices, this one was made up of sheets of parchment painstakingly hand bound with the same magical silk as the Amulet and Pfife cords. Running her thumb over the ridges of the binding, Faylene felt the same reverent thrill of power she experienced holding the Amulet.

She grabbed her suitcase and left the hotel room without a look back. Everything of importance lay ahead of her. The realization of a dream, sprouted back when she was a young Guardian watching over Drynfyre, would soon reach fruition.

Hailing a cab, she gave her destination to the driver and settled into the backseat. Her own Falcon Air jet would land in Baltimore just an hour after Elsbeth's.

In three hours, I will be one step closer to becoming the most powerful Guardian since Kareth.

As the Chicago cityscape rolled past the cab window, Faylene's mind returned to that life-changing day in 1969 when her grandmother shared her secret. It changed the way Faylene saw the Guardians, how she felt about her family, how she imagined her future.

The den's library held the largest collection of documents of any of the seven dens. The exhaustive task of transferring all the documents to microfiche had already taught her much more about her ancestry than her official childhood studies. Recruiting help from her little sister Elsbeth had helped, but even so, Faylene knew completion was decades off.

They hadn't been surprised to see grandma Nanette when she showed up, the former Prime loved to visit her granddaughter now that she'd started the microfiche project. She'd shown great interest in it, and Faylene soon discovered why.

She was there when Elsbeth found the hidden Codex. When the sisters read through it. She took them into her confidence and shared the real story of Hanna Vorman. She swore them to secrecy, and told them the power that awaited them at the end of the journey, if they did exactly as she said.

And they did. After all, Hanna Vorman stole the artifacts, Prime responsibility shifted to Nanette's family line, as first cousins, once removed. Hanna was an only child, and with her parents long dead by then, there was no one left to defend her honor. Or to demand retribution. Faylene and Elsbeth, Nanette told them, were more of the right mindset to complete the plan Vorman had thwarted. Their mother was too soft, and Nanette had never shared this with her.

This fact intrigued Faylene, as a sixteen-year-old who constantly battled with her Prime mother. What better rebellion could there be than to work behind the scenes on the greatest plan of all time?

A nagging thought plagued Faylene, and had since the call from Tiernan set this final phase of the plan in motion. How had the Amulet ended up with those meddling kids' great aunt? Could the woman possible be Vorman descendent? If so, then those kids were … Faylene shook the thought away. None of that would matter soon. The old woman was dead, both Amulets would soon be in Faylene's possession, and Nanette's glorious vision would be on its way to realization. Finally. After all these years, Vorman had failed to stop them.

Would the Whistler be an obstacle to Drynfyre? Faylene wasn't sure yet, but if Nanette was right, and if Faylene had interpreted the hidden Codex correctly, the Amulets would give her access to the one thing that would override any bond Willow had with the beast.

As her cab pulled up outside the private airport, Faylene peeled off a couple of twenties from a roll of bills and tossed them into the front seat, shorting the driver on the tip. A completely different life waited for her at the other end of this plane ride, and only thing standing in her way was an accidental Dragon Whistler.

CHAPTER 27

TIERNAN SUCKED ANOTHER deep breath from the oxygen mask and replaced it on the tank next to her, then gingerly held an ice pack to the side of her head, just about her ear.

"I need to update Belinda," Coreen said, sounding exhausted. "Tell me everything."

Ben, Willow, Thomas and Marcus were gathered around the conference room table where Coreen sat next to Tiernan in one of the two chairs nearest the door. Ben thought Tiernan probably wanted to sit as far away from the vault as possible. If he'd been the one bashed on the head and left to die an airtight iron closet, he wouldn't want to be anywhere near it either.

"This is all my fault," said Tiernan, slumping forward. "Elsbeth told me Faylene asked her to make sure the new Amulet was the real deal. That she thought it might be a fake. What was I supposed to say?"

"Elsbeth doesn't have authorization in the system to enter the vault," Coreen sighed. "She needed you to get in there."

"She was just so confident. I thought—" Tiernan's eyes filled with tears.

"You thought you'd be in trouble with Faylene if you didn't do what Elsbeth asked. I understand." Coreen put a hand on Tiernan's arm.

"I can't believe that woman," Thomas growled.

Coreen clearly agreed with her husband. "Faylene always butted heads with the Elders, but I don't think anyone doubted her loyalty," she said, shaking her head.

"Why would she do this?" Tiernan moaned.

"I think we might know," said Ben, pulling the journal from his backpack and exchanging a look with Willow to see if she thought it was okay to talk about this now. Willow nodded so Ben went on. "My dad found this with Aunt Matilda's things last night. According to this, Matilda was a descendent of Hanna Vorman."

The air seemed to go out of the room. Tiernan reached for the oxygen mask again. Coreen reached for the diary. Ben slid it across the table to her. "Look inside the front cover."

Coreen did, holding the diary out so she and Tiernan could both read it. "I don't believe this," Tiernan said, her voice muffled by the mask.

Ben's couldn't help feeling excited. "You see? Hanna was trying to protect the dragons from being used by the real traitors. They wanted to get something called the Dragon Treasure. Look at that page I marked."

Coreen flipped to the dog-eared page and scanned the page, then reading aloud to Tiernan: "It seems my lot to be the one believed traitorous, but if by carrying this burden I can keep the Dragon Treasure safe, it is a burden I shall gladly shoulder. Yet I know it is not just mine to bear. I must pass the burden like an heirloom to my daughters, and on to their daughters. Through them I will create new Guardians. Secret Guardians."

"Holy cow," Tiernan said, lowering the mask.

"What's the Dragon Treasure?" Willow asked.

Tiernan raised her eyebrows, her expression shocked and pale. "Just a legend." She lifted the ice pack to her head again. "Nobody believes it actually exists. Kareth never wrote about in any of her Codices, but we've heard stories about it, passed down, like … fairy tales." Goosebumps rippled along Ben's arms. Fairy tales were coming true all over the place lately.

Coreen looked up from the diary. "If what Hanna writes here is true, Nanette found something that made her believe she could use all seven dragons to find the Dragon Treasure." She handed the book to Tiernan, who read the passage.

Willow narrowed her eyes. "Could the Amulets be used to wake the dragons?"

"I don't … think so. I mean, that's what the Pfifes are for." Tiernan shrugged. "To bond each dragon with a Whistler at the Awakening so that this Guardian could protect them. And control them, if need be."

"But Nanette was Faylene's grandmother," Coreen said, thoughtfully. "It's quite possible she passed down whatever she learned about the Dragon Treasure to Faylene." She took a breath, exchanging a look with Thomas. "I have to call Belinda." She left the room and Thomas followed.

Tiernan put one hand on the diary. "Thank you for bringing this. And thank you for saving my life. If you hadn't showed up when you did …"

Ben felt his face go hot. He imagined ugly blotches popping up all over his neck. He glanced at his brother and saw the same kind of angry rash spreading across his neck.

Willow waved her words away like they saved lives every day. "So what's going to happen now?" Her eyes grew wide. "You aren't going to let Faylene take Drynfyre, are you?"

Tiernan's expression froze. "Faylene can't take Drynfyre …"

Willow looked confused, but Ben understood immediately. The pieces slipped into place like tumblers clicking in a lock. "If Faylene needs to wake all seven dragons to get this Dragon Treasure ... " He looked at Willow, eyebrows raised.

"Willow," Tiernan leaned forward. "Drynfyre is the only dragon bonded with a Whistler. Which means Faylene can't wake Drynfyre without ... you."

Willow became as motionless as if someone had magically turned her into wax.

Marcus stood up, panicked. "Are you saying this Faylene woman is going to come after Willow?"

Tiernan ignored Marcus, moving to squat beside Willow's chair. "Willow, I promise, we will not let her near you."

Ben scooted closer to Willow. What had seemed like a thrilling adventure a few moments ago now felt threatening. Marcus leaned against the wall, the heels of his hands pushing against his eyes. "This is wacko! I have got to call Dad. Aunt Amanda is going to kill me for bringing Willow here ..."

Tiernan put a hand on Willow's shoulder. "Here's the thing, if the Dragon Treasure does exist, then it must be important. We cannot let Faylene get to it."

She sighed and gave Marcus an apologetic look. "There's only one way to be sure that doesn't happen. We'll have to get to it first."

CHAPTER 28

ON A SMALL, uncharted island far out in Maryland's Chesapeake Bay, in Geldfyre's underground den, Portia Manelli struggled to contain her panic. These were her last days as Primary Guardian and she should be enjoying them. Her daughter Sophie would take over in less than a month when she turned sixteen. Unfortunately, it now looked like the transition might not happen as smoothly as Portia always believed it would.

"Everything's secure," said Sophie coming up behind her.

Portia fell quiet, proudly taking in her daughter's presence. She found herself captivated by her daughter so often recently. Her slight, petite frame. Her gray-blue eyes; identical to Portia's own, yet so much more striking with Sophie's flawless olive skin—courtesy of her father's European heritage. The girl's raven hair, cut blunt at her jaw line, framed a face that looked older than her years. But Sophie was just as beautiful inside. Her heart was as kind as her mind was brilliant. The girl studied continuously. Passionately. She probably knew more about draconian history than any other Guardian of her generation—if the honors bestowed on her by the Elder Council at her graduation last spring were any indication.

Portia kissed Sophie on the cheek. "Lockdown complete?"

Sophie put her hands on the desk and leaned over to look at the various screens displaying the den's high security features. "No one's getting in or out for another thirty-six hours." She crossed her arms across her chest, skeptical. "I still can't believe the missing Amulet was found."

Portia shook her head. "I can't believe it was stolen again."

"And by an Elder." Sophie's eyes narrowed with disgust. Portia peered through the Plexiglas at the sleeping Geldfyre. His golden scales shimmered, but a glance at the temperature gauge reassured her. Sleep on, beautiful beast.

Sophie went on. "Does Belinda really think Faylene might come after Geldfyre?"

"You heard her," Portia said, referring to the call that had initiated the lockdown. "Faylene is a loose cannon—"

A faint sizzling sound stopped Portia mid-thought. She spun, eyes searching for the source of the noise. Scowling, Portia pointed to a spot over by the elevator doors. "What is that?"

A dark spot of cloud formed out of nothing, growing to completely obscure the elevator doors. Thick smoke swirled and churned, alive with sparkles of magical radiance. Sophie gasped. "It's an Onyx cloud! I've read about them in the Codex. The Amulets can create them." She looked at her mother, eyes coiled with fear. "Mom?"

An opaque image of a face appeared in the cloud. "Faylene!" Portia snarled, striding toward the vaporous image. "Get out, traitor!"

The cloud thickened and Sophie ran up behind her mother. "Mom, she's using it as a portal," Sophie said. "We don't have much time."

Sophie sprinted down the corridor to the conference room vault as Portia raced back to the monitoring station. She tapped the side of her head, engaging the mic on her Bluetooth headset that connected her to Guardian headquarters. Faylene might have found a way in, but she would have a tough time getting out with a five-ton dragon. A sudden thought made Portia hesitate. Could Faylene use the Amulets to transport Geldfyre? Portia had no idea.

Someone picked up the call. "Winged Victory Insur—"

"Code red, I repeat, code red," Portia interrupted, her voice intense and firm.

She heard three clicks while the call transferred. Seconds later Belinda was on the line. Portia swallowed around the tight lump in her throat. "Faylene is using an Onyx Cloud. She's almost in."

"She didn't waste any time, did she?" Belinda growled. "The Pfife?"

"Sophie is on it." Portia tried to calm the shake in her voice. Portia squatted to unlock the cabinet beneath the console using a key that hung from a chain around her neck. Inside the cabinet she took out the three, loaded Magnum pistols. The guns would probably be no more help against the Amulets than pointing an index finger and cocking her thumb, but she had to try.

"Your loyalty will never be forgotten," Belinda's voice softened. "I've scrambled emergency squads, but ..." She didn't finish, as if thinking better of the words she almost spoke. Portia knew Kenneth and her other cousins would never make it to the island in time to help them. It just wasn't physically possible.

Portia stuffed one of the guns into her waistband, barrel-first. The cold metal pressed against her stomach, failing to calm the churning terror there. "Belinda, if the Treasure is real, you cannot let Faylene get it," she barked, knocking the Bluetooth from her ear. It clattered to the floor as she walked out of the monitoring station, a gun in each hand.

It would take a miracle for her and Sophie to make it through this alive.

In the thirty seconds it took to retrieve the weapons and alert Belinda, the Onyx Cloud had thickened and expanded considerably, but there was no sign of Faylene yet. And then, a white light beamed from the center of the cloud. Portia pointed both guns at the cloud as Faylene stepped out of the light, followed by her sister Elsbeth.

"You will not go anywhere near Geldfyre." Portia thumbed the hammers back simultaneously; hoping the threatening sound of two bullets sliding into two chambers would convey her seriousness.

"Portia. Dear. I really don't want to hurt anyone," Faylene said calmly, palms out in supplication. "Especially not your daughter."

Itching to let bullets fly, but fearful to discover they would do no good, Portia smoothed her stony expression, keeping fingers tight against the triggers. Control. Calm and cool. Do your job, she told herself. Do your job. When the time is right, take action. "I swore an oath to protect the dragons," Portia snarled. "The same oath you swore. Seems you didn't take it quite as much to heart."

Faylene's mouth tightened into a thin line. Her sister glanced at her, a flicker of uncertainty on Elsbeth's face, but if any hesitation crossed Faylene's mind it fizzled before taking root. She reached inside her blouse, pulling the black gems out by their cords. The stones pulsed in perfect harmony.

"I assume you know what these are," Faylene said, taking a step towards Portia.

"Of course I do. I also know what Elsbeth did to Tiernan at Cheyenne Mountain." Portia risked a glance at Elsbeth—nervously gnawing the nail on her pinky finger—before returning her gaze to Faylene who moved another step closer. "You two have made Hanna Vorman look like a hero. Oh wait. Plot twist. She is the hero."

Faylene paused, eyes narrowing. "How do you know about Hanna Vorman?"

"We know a lot more than you think," Portia said, lifting her chin.

Faylene shrugged, her wry smile returning. "Hanna Vorman may have stopped destiny once, but it won't be stopped again." Her smile grew hard and cold. "Now hand over the Pfife."

"Forget it," Portia said, her muscles shaking from holding the guns at arm's length for so long. She should have pulled the trigger before now, but some part of her struggled with shooting one of her own. She wanted Faylene to repent, to turn away from the dark side.

Faylene cupped her palms under the Amulets and a strange sense of disconnection swept over Portia. First, her arms gave out. She lowered the guns, and then consciousness slipped, and fear enveloped her heart. As she crumpled to the floor, she whispered a single word:

"*Sophie.*"

SOPHIE WASN'T SURE the deadbolt on the crawl space would hold against the Amulets' magic. She huddled against the back wall, knees pulled to her chest, neck bent low—Geldfyre's Pfife in one hand, music in the other.

She heard voices in the hallway outside the door to the crawlspace, their words undecipherable. Two voices, and neither her mother's. Sophie squeezed her arms around her knees, trying to quell her trembling.

Silence fell in the hallway.

Please, please, please.

She prayed they hadn't hurt her mother. That, after all this was over, she would feel her arms around her, hear her say Sophie had done just as she should. That everything would be okay.

The voices spoke again. Closer now. And Sophie could understand the words.

"The vault door is ajar," said a woman's voice. Faylene? It had been years since Sophie had seen the Elder, so she couldn't be sure. "The girl must have the Pfife."

"You didn't think they were going to make it easy, did you? Go check. Be sure." This voice was scratchy and harsh, older than the other. That was Faylene.

Footsteps faded away, then she heard a shout from another room. "The Pfife is gone. The music, too."

"I am sure little Sophie is tucked away in her hiding space; a location not on the blueprints."

It felt like they stood just beyond the closet door. "Look at the Amulets," said Elsbeth. Sophie's heart clutched as the Pfife's runes glowed hot against her palms.

"She's definitely close," said Faylene.

"Amazing," Elsbeth said, awe in her voice. "Grandmother was brilliant to strike lessons about Amulet powers out of the curriculum all those years ago. Think about it, when we deleted all those sections instead of translating them to microfiche, we must have missed one. Coreen and Tiernan searched the database and found it, realizing they could use the Amulet to track down the Pfife. A happy accident to be sure."

"We wouldn't have the Amulet otherwise," Elsbeth agreed.

"Oh, there we go. I think we're close." Sophie heard the storage closet door swing open. From inside the hidden compartment, she pictured Faylene's triumphant smile melting, and stifled a nervous laugh.

Faylene swore.

"Maybe she stashed it somewhere in this closet," Elsbeth growled. "Look at all the boxes! It could be in any of them!"

"No," Faylene said, in a tone that raised the hackles on Sophie's neck. "She wouldn't leave something so valuable unguarded." Silence fell. Sophie sensed Faylene's gaze like a laser beam, searching every inch of the closet.

Something that sounded like fingernails scratched along the closet walls. "Sophie, dear," Faylene sing-songed. "Come out, come out, wherever you are …"

Scccrrrrriiiiitch. Scccrrraaatch. "I know you're here somewhere …"

She's trying to find a seam in the wall, Sophie realized. She'll find the edges of the secret door. Sophie breathed in short panicked gasps as fear threatened to overwhelm her. There was nowhere for her to go. Nowhere to run.

She was trapped.

CHAPTER 29

"HOLD UP. ARE you kidding? You want me to wake Drynfyre ... again?" Willow's short, stubby fingernails dug into the chair's armrests, leaving crescent moon shapes in their wake.

"That's the idea," said Coreen, with a pained look. She gave Tiernan a slight nod, silently asking her to explain.

Tiernan spoke quietly. "If we want to find out if the Dragon Treasure is real, and where it's located, a dragon will have to help us."

Willow met Tiernan's gaze. This whole conversation was like riding that Rotor ride her Dad had told her about riding at Elitches when he was a kid: spinning around with your back against the wall until you were pinned, and the floor dropped out beneath you. Trapped by G-Forces until the ride was over. "Do I have to?"

"Faylene is going to come for Drynfyre. We'll need to move her to protect her. We can't do that without waking her," Coreen explained. "And we can also ask her about the Dragon Treasure."

Thomas leaned against the wall, arms crossed over his chest. He glanced down the hallway at Marcus, who stood near the elevators talking on the phone to his dad. "You know," Thomas said. "If all seven dragons are required to get the Treasure, you won't be able to get to it any easier than Faylene."

They all looked at Thomas, stunned. Then all heads swiveled to Coreen for her response. She took a deep breath, composing herself. When Tiernan had first explained her plan, Coreen had been against it, but after a discussion with the Elders she'd agreed it was the best approach. "Belinda thinks that, if the Treasure is real, and Drynfyre believes it's in danger, she will want to help protect it."

Willow pushed her chair back from the table. She just couldn't sit anymore. "You don't understand, Drynfyre was really mad at me when she realized I was going to put her back to sleep. I've felt horrible about it ever since. I'll wake her again if you want me to, but I don't think she'll help us."

Coreen stood and moved toward Willow. She looked pale and shaken. "I understand what you're struggling with. But I want you to understand, for us, much of this is just guessing. We're in new territory here. Everything we know about the dragons, the Amulets, the Pfifes ... it's all book learning. None of us have any real experience. It's knowledge that's been passed down about things that were decided fifteen hundred years ago! And the Dragon Treasure? Faylene could be off on a wild goose chase. We just don't know."

"But Drynfyre will," Willow nodded, trying to keep her knees from giving out. She picked up the small black box from the table and opened the lid. One glimpse of the Pfife brought back all the incredible joy she'd felt while playing it. To be honest, she was kind of excited to play it again, not to mention, getting another chance to look into Drynfyre's eyes. Fear and excitement swirled dizzily in her head.

Ben stepped up beside her. "You sure?" he asked.

Willow nodded, resolute.

"Then you'll need to learn the other songs," Coreen smiled, but Willow noticed her face was all sweaty.

Ben spread the sheets across the conference room table. "Can you read these? How do we know which does what?" he asked Coreen.

Willow stiffened.

"It's Illian," Tiernan said, tentatively. "There's a translation guide around here somewhere. Unfortunately, Faylene is an expert. Us ... not so much." She exchanged a look with Coreen.

Willow slipped the Pfife cord over her head, letting it fall cold and solid against her chest. "Um, guys? There's something I didn't tell you yesterday. I can read this now."

Every head in the room snapped in her direction. "You can read what now?" Tiernan's eyes widened.

"The words. The Illian," Willow said. "Before I figured out how to play the Pfife, I had no idea what they meant. But after ... I could just ... read them."

"It's because you're a Dragon Whistler," Tiernan said, unmistakable awe in her voice.

Willow mustered a lopsided smile and sifted through the parchment. "I guess so. This one is Awaken. And this one is Flight."

Coreen raised both eyebrows. "Very interesting."

Willow clutched the Pfife. "So, what if Drynfyre is still mad at me?" A wave of doubt rolled over her as she remembered the horrible sadness in Drynfyre's eyes. The flames of anger just beneath the sorrow. Tiernan and Coreen shared an uneasy look that did nothing to settle the butterflies jittering in Willow's stomach.

Ben put a hand on her arm. "How cool it is that you get to talk to a dragon. Again? Seriously, it's amazing!"

Willow relaxed a bit, her heartbeat slowing as his words sank in. Ben was right. Sure, this was all overwhelming, but she couldn't let a little fear overshadow the amazing parts. Hadn't she always considered herself a treasure hunter? Well, now she had the opportunity to find what had to be the most awesome treasure ever. Not to mention, she was the only kid on the planet who had carried on a conversation with a real, live, fireball-spitting dragon. Even if the dragon wasn't exactly happy with her.

"Okay," she said. "Let's do this."

THE WORKERS REMOVED the rest of the scaffolding covering Drynfyre and then gathered near the back of the room to watch. Tiernan shushed their excited chatter with a frown. "If you can't keep quiet you won't be able to stay in here. This is a dragon we're talking about!" Sheepishly, the crewmen complied.

Willow positioned herself near (but not too near) the dragon's head. Coreen had told them Belinda insisted they act fast, sot hey couldn't wait to wake Drynfyre until Mom and Uncle Josh got there.

Willow didn't need to look at the music to play the Awakening Song, it was the same one she'd played in the park that first time and there was no way she'd ever forget that melody, as long as she lived. After just the first few notes, an odd sense of confidence sizzled through Willow's veins. She felt like she could do anything. Her fingers hit each note perfectly, her breath just right to make each note zing. The tune filled the space around them with a magical sparkle, like happiness turned into sound. This was different than when she'd played in the park, maybe because she was closer to Drynfyre now? The sparkle poured from the Pfife, wrapping Drynfyre in a golden, twinkling blanket, alighting each scale before seeping in. The last notes hung in the air, doused one by one by the metallic rustle of Drynfyre's rousing. The dragon pushed up onto her barrel back legs, and lifted her body onto all fours. Her talons flexed, digging grooves into the earthen floor.

Willow glanced back at the group. In spite of her nervousness, she couldn't help but smile at Marcus' comically stunned expression. He looked like he'd just seen … well, a real-life dragon. Ben's eyes shone as if there might be tears in them. Tiernan's expression was serious and grim. Coreen looked even paler and sweatier than before. The rest of the workers stood against the back wall with their mouths hanging open.

Willow whirled back to Drynfyre. The thrill that tingled her spine was equal parts terror and excitement. Drynfyre stood to full height, tucking her massing wings. Her amethyst eyes shone bright with the last sizzle of the Pfife's magic, then it dissolved, her vertical pupils thinning to skinny lines.

To what do I owe the honor of a second Awakening?

Willow swallowed hard, standing as tall and straight as she could. Coreen had told her to act confident and strong, to look Drynfyre straight in the eye and take command. She was The Whistler. She was the one in control.

She sure didn't feel like it at the moment.

"I need your help," Willow blurted, her words trembling as she spoke aloud instead of in her mind. Coreen believed denying Drynfyre a private conversation would give Willow the upper hand. But the truth was, Willow didn't want to feel powerful. She wanted to make sure Drynfyre knew how sorry she was—about everything.

The dragon sank onto her haunches and swiveled her ears forward. *And why would I want to help a human who wouldn't help me?*

If she'd picked up on Willow's silent apology, she wasn't letting on.

"Someone is trying to get to the Dragon Treasure," Willow said, her voice stronger.

What did you say? Drynfyre's voice hissed icy cold in Willow's mind. Her long neck stretched toward Willow, the movement terrifyingly quick. Willow froze, heart slamming in her chest.

"I said … the Dragon Treasure is in danger." You're in charge, she thought. Act like you're in charge!

What do you mean by that?

Interesting. Drynfyre hadn't asked what Treasure she was talking about. Maybe it was real. "A Guardian is trying to steal the Dragon Treasure."

I thought The Guardians are our protectors. Her tone was edged with sarcasm. Like she'd never really believed these words. *Kareth assured us.*

"Well, humans make mistakes sometimes," Willow gulped. She glanced behind her. Tiernan nodded with encouragement. "And some of us, you know, make better choices than others." It sounded like something her mother would say, but the words seemed to give the dragon pause.

You speak the truth.

"So, okay, here's the deal," Willow said, summoning up her best take-charge kind of voice. "One of the big-boss Guardians thinks if she wakes all the dragons, she'll be able to find this secret Treasure that nobody is sure really exists, but I guess it must or you wouldn't have looked at me that way." She wondered if Drynfyre would stop her, but the dragon just blinked. Willow took this as permission to continue.

"So, yeah, this big-boss Guardian—her name is Faylene, by the way—stole both Amulets and took off with them. Nobody knows where. Plus, if she needs all the dragons, that means she'll need you, too. And since I'm your Whistler, she'll also need me."

Drynfyre's expression remained the same, so Willow plunged ahead. "Coreen and Tiernan think if we can get to the Treasure before the bad Guardians, then we can help protect it from, I don't know, whatever

Faylene plans to do with it." She paused, leaning toward the dragon conspiratorially. "What is the Treasure anyway?"

Drynfyre didn't respond, swinging her head toward the back of the cave. She snorted a ball of flame. Willow shrieked. The work crew scattered as the fireball exploded against the back wall, high over their heads. Drynfyre shook her head like a horse. *Sorry. I had a tickle in my nose.*

Willow glanced back over her shoulder at the remaining group. Everyone but Coreen, Thomas, Marcus, Ben and Tiernan had fled.

"Um, bless you. So is the Treasure real?"

Yes. It is. Drynfyre looked down her snout at Willow, her tone of voice not quite as sarcastic as before.

"She says the Dragon Treasure is real," Willow relayed the dragon's thoughts, then turned back to Drynfyre. "Why would Faylene want to steal it?"

Drynfyre inspected Willow before answering.

The same reason any human desires what doesn't belong to them. Power.

"But, how would this Treasure give Faylene power?"

Drynfyre hesitated. The silence in her mind told Willow two things. First, that the dragon didn't trust her. And second, she had the ability to mask her thoughts from Willow when she wanted to. Willow wished she could do that herself.

I would like to know why the Guardians sent a child to awaken me. A glimmer of something Willow hadn't seen before shone in Drynfyre's eyes. *Am I not worthy of a full-grown human?*

"Of course you are!" Willow blurted. "It was an accident, me waking you up. I didn't know what I was doing. See, your Pfife was stolen a long time ago—well, not so long compared to how long you've been asleep, I guess. Anyway, someone was trying to steal the Dragon Treasure back then, too." She felt herself going into rambling mode, talking fast like she always did when she was nervous. "One of the good Guardians—her name was Hanna Vorman—she found out what the bad Guardians were doing and she stole your Pfife and one of the Amulets. To keep them safe. For a really long time the Guardians believed Hanna Vorman was a traitor, because they didn't understand why she took the Pfife and Amulet, but then last week, me and my cousin Ben—that's him back there—" Willow pointed over her shoulder at Ben who lifted his hand tentatively in a wave at Drynfyre. "We were poking around in this old hotel and we found the Pfife hidden in the attic. We found the music too. I wanted to try and play the thing and so I was just messing around trying to figure it out and, well … I guess I figured it out."

Willow sucked in some breaths. Drynfyre just looked at her a minute, like she was trying to absorb all the information Willow had just dumped on her. *You weren't taught to play the Pfife or to read the music? You just … figured it out?*

"It wasn't hard." Willow looked over her shoulder at Ben again. Then back at Drynfyre. She sighed. "I have perfect pitch."

Drynfyre tilted her head like she wasn't sure what Willow meant.

"So … about the Dragon Treasure. Can you take us to it?" Willow asked.

Drynfyre hesitated then lowered her head, staring intently into Willow's eyes. *No good can come from a human possessing the Treasure.* Willow felt the same tingling she'd felt when playing the Pfife before. *I will help you stop this Guardian.*

"Oh, that's awesome! I mean, I was afraid you wouldn't help because I thought maybe … well, you seemed kind of upset with me before." She stopped herself, squeezing her eyes together and giving her head a shake. "I really am sorry about all that. Truly." She looked back at the monitoring station again. "Can they come in and talk to you?"

I will not harm them. Drynfyre's voice felt softer and kinder now. Willow was glad she'd apologized, even though Coreen had warned her against it.

"Come out, guys. Drynfyre is going to help us!" Willow dashed back and forth between the doorway and Drynfyre, charged with relief and excitement. "I'll translate," she said as Tiernan and Coreen tentatively approached. Coreen really did not look good. She had one hand over her stomach, like she felt sick.

Thomas remained by the door. Marcus and Ben hovered just inside the room, looking unsure about moving any closer.

Coreen touched her forehead with two trembling fingers. "Thank you for giving us audience, great one."

Drynfyre gave a slight nod, but Willow sensed that she liked Coreen's respectful way. She turned to Willow. "We just learned Geldfyre's den was breached. Thankfully, the Primary and her daughter survived." Coreen paused. "But Faylene got the Pfife. Geldfyre is gone."

If this Guardian used the Pfife, Geldfyre would be unable to resist her, Drynfyre thought. *She is now his Whistler. He is compelled to do this Whistler's bidding, just as I am compelled to do yours. He will fight any who oppose her. Even me.*

Willow relayed Drynfyre's words to the others. "Drynfyre thinks she'll make Geldfyre fight us," she said, worried.

The others will as well, if she wakes them. I may be able to defeat a single opponent, but no more than that.

"We need to get to the Treasure first to protect it," Coreen said, after Willow put Drynfyre's thoughts into words. "Can you take us there?"

The better course would be to go to Mysendrake first.

"Mysendrake?" Willow asked, looking at Tiernan. "Isn't that the English dragon you told us about? Kareth's dragon?"

He is the Seventh Dragon, Drynfyre corrected.

"Drynfyre calls him the seventh dragon," Willow said. "We need to get him before going after the Treasure."

"Why?" Coreen asked, her voice weak.

Drynfyre considered Coreen, then looked at Willow. *He is essential to the Treasure's protection. That is his story to reveal, should he choose to do so.*

Coreen doubled over, hands on her stomach. "I'm fine, it's okay," she said, waving off Tiernan's concern. "Drynfyre, if Mysendrake is the key wouldn't Geldfyre tell her?"

Only if she asked him directly. He is compelled to follow her orders, but he would not volunteer information.

Tiernan kept her eyes on her aunt, worry etched deep in her expression. "So assuming Geldfyre hasn't told her, and assuming Faylene doesn't somehow already know she needs to go after Mysendrake, then she's probably headed to the Greenland den. It's the next closest one. If we went straight to Mysendrake, and we do it fast, we could beat her there."

"I'll call Gert in England. Let her know we're coming," Coreen said, then doubled over again. Thomas grabbed her arm, but she pushed past him, out the door. "I'm fine!" she croaked.

Tiernan gave Drynfyre a small grateful bow. "Thank you, Drynfyre. I believe you just gave us our advantage."

CHAPTER 30

TIERNAN STUCK WATER bottles in the side pockets of Ben's backpack. Her heart thumped wildly, but she still wasn't sure if it was from excitement or absolute terror. She was beginning to think there wasn't much difference between the two.

Coreen returned to the conference room with a box of granola bars and some beef jerky sticks from the kitchen. She seemed a little better, but Tiernan still worried about her. Her skin was pale and sweaty; her hands shook as she pulled the granola bars out of the box. Tiernan exchanged a concerned look with Thomas but he shook his head. Coreen was stubborn. If she didn't want anyone fussing over her, you'd better not fuss.

"Drynfyre's almost finished eating," said Coreen, tucking the snacks into the backpack. "Those frozen steaks didn't seem to give her a problem, but she'll need more than that to fly across the Atlantic." Maybe Coreen was just worried. They certainly had good reason to be. None of them had any idea what they were doing, or what they were dealing with. They also didn't have a choice. Mysendrake was their best shot and they had to get to the English den quickly. According to Willow, riding Drynfyre was their best chance.

Tiernan checked the pack's inventory. "Flashlight, rope, binoculars, water, snacks, first aid kit, the com set, and my phone in case the com set doesn't work ... Looks like we're ready. We even have a pair of fuzzy drumsticks." Tiernan winked at Ben. She looked at Marcus. "Your dad almost here?"

"I think so," Marcus said, checking his cell phone. "I thought they'd be here by now."

Willow ran in, eyes bright, parchment in hand. "Okay, there are the two pieces of music that should help us. Drynfyre thinks this one will let us ride her, and this one should make her invisible." She handed the music folder to Tiernan, who slipped it into the pack and zipped it up. Good thing they didn't need anything else, there wasn't much room left.

"Excellent. You have the Pfife?"

Willow pulled the string from her shirt and dangled it in front of Tiernan's face. "Okay, then. I guess we're ready." An apprehensive chill wrestled in Tiernan's belly with a sparkle of excitement. Tiernan had studied dragons her entire life, had grown up knowing magical creatures actually existed, but this was really happening. Not just words in a book.

Imagine the things they could learn from Drynfyre! Answers to questions they'd wondered about for so long … about Kareth, and magic and—

"Coreen!"

Tiernan whirled at the alarm in Thomas' voice as Coreen collapsed to the floor.

CAREFLIGHT WAS ON the way. Thomas suspected appendicitis. Tiernan sat by her aunt, holding her hand. "You'll have to go without me," Coreen said. "You can do this."

"But …" Tiernan's heart hammered like a metronome pegged at 208. "I can't go without you." Tendrils of panic wound around her lungs making it near impossible to breathe.

"You can. Go!"

Thomas' crew had already removed the tarp covering the hole in the den's roof. The hanger door, originally intended for such a departure, was damaged from the previous day's escape so Drynfyre would have to go out the way she had yesterday.

"My dad and aunt aren't here yet. We can't just leave," Marcus said, following her into the den. "What if they don't want us to do this?"

"Marcus, we don't have time to wait, or frankly, to argue about it with them. I have to go. And so does Willow."

"If Willow's going, I'm going," Ben said.

"Dad is going to kill me," Marcus muttered, looking ill.

Willow groaned, sinking to the floor by Drynfyre. "If we don't go soon, I'm going to lose my nerve." She placed the first piece of parchment on the ground. Pfife in position, she looked at Tiernan. "Are we ready?" At Tiernan's nod, Willow put the Pfife to her lips. The blanket of music eclipsed all other sound in the cave, weaving its magic. It was difficult to rush such beauty, but Willow knew she must. At the end of the second stanza, Drynfyre evaporated into nothingness.

Ben let out a whoosh of breath. "It worked."

"You might have wanted to play the other song first," Marcus raised his eyebrows at Willow. She looked at the invisible dragon, then back at them.

"Yeah, that might have been better."

Marcus took a step forward. "So how do we board this flight when we can't even see her?"

Willow paused, listening for a second. Tiernan was beginning to understand when Drynfyre was speaking in Willow's head from the telltale far away look on her face. "Make a chain," Willow instructed, taking Ben's hand.

Marcus took Ben's other hand and laced his fingers through Tiernan's. Hopefully, he didn't notice the warmth rushing to her cheeks. Willow reached her free hand toward Drynfyre until suddenly the dragon bloomed into sight as if someone had ripped away a veil of invisibility.

"As long as we have physical connection to her, we can see her," Willow said. Tiernan didn't let go of Marcus's hand, but moved closer to Drynfyre, running the fingers of her other hand along the dragon's familiar, smooth scales. A warm tingling spread up her arm. It seeped through her body, filling her with a friendly, comforting feeling. It was like being pumped full of tiny bubbles. Odd, but not uncomfortable. Ben and Marcus did the same, dropping their linked hands.

"When we're touching her, we're invisible too," Willow said.

"So cool," Tiernan murmured, grinning at Marcus. "How do we get on?"

Drynfyre sunk down onto her belly and extended her right front leg, claws curled upward. Willow scrambled into the middle of the paw and Drynfyre gently lifted her high enough to jump easily to the dragon's upper back. Then Drynfyre returned her paw to the ground.

"C'mon, Ben, it's so cool up here!" Willow called.

"I can't believe I'm doing this," Ben muttered, blowing out three puffs of air to work up the nerve to move between Drynfyre's claws.

Once Ben was on Drynfyre's back, her paw returned for Marcus and Tiernan. "Ladies, first," Marcus swept his hand in a majestic bow.

"Such the gentleman." Tiernan tried to keep her voice steady as she climbed between the talons. They were as long as she was tall, sharp and gleaming. She could see why Ben was nervous. When Drynfyre lifted her, the movement was like taking off in a rocket. The paw stopped and she quickly jumped off Drynfyre's paw and onto her back.

Willow grabbed her arm. "You okay?" she asked, a concerned look on her face.

"Yeah, I'm great," she said, shaking off the fear and standing up. *Pull yourself together! These kids are handling this better than you are! You're a Guardian!*

With a lift of Drynfyre's paw, Marcus had joined them.

"Okay, just one more song and we can get out of here," Willow said, handing Ben a piece of parchment. "Could you hold this up for me?"

The Riding Song made Tiernan imagine dipping and spinning through clouds, diving towards rivers and soaring over treetops. The last notes faded away leaving Tiernan a bit dazed. "Did you feel that?" she whispered.

"That was so cool," Marcus and Ben said simultaneously.

Willow tucked the Pfife into the neckline of her shirt. "You ready? Because Drynfyre is."

They sat down on a flat patch of scales across Drynfyre's thick shoulders, wide enough to seat a couple dozen people. It was like sitting on smooth chain mail. "What, no seatbelts?" Ben asked with a nervous laugh.

"Don't worry," Willow said. "The Flight Song will protect us. We literally can't fall off."

"Right," Ben said, working his fingers under the edges of his scale.

"Don't worry. Drynfyre won't do anything to hurt Willow," said Tiernan.

"It's more than just me," Willow said. "Drynfyre feels protective of us all. I can feel it."

When Drynfyre pushed up onto her feet, the tingling sensation from before swelled like soda bubbles shaken up. Tiernan swallowed. This was it.

Willow looked at them. "Everybody ready?"

Marcus nodded, but he didn't look ready. Ben squeezed the edges of his scale so hard his knuckles turned white. "Ready," he squeaked.

"Me, too," Tiernan said.

Drynfyre launched herself into the air.

CHAPTER 31

"THERE THEY ARE!" Ben yelled as they soared into the twilight. Marcus craned his neck to see their dad's car pulling into the parking lot below them. He groaned.

"Great. I left dad like ten voicemails, but they're still going to be mad." He shot a look at Ben. "Of course they're going to be mad. What parent wants his kids flying across the ocean on the back of a dragon to wake another dragon to protect it from being kidnapped by a psychopath?" He groaned again.

"Psychopath is a strong word," Tiernan muttered.

"Why do I have the feeling this was a bad idea?" said Marcus.

Ben was surprised to find flying on the back of a dragon was nothing like flying in an airplane. There was no picking up speed as you raced down a runway. One minute you were on the ground, the next you were flying. That sounded scary, but it wasn't, actually. Maybe it was the Riding Song's magic, but he could barely feel the motion of flying at all. It was more like floating.

The other surprising thing about dragon riding was the lack of wind. Ben figured they'd have to hang on for dear life as gale-force winds tried to rip them from the dragon's back, but there was nothing like that. It was like flying in a bubble.

He was kind of glad they'd flown away before his dad and Aunt Amanda arrived, because his dad would never have let him go on this absurd adventure. He couldn't even believe he'd agreed to go himself.

Drynfyre pushed her wings forward then pulled them back, each stroke moving them higher into the sky. They were above the mountain peaks in moments. While flying seemed much safer than Ben expected, a thought suddenly popped into his head that scared him to death.

"Hey! What about airplanes!" he gasped. "What if we—"

"Chillax, cuz," Willow said, calmly putting a hand on his arm. "I told Drynfyre all about them."

"But they go like five hundred something miles an hour! And I have no idea how fast we're flying! And they can't see us!"

Willow patted his knee. "Drynfyre can sense the sky for miles around us. She'll know when an airplane is coming way before it gets too close. She must have some sort of radar thing, like bats only with a bigger range. It's okay, Ben. Really."

"It's okay?" He swallowed hard.

"It's okay," Tiernan agreed.

And it was. They flew into the deepening twilight, the rhythmic stroke of Drynfyre's wings lulling them all into silence.

Ben finally released his grip on his scale. It wasn't like he needed to hold on, even when Drynfyre dipped her left wing, tilting northeast. There was no sensation of turning or falling or anything. The shifting horizon was the only thing that told Ben they were changing direction.

"Whoa, check it out!" Willow cried, scrambling to her feet and moving closer to Drynfyre's neck to peer over her shoulder. "It looks like some big huge snake!"

"Snake?" Ben tensed.

"Relax, it's just a river," Marcus said.

"Must be the Mississippi," Tiernan said, moving off her scale to join Willow. "Ben, come see."

"Nah," he said with an emphatic shake of his head. "I'm good, thanks." He was fine sitting here, but standing up? That was a little much.

"C'mon," Willow whined. "Look! Nothing's going to happen. I can jump up and down, and I won't fall off." She bounced around to demonstrate, sending Ben's heart into a tizzy of terror.

"Please, don't do that!"

"I told you! Drynfyre said we can't fall off," Willow chided, hands on her hips. "Even if I tried to jump off I don't think I could."

"Please do NOT test out that theory!" Ben yelled.

"I promise, but only if you come over here and look at the darn Mississippi River!" Willow yelled back.

"Guys, stop," Tiernan said. "Ben doesn't have to look if he doesn't want to. Nobody is going to make anybody do anything that makes them uncomfortable on this flight."

"You mean, other than going on the flight in the first place?" Marcus snipped.

"If no one can do anything uncomfortable, then Willow won't have any fun at all!" Ben snarled, his emotions accelerating. Feeling mad sure was better than feeling scared; in fact, it felt so much better that Ben let it swell up like a monstrous blob in some old horror movie. "Willow loves asking people to do things that make them uncomfortable!"

The wounded expression on Willow's face plugged the flow of words from his mouth like someone had popped in a cork. Her eyes glistened with tears and her bottom lip quivered. Ben's cheeks flushed with heat. Why had he said those things? "I'm sorry, Willow. I don't know why I said that. This is all so strange, like some totally wacked out dream I can't wake up from." He put the heels of his hands against his eyes. "I didn't mean any of it. I'm so sorry."

Marcus silently squeezed his shoulder.

"No Ben." Willow's voice sounded worried, when she should have been angry and irritated. She sat down next to him. "Don't be sorry. You're kind of right," she said. "I talked you into exploring that hotel. I got you to help research the Pfife ..."

Ben dropped his hands. "Nah, I was just as curious about it as you were. I guess I'm just scared about what's going to happen when we get where we're going."

Willow threw an arm over his shoulder. "We're going to do great. Don't worry."

"Okay, then," Tiernan said. "Glad that's settled." She pulled her cell phone from her back pocket. "I wonder if I can get a signal up here." She sighed. "Yeah, didn't think so. We're going to land for a few minutes when we reach the coast to let Drynfyre eat some more before we head across the ocean."

"Good idea," Willow nodded. "She's hungry."

"I didn't think those frozen steaks would be enough. We can call Thomas and check on Coreen. And let your folks know you're okay."

"They're going to kill me," Marcus muttered again.

Evening was already on them. Ben looked out over the dark smudge of the Atlantic just beyond the last clusters of lights scattered across the land's edge. "Drynfyre's looking for a place to land," Willow told them.

Ben grabbed the edges of his scale seat as Willow gave him a grin. Drynfyre touched down with only a slight bump. "We know you don't have a lot of choices when it comes to dragon air travel," Marcus quipped, "but we appreciate you choosing Drynfyre airlines." Tiernan gave him a crooked grin as she climbed to her feet.

Ben breathed in the salty air. "Where are we?" he asked. "I mean, we're obviously by the ocean, but which state?"

Tiernan looked down at her cell again. "Got full bars now, let me check GPS." She tapped the phone. "Moving slow, hold on."

Marcus looked at his own phone. "It's 8:45. Are you kidding? We crossed three time zones in about 15 minutes."

Moonbeam-lit whitecaps reached ghostly fingers toward the beach. Swaying grasses whispered welcome all around them. A picturesque two-story lighthouse perched on a distant cliff.

"I'll show you how to get off," said Willow, moving closer to Drynfyre's shoulder. She put one hand on the dragon's neck and sat. "Okay, I'm ready." Drynfyre's scales shifted, fitting together perfectly to convert her forearm into a chink-proof slide. Willow slid neatly to the ground.

She looked up at them. "Even more fun than getting on! C'mon!"

Ben didn't hesitate. He slid down and stumbled off the end of Drynfyre's paw, tripping out of the bubble of magic. As soon as Ben lost physical contact with Drynfyre, she—and Marcus and Tiernan—became invisible. Ben watched as the two of them appeared out of nothing as they reached the bottom of Drynfyre's leg.

"She's going to ... um ... find something to eat," Willow told them. A whoosh of air indicated Drynfyre's departure. "She says she wants to hunt in the ocean." Willow looked slightly nauseated.

"Hmm," Marcus raised an eyebrow. "Dragons like seafood."

"And goats," Tiernan said, distracted. She looked around. "I guess we can hang here for a bit. It's nice and deserted. Probably why GPS is having trouble loading." It was almost fully dark and the lack of civilization made it hard to see their surroundings. They huddled close in the circle of light from Tiernan's phone.

"Finally!" Tiernan's voice brightened. "GPS kicked in. Apparently we are on the northern part of an island off the coast of Rhode Island. No developments around here. It's like a big park. So if we travelled halfway across the country in only fifteen minutes, getting to England shouldn't take much longer than an hour." Tiernan tucked her phone back in her pocket. "Hopefully Faylene didn't head straight for Mysendrake, too. If she did, she'll beat us there."

"I'm starving," Willow said. "Anyone else hungry? How about a snack?"

Tiernan unpacked a blanket from Ben's backpack and spread it on the ground. She pulled out a couple of flashlights and handed out granola bars and jerky sticks as they settled on the blanket. "Will Drynfyre be able to find us again?" Ben asked, peering upward and hoping that if and when she did, she wouldn't accidentally land on them.

"She knows right where I am, I mean, where we are," Willow said. Ben sensed the blush behind her words. He felt like he needed to reassure her, after his outburst before.

"It's okay, you know."

"What's okay?" she asked, peeling the wrapper from a granola bar.

"That you and Drynfyre have a special connection," Ben said, nudging her with his shoulder. "You don't have to act like you don't."

Willow painted slow figure eights with the flashlight beam as she chewed. "Yeah?"

"In fact, I'm glad it's you. I probably couldn't deal with it."

Tiernan handed out small bottles of water. "Yes, you could," she said, her voice tight. Maybe Tiernan wished she had the connection with Drynfyre instead of Willow. "Kids can handle a lot more than grownups give them credit for. Or they give themselves credit for."

Ben unwrapped a jerky stick and gnawed it thoughtfully. "I don't understand why it's so important we get to Mysendrake first," he said.

Tiernan took a long drink from her water bottle before answering. "Mysendrake has always been thought of as the most important dragon of the seven. He was very close to Kareth, the last one to be put into hibernation. He played a big part in convincing the other dragons to trust the hibernation idea."

"Yeah, I bet they weren't real keen on it," Marcus said.

"Drynfyre sure wasn't happy about it," Willow muttered. "The first time, or the second."

A huge thump a few yards away made Ben lurch to his feet. He clutched his chest, panting. "Jeez, that scared me to death!"

Willow clapped him on the shoulder. "Relax. It's just a dragon."

Marcus stuffed the blanket and the leftover snack items into Ben's pack. "Do you want to call your folks before we take off again?" she asked Marcus.

He hesitated. "Um, you know, maybe just ask Thomas to let them know we're okay? I really don't want to deal with my dad right now." He gave Tiernan a convincing grin.

She raised an eyebrow. "All right then." Tiernan tapped her phone.

Ben slid into the backpack's straps and followed Marcus and Willow in Drynfyre's direction. He was far from ready to re-board for the next leg of their journey, but surprised at the strange sense of comfort that settled over him as he felt the dragon's scales under his fingertips and Drynfyre flickered into view.

CHAPTER 32

GELDFYRE ZIPPED THROUGH the underwater tunnel of the Chesapeake den and up through the deepest part of the bay at a mind-bending speed. The Flying Song protected her from the water, a bubble of magic around a missile. As a Whistler, she swelled with invincibility. Playing the Songs, commanding the dragon, all of it was exactly as she'd dreamed. She was powerful. She was beautiful.

They reached their destination a mere ten minutes after launching from the Bay. Located deep within the thick ice of the Petermann Glacier, the Greenland den was the only thing more difficult to access than the Glacier itself. Although parts of Greenland could reach 68 degrees during the summer, the temperature on the Ice Sheet was still well below freezing, making the winter jackets Elsbeth purchased at the outlet mall between the Baltimore airport and the Chesapeake den even more necessary.

Geldfyre landed with a spray of snow and ice near a tall cliff not far from a small wooden ice-fishing shack that doubled as the den's entrance. In the icehouse, Faylene and Elsbeth stood side-by-side in the small room as Faylene wrapped her fingers around the Amulets, chanting the Illian words that summoned the Onyx Cloud.

Nothing happened.

Elsbeth looked at her, confused. "What's wrong?"

Faylene stared at the Amulets. "I'm not sure."

Before she could wonder further, a stainless steel elevator car rose out of the circular hole cut into the ice. The doors slid open. "Quite hospitable of them," Faylene said, raising an eyebrow. Elsbeth looked uncomfortable, but followed her into the car. The door automatically closed and the windowless tube plunged down into the ice.

Faylene wondered why she wasn't able to create the Onyx Cloud. She must have pronounced something wrong this time. Surely it wasn't a one-time-use thing. The pages Nanette gave her hadn't been preserved as well as the rest of the Codex, so some parts were undecipherable, some things still unknown. But the Onyx chant had worked once. She pressed her lips into a tight line, angry, mind spinning. She had counted on the gems providing access to all the dens. But it looked as if she might have to improvise.

Down, down, down the elevator sank and the lower they went, the more the Amulets tingled in Faylene's hands. As the elevator slowed, they began to pulse. The Pfife was near.

As the doors slid open, Faylene registered the mistake immediately. There was no time to move, but there wasn't anywhere she could have gone anyway. The Primary didn't hesitate. Faylene heard a loud pop that slammed her against the wall of the tube. It felt like a horse kicked her in the chest. The old saying "as easy as shooting ducks in a barrel" popped into her mind. Sadly, in this case, she was the duck.

Elsbeth dove out of the elevator, tackling the Primary, but the damage was done. Faylene's knees collapsed and she slid to the floor. Tugging down the zipper on her parka, she put both hands to her belly and moaned. The blood welled beneath her palms, seeped through her fingers.

How did this happen?

It was an ambush, and a blatant one at that. She thought the Amulets would make her untouchable. How could she have been so stupid and careless? Cockiness, it was always her Achilles, wasn't that what grandmother had said? She'd assumed a lot about the Amulets' powers—too much, apparently—and now everything was over before it truly began. A sweeping sadness brought tears to her eyes.

"Oh, Fay!" Elsbeth cried, rushing back to her side. The Primary lay unconscious on the floor behind her.

"Anyone else?" Faylene's voice was little more than a croak.

"No, she was alone. And she won't hurt you again, I promise."

Not unconscious then. Faylene closed her eyes. Now Elsbeth had killed for her. For a failed mission. She hadn't intended for anyone to die. They had left Portia and Sophie alive at Chesapeake, she thought the Guardians would see that she hadn't taken the opportunity to do them permanent harm. But it seemed they had authorized the Primaries use whatever force necessary to stop Faylene and her sister.

"Hurry," Faylene moaned. "Find the Pfife. No, it's okay," she said, when Elsbeth protested. "Go. I … I'm actually feeling better." It wasn't a lie. The pain was subsiding. And she could swear the bleeding had stopped.

"How? Are you in shock or something?" Elsbeth tugged Faylene's hands away, exposing the site. "There's so much blood, but …" Elsbeth's wide eyes met hers. "Oh my … Fay?"

Faylene scooted up to lean against the wall, shrugging out of her coat. She unbuttoned her blouse to see the wound. Elsbeth gasped. Faylene's skin was wet with the bloody residue of an injury undone.

They stared at each other. "Goodness," Faylene said, poking the wounded area with her fingers. Unbelievable. There was no wound, at least, not any more.

Elsbeth helped her to her feet and something clinked to the floor of the elevator. A silver, bloody slug. Had the bullet gone clean through her? Or had the magic dispelled it from the wound as it healed?

"The Amulets protected you!" Elsbeth breathed, a wide grin on her face. Her sister blew out an enormous sigh and placed a shaking hand to her forehead. "Sheesh, I thought you were a goner." They looked at each other, then burst out in relieved laughter.

Faylene re-buttoned her shirt and slipped back into her coat. She was sore but whole and definitely not dead. It was almost like nothing had happened at all. She caressed the Amulets and tucked them against her skin, zipping up her coat.

Elsbeth grabbed the fallen Guardian by the armpits and dragged her down the hall after Faylene, who didn't bother to offer any help. "I'm not sure if this is the Amulets doing or not," Faylene pondered. "It may be because I am Geldfyre's Whistler. It would make sense for the bond between dragon and Whistler to contain a magical healing property. It would be to the dragon's benefit." By time they reached the conference room, Elsbeth was panting.

Each den was designed in a similar layout, so finding the vault was no problem, but they needed the Primary Guardian to open it. Specifically, her finger.

Faylene helped Elsbeth lift the woman and they placed her index finger on the scanner. A red light whirled and the lock disengaged behind the thick metal door.

After propping the Guardian in the corner, the sisters exchanged a look. Faylene nodded. "You ready to be a Whistler, too?"

Elsbeth's eyes glowed. "Absolutely."

Faylene swept open the vault door and Elsbeth snatched the black velvet box from the shelf. She opened it with a flourish. "Oh, Völsendrake, we are going to have such fun," she cooed, running a tapered fingernail along the smooth white surface.

"Don't forget the music," Faylene reminded her before heading back down the hallway to the monitoring station. Elsbeth followed her, glancing at the sleeping dragon before turning her attention to the inscriptions atop each parchment. "Once you waken her those will be easier to read, apparently," Faylene reassured her. She sifted through the parchments and found the right Song. "Here, this is the one. Remember, playing a real Pfife is different than the one you practiced on." The training Pfifes simulated fingering, but as Faylene had discovered in

Geldfyre's den, playing an actual, magical Pfife was a whole new level of amazing.

Nodding, Elsbeth moved her fingers into the proper position for the first note. While Faylene had taught her how to play, Elsbeth hadn't had the opportunity to practice this particular tune, as each dragon's music was unique to its specific dragon. There were no copies of the music, so she was seeing these Songs for the first time. "Once she wakes, she'll know your every thought," Faylene said, looking her sister in the eye. "Keep your guard up."

"I know," Elsbeth snipped, taking a deep breath. She stared longingly at Völsendrake with hungry eyes. Then she began to play.

Like before, Faylene was emotionally overwhelmed by the Pfife's music. Memories swirled like snapshots from the past: studying to become a Guardian, taking her vows, Grandma Nanette revealing the secret book …

Völsendrake stirred. She woke much more calmly than either of the other dragons; lifting her neck, stretching, her deep red scales rippling like a wave of metallic blood. When she pushed up from her straw-covered icy bed, the spikes of her ears nearly brushed the ceiling. Völsendrake tried to extend her wings but the tips hit the walls of the den. With a grunt of frustration she sank down onto her haunches, eyes on Elsbeth. Faylene watched their silent communication. The inner voice of a dragon invoked powerful feelings and she wasn't sure how her sister would react. At first, Geldfyre's voice had made Faylene feel like her brain had been soaked in warm honey, each neuron hungrily soaking in his every thought. In the midst of this emotional upheaval for her, she'd had to retain control once Geldfyre realized her intentions. No doubt Völsendrake would also attempt to violate the bond if she understood why Elsbeth had awakened her. These first few moments were crucial.

"I have her," Elsbeth whispered. "But she's really angry." Elsbeth looked at Faylene, eyes large. "She is trying to make me kill you right now."

Faylene raised an eyebrow. "Is that right?" Turning to the dragon, she crossed her arms across her chest with a serious scowl. "You will obey your Whistler without question, as Kareth commanded," she ordered.

A snort of fire billowed from Völsendrake's nostrils. Fireballs skittered across the ground and sizzled at their feet. The preciseness with which the dragon could control her flame was astonishing if, indeed, she hadn't actually intended to scorch them. Was Völsendrake more determined than Geldfyre, or was Elsbeth not strong as Faylene?

"Let's get moving," Faylene snapped, irritated by the dragon's impertinence. "Ask her how we get out of this sunken ice cube."

"Here," Elsbeth answered, hitting a button on the console. A large iron door in the wall behind Völsendrake cranked upward revealing a metal tunnel that snaked back into the ice before ramping upward.

Once they had traveled up through the tunnel and she was back on Geldfyre, Faylene finally relaxed. The two dragons soaring side by side through the Arctic sky, and she stretched out, taking in the sea of stars dusted across the inky sky.

Just before she drifted off to sleep, she sent Geldfyre a mental message.

Wake me when we reach England.

CHAPTER 33

WILLOW SAT UP with a start, the dream evaporating. Her mind stretched out after it, but the tendrils slipped away leaving a vague memory about dragons and England and—

Reality rushed in as her sleep-addled mind registered her surroundings. She was on Drynfyre's back. Ben lay next to her using Marcus' leg as a pillow. Tiernan stretched out at Ben's feet, hands behind her head, staring up at the dark sky. She glanced over at Willow. "You okay?" she whispered.

"Yeah," Willow said quietly, rubbing her face briskly with her palms. "Argh, I shouldn't have fallen asleep. Now I feel all funky."

"I'm not a good napper either," Tiernan said, returning her gaze to the stars. "Always makes me feel worse for some reason."

"I couldn't help it. It was just so comfy. I was just watching the stars go by and then ..." Willow made a long, drawn-out snoring sound. Marcus chuckled. Willow hadn't realized he was awake.

"You've only been asleep for about ten minutes," he said. "I've found it hard not to drift off, too. But the view is just too fantastic."

Willow looked up. "I've never seen so many stars." It was like someone had sprinkled glowing salt across night water. How could it be that they were thousands of feet above ground, traveling who knew how fast, when it barely felt like they were moving at all?

Tiernan pulled her phone from the belt at her waist, illuminating it with the push of a button. "We've been flying almost an hour. Willow, could you check in with Drynfyre and see how close we are?"

"Okay." Willow looked off Drynfyre's side, catching glimpses of light in the spaces between wing flaps. "I think I see land!" she reported then reached out to Drynfyre with her mind: Are we there yet?

Soon, child.

Do you think Mysendrake will help us?

We will discover the answer to that question when we wake him. He may not be pleased.

But we're trying to protect the Treasure!

Perhaps, but this was not part of Kareth's plan. And Mysendrake never questioned Kareth. He followed her blindly. Love makes creatures do foolish things.

A dragon was in love with a Guardian?

Willow felt Drynfyre hesitate. *He believed she wanted to protect us. We all believed that to some extent, or we would not have agreed to the great sleep.*

Her words gave Willow a strange feeling in her stomach.

Do you still believe that?

Again, a hesitation. *When you woke me, and I realized how much time had passed* ... Drynfyre didn't complete the thought and Willow felt that invisible wall go up again.

I'm so sorry about before. Making you go back to sleep and all. When Drynfyre didn't respond, Willow turned back to Tiernan. "She says we'll be there soon."

Ben stirred, snorted a couple of times and sat up slowly, eyes heavy with sleep. "Where ..."

"It's okay, buddy," Marcus patted his shoulder. "We're just flying across the Atlantic on the back of a dragon, headed to the cave of another dragon. Perfectly normal evening."

Ben gave an involuntary shudder and rubbed his eyes. "How could I forget?"

Why did Ben have to be so negative all the time? She didn't understand him. Sure, this was a little overwhelming, but it was also a true adventure. Besides, what they were doing was important. If they could stop Faylene, they'd be heroes! For real this time.

"Ben?" Willow asked, choosing her words carefully. They'd come a long way in their relationship this week and she didn't want to blow it. "If I ask you something, do you promise not to be mad?"

Pulling his backpack into his lap and wrapping his arms around it, he shrugged. "Okay."

"Coreen getting sick wasn't good," she smiled thinly at Tiernan who had never had gotten a call to go through, so they weren't able to get a message to her mom and Uncle Josh, and they still didn't know how Tiernan's aunt was doing. "But other than that, I think this is, most definitely, the coolest thing that's ever happened to me in my whole life. Don't you think so, too?"

He stared at her, his expression blank.

Willow spread her arms out wide. "I mean, sure, it's terrifying, but look at us! Riding a dragon, going to England in search of a secret treasure—"

Ben shifted uncomfortably and dropped his eyes, mumbling something she couldn't hear.

"Yes, our parents are going to be mad, and yes, this is probably really dangerous but can't you just enjoy it?" Willow said. "You are riding on a real. Live. DRAGON! I can hardly even believe it's true. It's like a dream."

Ben suddenly looked at her. "No it's not, it's like a nightmare!" Then the words spilled out of him. "I wish I thought all this was the best thing ever," he spread his arms out, mocking the gesture she'd made before.

"But all I can think about are the 'what ifs'? And whatever comes after the 'what ifs'. Because in my experience, what comes next is always bad! What if the spell wears off and we fall into the ocean and get eaten by sharks? What if we get to England and this other dragon attacks us? What if Faylene gets there first and she takes over the world and she's like Hitler on steroids? What if something happens to me or my brother or you or Tiernan? Bad things happen, Willow. I know they don't usually happen to you, but they do to me!" His voice cracked as he fought back tears.

Willow glanced at Tiernan who hadn't moved since Ben started his rant. She raised her eyebrows at Willow in a gesture that said, well, you asked. She was right. Willow had asked. And now she had an answer. She cut her eyes at Marcus.

"Ben, it's okay—"

"Oh, right," Ben huffed, shrugging his hand off. "No matter what happens, Marcus never gets freaked out. Always cool as a cucumber. Remember? That's what mom always said."

Marcus' face shifted from concern to shock to hurt. Willow and Tiernan exchanged a look. That's what Ben meant, of course. About bad things happening. He meant what had happened to his mother.

"Ben, I'm really sorry," she said. "I know this year has been hard—"

"You don't know anything!" Ben exploded, red-faced. His chin quivered with emotion. "You have a mother! She cooks you breakfast and makes you take a shower and gets mad at you for breaking the rules. My mother is GONE! She can't do any of that anymore. And I miss her. I miss her so bad! I even miss her yelling at me to pick up my room!" Ben crumpled as deep sobs erupted from him. He pulled his knees up and tucked his head. Instantly, both Tiernan and Willow crouched by his side, hands around his shoulders. Marcus rubbed his back.

"I'm so sorry," Willow gushed, the lump in her throat like a wedged tennis ball. "I know I didn't make moving in with us easy. I don't know what my deal was. I was such a brat."

"What's going on with your folks is tough, too," Marcus said softly and Willow was surprised at the emotion in his voice. She nodded.

"Yeah, but it's not the same. If I lost my mom or dad, I don't think I could be as brave as you guys."

"I'm not brave," Ben sniffled.

"Are you kidding me? Going through all that without turning into a horrible, nasty person?" Willow sat back, the truth of her words ringing in her ears. "I don't have such a good reason for being nasty, and I can be awful."

Ben looked at her, but said nothing.

"Y'know, it's fine if you want to deny that," Willow grinned, happy to see Ben grin back.

We are here.

Drynfyre soared over thick rock pillars jutting up from the breakers and landed on the crescent-shaped beach. Tall, chalky-white cliffs towered behind the beach, ghostly in the light of the full moon. Waves crashed against boulders clustered between the cliffs and the sea, spraying foamy mist into the air with their thunder. The mouth of a cave yawned at the base of one of the cliffs.

When they were all on firm ground, Willow pulled two flashlights from Ben's backpack. Tiernan checked her phone. "Dang it. No bars. If I figured it correctly, it's around three in the morning here. Anybody tired?" She grinned.

Willow shook her head. "Not at all."

Ben refused to look at Willow. "Me either."

Tiernan held her phone up like that might help get a signal. With a sigh, she gave up.

"I'm sorry," Marcus said quietly. "I'm sure she's—"

"Yes! Coreen is going to be okay. She has to be. It just would be nice to know for sure." Her tone was strained, and snappish. She heard it, too. "I'm sorry, I'm just really worried." She looked around, tucking her phone back into her tool belt. "I was hoping we'd have a welcoming committee." Taking one of the flashlights, she directed the beam at the mouth of the cave and headed across the rocky beach toward it.

Turning to Drynfyre, Willow whispered, "What if Faylene shows up while we're in there?" The thought made her stomach lurch.

Drynfyre lowered her muzzle toward Willow's head, her gaze soft in the moonlight. I will sense when the other dragons' near. I will warn you.

"Okay," Willow said. Then, impulsively she laid her cheek against Drynfyre's snout, stretching her arms around her muzzle as best she could. Then she turned and ran to catch up with the group.

The ceiling of the cave loomed hundreds of feet above them, the rocky surface slick with moisture. The flashlights' feeble beams hardly penetrated the gloom. Tiernan aimed her light toward a back wall. "There! A reflector. Look around, maybe there's another one," she suggested.

They found nothing but rocks and dirt. Tiernan worked the reflector with her fingers, but couldn't turn it or pry it off.

"Why else would there be a reflector?" Marcus muttered. "It must mark the entrance, somehow."

"Look!" Ben shone his flashlight deeper into the cave. They followed the beam to a white reflector. "Reflector breadcrumbs?" Ben asked.

"Maybe," Tiernan said, shining her light farther into the cave. Ben joined his beam with hers. The cave continued far back into the darkness but, along the right side, a red reflector winked at them.

"There!" Ben cried, excited. They hustled toward another white reflector farther back in the cave. They moved as quickly as the uneven floor would allow, kicking up loose rocks, catching each other when they stumbled. When they reached the reflector, Willow spun around searching for another. A need to hurry pressed on her. Faylene could show up at any minute.

Ben and Tiernan trailed their flashlight beams slowly along the walls, moving from high to low, back and forth. Nothing. "What now?" Ben collapsed onto a thick round rock near the cave wall. It looked solid enough, but as soon as he sat on it, it sunk into the cave floor. Ben launched himself off the moving rock as a section of the cave slid away to reveal a white-tiled passageway.

"Holy dragon wings, Batman, you found it!" Marcus cheered.

"Nice job, my friend." Tiernan held out her fist and Ben bumped it coyly.

Nudging him with her shoulder, Willow grinned. "I told you we couldn't do this without you!"

CHAPTER 34

THE HALLWAY SLOPED gently downward away from the shoreline finally stopping at a tall gray metal door with a keypad in the wall beside it. Tiernan put her hands on her hips, examining the area. "Okay, how are we supposed to get in?" she asked out loud. There was no speaker or phone or anything they could use to communicate with the Guardian inside. "She knows we're coming. You'd think she'd be waiting."

"Should we knock or something?" Willow asked.

"Worth a try." Tiernan banged her fist on the smooth metal and the sound reverberated through the passageway. Nothing. Tiernan was about to knock again when the lock disengaged and the door opened with a horrible metallic screech. A tall, pale woman peeked out.

"Apologies! Been here sooner but the lift's out. Had to walk up all those stairs when I saw ya land on the CCTV."

The husky woman's British accent was thick and her red, knit work shirt and trousers looked like she'd slept in them. She had short, straight black hair that was heavily streaked with grey. Gerta was one of the older Guardians, but Tiernan hadn't realized how much older—she looked to be in her late sixties.

"I'm Gerta. Pleased to meet cha."

Tiernan cut her eyes at Willow as she stepped forward to shake Gerta's hand. "Hold up." A worrisome feeling spun in her gut. Something wasn't right here.

Gerta's eyes sparked with either amusement or irritation, Tiernan wasn't sure which. "Ah, well. Y' not sure I'm with ya or against ya? Understandable given what's gone on today, but you can trust me. We're all in this together, eh?"

Tiernan's heart beat a speedy thrum in her chest. There was no way to test Gerta's loyalty, so they'd have to risk it. Tiernan gave Marcus what she hoped was a warning look and he nodded in return, receiving her wordless message.

The door clanged shut behind them.

They followed Gerta down the hallway. The shadowless glow of fluorescent light made them all look pale and worried. Tiernan walked beside Marcus, keeping Willow and Ben in front of them where she could see them. She wasn't the only one who'd picked up on Gerta's strangeness. Ben looked like he might throw up and Willow snuck a glance over her shoulder, mouthing *what's wrong?*

Tiernan shook her head slightly, cutting her eyes toward Gerta as she raised her eyebrows. *Be careful*, she mouthed back. Willow hesitated, then nodded.

Gerta's hard shoes clomped to the end of the hallway where she unlocked another door to a stairwell. They circled down a stone staircase, each turn illuminated by yet another electric torch. The gloomy interior of the stairwell was a sharp contrast from the sterile hallway. Tiernan guessed this was the original entrance to the den, probably dug by hand thousands of years ago.

The farther down they went the more nervousness Tiernan became. Gerta's silence was unsettling. Marcus seemed to feel it, too. "How much farther?" he asked Gerta.

Willow and Ben sank onto a stair as the Guardian paused; sweat standing out on both of their foreheads. "Whew, I see why it took you so long to let us in," Willow panted.

"Buck up, poppets, we're almost there," Gerta replied, then disappeared around the next turn. Marcus raised his eyebrows at Tiernan. She shrugged wearily. They had to keep going. Reluctant, Willow and Ben stood up. Tiernan grabbed Marcus' hand and pulled him closer. "I don't trust her," she whispered into his ear.

"Me either," he whispered back.

"You coming, then?" Gerta's voice floated up the stairwell. They circled three more turns until they found Gerta waiting for them at the bottom. Behind her was an ancient wooden door with dark metal fixtures. "Shall we go see if Mysendrake's ready for his wake up call?"

Gerta pulled an old-fashioned keychain out of her pocket and unlocked the door. After a solid nudge from Gerta's shoulder, it swung open. She let them enter the enormous cavern first. Tiernan ushered Willow and Ben through, but put a hand on the door before following them. "After you," she said to Gerta, well aware that the smile on her face didn't reach her eyes. Tiernan felt Marcus tense behind her, waiting for Gerta's reaction.

"Suit y'self," Gerta said and followed the children into the den. Marcus left the door standing open.

"So, you want to beat Faylene to the Dragon Treasure," Gerta continued, a trace of disbelief in her voice. "Course t'aint no such thing, this Treasure, but that Faylene, she was always one t'ignore facts." Gerta entered the monitoring station and punched some buttons on the console. Light fixtures in the ceiling winked on, revealing a sleeping Mysendrake.

He was somewhat smaller than Drynfyre and, instead of shimmering silver scales, Mysendrake's shone a deep emerald green. His long, forked tail curled completely around the perimeter of his body like a giant sleeping dog. Willow smiled. "He's so cute!"

"Cute?" Gerta snapped, clearly offended. "Won't think he's so cute when yer burnin' t'death. I'll git the Pfife. We don'ave much time."

A suspicion thick as sulfur hung around Tiernan. As soon as Gerta left the room, she ran to the desktop communications unit in the monitoring station and keyed in her passcode. Scrolling through the most recent communications, Tiernan saw the incoming call from the Cheyenne Mountain den, the one Coreen made before they left. The next call was, unfortunately, from a very familiar number.

Faylene's personal cell phone.

Tiernan's stomach turned to ice water. She jerked her head around to look for Gerta, but the Guardian had not returned. "Stay with the kids!" Tiernan hissed at Marcus, shoving them all into the monitoring station.

Tiernan slipped the crossbow off her back and toed off her shoes. Her bare feet silent on the tile, she crept around the corner and toward the open conference room doorway.

When Gerta turned away from the vault, Pfife in one hand, music case in the other, she was shocked to find an arrow pointed at her nose. "How long did it take you to turncoat when Faylene called? Or were you a part of this all along?" she growled.

"I'm sure I dunno what you mean." Gerta's voice cut cold and harsh through the stale air. "Now put that thing down before yeh do summat you'll regret."

"Unfortunately, I've already done that," Tiernan spat. "I trusted you to be a loyal Guardian."

Gerta's eyes narrowed. "Loyal Guardian, hmmm, well whot 'xactly is that? Is it blindly following rules written ages ago? Or changin' the world?"

"You said you didn't believe in the Dragon Treasure," Tiernan said, the tip of the arrow inches from Gerta's nose.

"Pffft." Gerta's spittle flew far enough to make Tiernan blink, but before her disgust had a chance to register, Gerta knocked the crossbow out of Tiernan's hands. Dang, the old hag was faster than she looked, Tiernan thought as the arrow zipped past Gerta's ear and thwunked into the wall behind her.

"Now wha'cha gonna do, missy?" Gerta sneered.

Tiernan let her training kick in. Literally. She spun and swept a foot at Gerta's knees. The Guardian crashed to the floor. Tiernan jumped on top of her, straddling her belly. Gerta rolled, but Tiernan knew that trick and rolled along with her, pulling her legs in and sliding them under Gerta's chest. With a powerful thrust, she launched Gerta into a line of conference room chairs that scattered like bowling pins. Tiernan scrambled after her, twisting Gerta's arms behind her, shoving her face down against the tabletop.

"That's what I'm gonna do," Tiernan grunted. "Missy."

Marcus, Willow and Ben appeared in the doorway. "What happened?"

"She's working with Faylene," Tiernan panted, digging an elbow into Gerta's back.

"Yer too late!" Gerta snarled. "It won't be long, then yeh'll see what true power really is!"

Tiernan clapped one hand over the woman's mouth, smothering the rant. "There should be a storage cabinet just inside the door to the main den. Look around for something to tie her up with. Some duct tape would be nice, too."

Marcus returned half a minute later with a coil of rope and a roll of silver tape. Once Tiernan had Gerta tied in the chair, she bent down to look her straight in the eye. "How soon will Faylene be here?"

Gerta glared, eyes bright with defiance.

"Fine!" Tiernan growled, grabbing the music and the Pfife and handing them to Marcus. "Hold these, we're going to use them in a second." She rolled the chair backwards toward the open vault.

"Tiernan, no! She won't be able to breathe!" Willow cried. Tiernan stopped at the vault's threshold, eyes locked with Gerta's. Did she see fear there? No. More like triumph.

"Tiernan, please! We're the good guys," Willow's voice was firm. She put a hand on Tiernan's arm.

"Tell you what," she sighed. "I'm betting there's about an hour's worth of air inside that vault. At least, it was almost an hour before my friends got me out of the Cheyenne Mountain vault when Elsbeth locked me in there. Have to say, the air was pretty thin by that point. So if Faylene should be here within an hour, you've got nothing to worry about. I'll even leave her a note telling her where you are. 'Course, if she's not ... well, things could get ... tricky."

Gerta's expression faltered. She cut her eyes at Willow, perhaps hoping she'd start talking about doing the right thing again. Tiernan could almost see the wheels turning in the woman's head as she considered her options. "I ... I don't know when. Don't put me in there, please!"

"I see. No wonder you've been stalling ever since we arrived. The broken elevator? That long walk down the stairwell? Maybe you planned to lock all of us in the vault." Tiernan glanced over her shoulder at Marcus and Ben. She looked at Willow. "Do you really think she'd show us the same kind of mercy you're proposing?"

Willow spoke to Gerta. "I don't think the dragons would like what you're doing very much." She turned to Tiernan. "Maybe we should ask Mysendrake what to do with her?"

"Great idea. Let's go ask him." Tiernan spun the chair and wheeled Gerta toward the hallway.

"Yeh can't wake him!" shouted Gerta. Ignoring her protests, the strange parade filed down the hallway to the den where Tiernan placed the chair near Mysendrake's head.

"The Pfife, if you please," she said to Marcus. Willow sifted through the parchment until she found the proper Song, holding it at eye-level so Tiernan could see.

It had been a long time since Tiernan had practiced the Pfife. And, of course, the only Songs she'd studied were Drynfyre's so Mysendrake's required some sight-reading, which she was never very good at. She studied the stanza, working through the fingering a couple of times. "Okay, I think I've got it." As she put the Pfife to her lips, Gerta's voice took on a frantic tone.

"Wait! Yeh have no idea wha' yer doin'!"

"Your Jedi mind tricks won't work on me," Tiernan quipped, returning the Pfife to her lips. The melody was wistful and dark, full of mystery.

The air stirred around Mysendrake, sparkles streaking around his body. Tiernan backed away, pulling Willow and Ben with her. This hadn't happened when Drynfyre awakened. What was going on? Three bright flashes erupted in the magical storm, making them all shriek and shield their eyes. Finally, the wind calmed. Tiernan lowered her hands, and blinked.

An elderly man stood where Mysendrake had slept only moments before. An elderly … *naked* man. Willow gasped and Marcus clapped his hands over her eyes. Ben giggled as Tiernan felt her cheeks grow hot.

The old man said something in a language that might have been Irish or something older. It wasn't English and it wasn't Illian. He looked at them, confused.

"I'm sorry," Tiernan said. "We don't understand."

This seemed to register with him. "English, then, yes. I will use the King's English. Who are you? And what have you done with my tunic?"

CHAPTER 35

BEN RAN BACK into the den with a blanket from the monitoring station storage cabinet and draped it over the old man's shoulders.

"I'm one of the Guardians," Tiernan explained. "This is Willow, she's a Dragon Whistler. Who ... are you?"

Ben tried to ignore the pang of fear twisting in his gut. "And what happened to the dragon?" he asked.

"Silly boy," Gerta cackled. "He IS the dragon."

Willow and Ben exchanged confused looks.

This was no dragon, just a wrinkled, thin old man with silver hair and beard so long it brushed the floor. His gnarled fingers held the blanket closed and, although his face twitched nervously, his dark blue eyes twinkled. He cleared his throat. "That is not exactly true. I am not a dragon," he croaked. "I am a wizard hiding in the shape of a dragon."

"What?!" Tiernan put her hands on her head. "No! You are supposed to be a dragon! We need a dragon!"

"Tiernan ..." Marcus stepped toward her.

"Marcus, do you not get this? Faylene is almost here, and she probably has two dragons under her control already. We have only one. With two, we might have stood a chance—" Tiernan whirled on Gerta. "You knew, didn't you? Of course you did. Why did you try to stop us? Was this all some sort of trick?"

Gerta just shrugged and said nothing.

"What about Faylene?" Tiernan demanded, putting her face right up in Gerta's. "Does she know about," she jerked her thumb over her shoulder. "Him?"

"None of the Elders knew. Couldn't tell even if I'd wanted to. Kareth's spell keeps our secret. Faylene ordered me to stop yeh from wakin' him. I did m' best."

"Why did you wake me?" he demanded, eyes filled with confusion. "Is it finally time for the Awakening?"

"No, it's kind of a long story," Tiernan sighed.

"Drynfyre told us we needed you," Willow said.

"So, wait," Tiernan interrupted, hands on her hips. "Faylene needs seven dragons to get to the Dragon Treasure. But she has no idea that the seventh dragon isn't a dragon at all, but a wizard."

The old man's eyes grew wide. "Someone is after the Dragon Treasure?"

Tiernan nodded. "One of the Elders."

"Then we must depart at once," he said, pushing past Tiernan and stooping to pick up an extra length of rope from the floor. He wrapped it around his mid section, securing the blanket, leaving space for his arms to stick out the sides like a strange sort of toga. Then he raised one finger in the air. "But first, I need use of a chamber pot."

GERTA HAD LIED to them about the elevator; it was working perfectly fine. This made Ben feel a little less guilty about leaving her tied to the chair.

They ushered the wizard into the elevator and sent it rocketing toward the surface. He clung to the handrail, terrified either by the rapid ascent or the fact that an iron box was moving up through the earth of its own accord. It must be pretty freaky to wake up hundreds of years in the future. "It's okay," Ben said, reassuringly. "It's an elevator. It's the fastest way to get up to the cave."

"Soooo, what's your name?" Willow asked, hands defiantly crossed over her chest. Obviously, she wasn't sure they could trust him.

"I am Nordale."

"Okay, Nordale. Why were you disguised as a dragon?"

Marcus leaned against the side of the elevator car. "This is completely ridiculous."

Nordale held up a thin finger. "I believe I can answer all your questions, but we must first get as far from this place as we can before the traitor arrives."

The elevator jerked to a halt and the doors opened near the door where Gerta had let them in. Ben guided Nordale by the elbow up the hallway and out into the cave. The group carefully made their way across the rocky terrain, the soft glow of morning light making their flashlights unnecessary as they reached the mouth of the cave.

Willow froze, eyes wide and panicked. "Drynfyre says Faylene is coming! She's close!"

"Let's move! Move! Move!" Ben could tell Tiernan was trying to remain calm but her orders were barked as strong and stern as any drill sergeant he could imagine. Marcus swept the old man up in a fireman's hold and sprinted down the beach. Tiernan's look of surprise melted to admiration. She took Willow and Ben by the hands and they stumbled to keep up.

168

They ran through the misty morning air, accompanied by the crash of waves on the rocky shore. "Where is she?" How were they going to find the invisible dragon?

Willow glanced skyward. "Hurry!"

Face beaded with sweat, Marcus lowered Nordale to the ground as a whoosh of air stirred up the sand into tiny cyclones. "Cover your face!" Marcus yelled. When the sand settled, they could see the imprints of Drynfyre's paws. "There!"

Willow dropped Tiernan's hand and ran toward Drynfyre with her hands extended, turning invisible the moment she touched her dragon. Nordale didn't seem shaken or amazed by any of this, as Marcus and Tiernan helped him toward the invisible dragon.

With his hand on Nordale's arm, Ben touched Drynfyre and she appeared to both of them.

Nordale's smile was huge. "Oh, my beauty."

Ben couldn't hear Drynfyre's thoughts the way Willow could, but he'd learned enough about the dragon's body language to guess that Drynfyre wasn't as happy to see Nordale as he was to see her. Her pupils thinned to purple neon lines. She tossed her head angrily before placing out a paw, talons up.

Willow was already on board. "C'mon!" she yelled.

"Nordale first," Tiernan edged him between the talons. Drynfyre lifted Nordale a little too quickly and he nearly tumbled off.

Once everyone was seated, Drynfyre extended her wings, lifted her head and tensed her muscles. Ben could feel the energy building for the leap into the air. They were airborne before he could take a full breath.

"Where do we go?" Willow asked.

Tiernan looked to Nordale for the answer. His eyes were closed, head back. He looked like he was meditating.

"Nordale! Where do we go?" Tiernan reached over and shook his.

He didn't open his eyes, but answered blissfully, "Toward the setting sun, follow the land's edge. When we get nearer, Drynfyre will know."

"What exactly is our destination?" Tiernan asked Nordale in a tone brimming with suspicion.

"You're taking us to the Treasure, aren't you ..." Willow whispered.

Nordale smiled at her, and then simply gazed out at the coastline where the morning sun bathed the seaside landscape in warm orange light. "Oh, how I have missed mornings. It is my favorite time of day."

Tiernan looked behind them as Drynfyre banked inland. "Look! There they are!" They all turned to stare in horror at the two specks pursuing them.

"Why aren't they invisible?" Marcus asked. "Do they want us to see them?"

"They are invisible to anyone else," Willow explained. "Drynfyre says we can see them because we are inside her magical sphere. And they can see us as long as they are protected by their dragon's magic."

Nordale reached for Willow as Tiernan dug the binoculars out of the backpack. "Tell her to turn back," he warned. "If Drynfyre gets too close to the Treasure, she will not be able to resist and we will lead the traitor right to it."

Tiernan considered Nordale's words, jaw dropping in shock. "Yes, Willow, tell her to change course." Then, she asked Nordale, "Should we go east towards London or back toward the coast?"

"Over the sea! We must lead them away from the Treasure," Nordale urged.

Drynfyre banked left but immediately tilted right again to return to her original heading.

Willow groaned. "It's too late. She's locked onto the Treasure."

"They're getting closer!" Tiernan warned, looking through the binoculars.

"We're just going to lead them right to it?" asked Marcus.

"We have no choice now," replied Nordale, his eyes closed in resignation.

"She's trying, but she can't stop!" Willow explained, tears filling her eyes as if she felt Drynfyre's frustration. Drynfyre roared and shook her head side to side, but her wings kept a steady beat, a slave caught in a magical tractor beam.

Her altitude steadily dropped until she banked left, her head dipping toward the ground. Ben saw where they were headed and he couldn't help but be thrilled.

"Stonehenge?" Tiernan cried in confirmation. "That's where we're going?"

"The holy circle of stones," Nordale said, his voice sad but resolved. He looked at each of them, his voice deadly serious. "Whatever happens now, we must protect the Treasure. At any cost."

Ben stared at the wizard, his stomach tight. He'd always wanted to see Stonehenge, but not like this. What exactly would happen if Faylene got the Dragon Treasure? What could she do with it? He wished he understood how bad this was, but it was probably better that he didn't.

"Nordale, please, what is the Dragon Treasure? How can we protect it if we don't know what it is?" Tiernan demanded.

Nordale remained silent, staring ahead as the grassy plain and the stones grew closer. Drynfyre banked again, soaring over an empty parking lot and across a two-lane road to circle the prehistoric monument. From the air, Stonehenge looked like a giant had thrown a temper tantrum in the middle of two circles of tall stones, knocking them around and breaking them. The stones reflected the glow of the rising sun, shifting from silvery grey to flecks of orange and pink. Ben mapped the outer circle of rectangular stones like a clock face—from 12:00 to 4:00 stood four stones with three long stones laid across their top. Next stood a single stone then, completing the half circle at 6:00 were two sets of arches: each set made from two standing stones topped with a single. Other than another arch at 10:00, the stones remaining in the circle's "clock" were toppled.

The stones of Stonehenge's inner ring stood taller. This smaller circle was made up of three sets of arches, but these standing stones were closer together making for a thinner passageway beneath the arch. Two single stones stood by themselves and the rest had toppled over so long ago that grass had grown around them like fingers dragging the rock down into the earth.

From the sky, it was hard to tell the size of the monument's stones but as Drynfyre landed on the grassy plane beside the monument, Ben got a better perspective. The hulking rocks loomed like massive sentinels, as tall as three grown men standing on each other's shoulders.

"Everybody off!" Tiernan yelled. "Remember, once we leave Drynfyre, we won't be able to see the other dragons."

"To the circle!" Nordale called. Marcus grabbed Ben's hand and pulled him toward the circle. Nordale moved more quickly than Ben anticipated considering Marcus had had to carry him out of the cave. Maybe he'd recovered from turning back into his human form or something. Ben could imagine something like that was probably quite traumatic for an old guy, physically speaking.

Willow grabbed Tiernan's arm. "I should stay with Drynfyre."

"No way!" Tiernan refused. "It's too dangerous!"

They vaulted over the small fences put up to discourage tourists. "I should have stayed with her!" Willow moaned.

"What? No way! There's about to be a dragon battle!" Tiernan screamed. "And Drynfyre's magic might not be able to protect you against the Amulets!"

As they reached one of the solitary stones of the inner circle, a car horn blasted from behind them. A small car swerved into the grass by the side of the road, its driver leaning out the open window as he laid on the horn again. "Hey! You can't be in there!" He shouted between honks. "Hullo! You there!"

There was no one else on the road at this hour and since Drynfyre was invisible, all the guy saw was four kids and a half-naked old guy violating the "stay-on-the-path" rules.

"Just ignore him!" Tiernan urged.

Nordale glanced over to where they'd left Drynfyre who, of course, was invisible to them now as well. He searched the sky. Ben glanced up, too, but he couldn't see the other dragons because they were outside of Drynfyre's bubble. "There is no more time to waste," Nordale said, moving to a nearby arch as they gathered in the center of the middle circle. "Stay here, all of you," he ordered.

Ben paused, but followed him as he moved away. What was Nordale doing? He seemed to be looking for something. "Maybe this is the one?" he murmured, touching each standing stone in turn.

"The one for what?" Ben asked.

"You were told to stay in the circle!" He ran his hands over the stone's rough surface, its deep grey and white texture looking like a giant sugar cube dipped in a cup of time. Nordale circled the stones, moving between the gaps, searching with his fingertips. Ben followed, noticing that one side of the rock looked fuzzy with gray growth. "You should go back," Nordale grumbled, his voice tinged with panic.

"Look out!"

Ben whirled at Tiernan's shout. A suddenly visible Drynfyre flew backwards across the grass, struck by a dragon they couldn't see.

Ben gulped. The dragon battle had begun.

CHAPTER 36

WILLOW DUCKED AS A stream of flame spouted at them. It flattened against some sort of invisible barrier created by the inner circle of stones. Thank goodness, or they'd all be barbeque. Tiernan let out a huge breath, clutching one hand to her chest. "I guess that's why Nordale said to stay in the circle," she said, hugging Willow in relief. Marcus turned in a circle, searching.

"Where's Ben?" he asked, panicked.

Behind them, the sound of squealing tires told Willow the man trying to keep them off the grass had seen enough now that Drynfyre had appeared.

Ben ran back to join them. "What happened? Why are the dragons visible?"

"Where did you go?" Marcus grabbed him by the arms and shook him. "Do NOT leave this circle, do you hear me? Stay right here!"

"Okay, okay! I just wanted to see what Nordale was looking for."

Marcus's expression froze as a golden dragon materialized in the spot from which the flame had erupted. Faylene sat on its back, her grin triumphant. Willow looked up. The dark red dragon circling above was now visible, too. Her body went cold as ice even though she was sweating profusely.

Drynfyre! What should we do?

Do as Nordale says. Stay in the circle! Drynfyre answered as she charged the fire-breather with a roar. The dragons collided in a blur of silver and gold, a giant ball of wings, talons and teeth that tumbled toward the two-lane road with Faylene protected by what Willow assumed was the same kind of Song that had protected them while riding Drynfyre.

Ben grimaced with every bite and claw and snarl. Tiernan focused the binoculars on the red dragon above. It flew lower, circling the dragon fight. Another woman, who must be Faylene's sister Elsbeth, sat on its back. "Willow, Elsbeth is thinking about joining in. Warn Drynfyre!" Tiernan yelled.

Willow's brain instantaneously connected with Drynfyre's. Her dragon's reaction was just as instantaneous. One moment she seemed to be locked tooth and claw in a death grip with the golden dragon and the next she had disengaged and launched herself backward, narrowly avoiding a diving attack from the red one.

Drynfyre bulleted into the air and the chase was on, red and gold barreling after her. She headed in the direction of the ocean, back the way they'd come. "Where are you going?" Willow cried aloud, but Drynfyre heard her anyway.

Stay in the circle, the dragon's voice rang in her mind, but the thought felt weak and distracted.

"Don't worry," Tiernan reassured her, letting the binoculars hang from the strap around her neck. "Drynfyre had time to rest at Nordale's den. Those others just flew all the way across the ocean."

"Why can we see them now? Is the magic wearing off?" Willow asked.

"Honestly, I'm not sure," Tiernan shook her head.

"Nordale!" Marcus grabbed Ben as he started to run back to where he'd left the old wizard.

"Oh no you don't, you're staying right here."

In the center circle, Nordale pushed against the left stone of one of the arches like he was trying to knock it over.

Ben yanked himself free from Marcus's grip and ran to the center circle. Willow raced after him with Tiernan and Marcus close behind. As they neared, they heard Nordale chanting softly in some unrecognizable language. Switching to English, he murmured just loud enough for them to hear. "The Flame must be protected." He stared hard at a spot on the stone. "In the name of the Creator ..." he muttered, then started in with the funky language again.

"Whoa," Ben gasped. The stone around Nordale's splayed fingers began to glow and his hands sank into the stone as if it were made of pudding. Willow's heart lurched and she stepped back in horror. What was happening?

Nordale was up to his wrists when a tiny sunburst sparked to life on the arch's right side, growing like some inner light had punctured the stone. As Nordale's hands sank further into the sister stone, the light expanded until the beam formed first a square, and then a rectangle that stretched to the ground.

"It's a doorway!" said Ben in wonder.

Tiernan moved to put a tentative hand on Nordale's trembling shoulder. "Nordale? Are you okay?"

He looked at her with foggy, unfocused eyes. "Go through. I shall follow." His voice sounded like it was coming through some strange old radio, all crackled and thin.

Without hesitation, Tiernan moved to the doorway and peered into the light. "You guys stay here—"

"Hold on," Marcus grabbed Tiernan's arm. "You don't know what that is! What if it takes you somewhere and you can't get back?"

174

"You can't leave us here," Willow added. "Nordale wants us to go with you, right Nordale? Maybe the Dragon Treasure is in there!"

Nordale didn't answer, fully concerned with his spell. Tiernan hesitated, staring at Marcus. His face was ghostly pale. He shook his head. Ben looked from Willow to Marcus, his eyes wide and scared. "Marcus is right," Ben said. "We don't know what's down there. What if it's … bad?"

Marcus let go of Tiernan's arm, closing his eyes for a moment before heaving a huge sigh. "No, Willow is right. Nordale opened this for us and we should go in. I don't know why, but I trust him."

Something glimmered in Tiernan's eyes. She pulled an arrow from her quiver and slipped the bow off her shoulder. "Me too. Whatever is in there, we'll find out together." She nocked the arrow and nodded at Ben. "Okay?"

Willow's heart swelled at Tiernan's fierceness. Whatever being a Dragon Whistler might mean, should she get through all this, Willow hoped she could be a Guardian like Tiernan someday. She'd never known anyone so completely fearless before.

Willow took Ben's hand, smiling at Marcus. His palm was sweaty but his grip more solid and confident than she'd expected. "Ready?" Tiernan asked. Ben took a deep breath and gave them a quick nod.

"Let's do this," Marcus nodded.

Tiernan glanced at Nordale, his arms still embedded in what now looked like soupy stone. He turned his face to them, eyes glowing with the same white light of the doorway. He seemed to focus for a moment. "Go!" he barked. "I will try to follow."

As they stepped in, he continued weakly. "If I can not, please, tell her I love her."

CHAPTER 37

BEN BALKED. HE couldn't stop thinking about what Marcus said—what if they couldn't get back? His confidence guttered, like a candle flame drowning in its own melted wax. He yanked his hand free from Willow's grip, turning to double back, but the glow had already enveloped him with a cloud of liquid sunshine. Alone in the blinding light, his mind spun in a thousand different directions, splattering him with a mishmash of emotions and memories.

Willow playing the Pfife.
Tiernan racing up to them at the park.
The first time he beat Marcus at NBA2K on Xbox.
Driving away from their home in Texas that last time.
Blowing out the candles on the Star Wars 9ᵗʰ birthday cake.
Watching SpongeBob on the couch between his parents.
His mother's face looking down at him as he snuggled in her arms.

An intense, amazing feeling of love embraced him so tightly it squeezed a sob from his lips as the images evaporated, leaving him standing next to Willow, Marcus, and Tiernan in a completely white room. Actually, room wasn't the right word; it was more of a white space. He saw no walls, no ceiling, no floor beneath his feet, although he didn't feel like he was floating. There was simply a sense of place. A place made of light—super bright, yet not blinding. It was all very ethereal and Heavenly.

Before them stood a thin, white pillar, about four feet tall. A thick orange flame flickered in mid-air above it. On the other side of the pillar stood a stunning red-haired woman draped in white so pure she almost blended into the space around her.

Ben gasped as every muscle in his body froze in shock.

The woman looked just the way he'd pictured the angel in *Widershins*, except without wings. He thought about the words used in the book to describe her, words he'd read thousands of times: soft corkscrews of auburn curls, eyes as blue as a midday sky, milky smooth skin tight over high cheekbones.

In the split second it took for all these observations to register in Ben's mind, the woman changed. Her complexion darkened. Her hair shortened into black, tight crimps. Her blue eyes deepened to navy, then brown. Only her white robes remained unchanged.

Instantaneously, another alteration began—now she had almond-shaped eyes. Straight hair. Olive skin. This shifting continued; change after change. Ben wasn't the only one in awe over this. He saw expressions of wonder on the other's faces as well.

"Nordale," cooed the angel, her voice soft with some kind of lilting accent Ben couldn't place. Then she spoke in a language he didn't understand or recognize, but it was beautiful, like a combination of French and something maybe Middle Eastern? He couldn't quite place it, but it was captivating.

Ben followed the woman's gaze. Nordale approached from the vast whiteness behind them. There was no sign of the bright light they'd entered through. Nordale's face looked even more drawn and aged, as if the effort to open the doorway had taken a toll, but his eyes shone bright with energy, adoration and relief.

"Nordale," the woman said again. Then she looked at the group and shifted to English. "I speak so you can all understand. I sensed the Awakening." She paused, moving through two full shifts before finishing. "Has the time finally arrived?"

Nordale's expression fell. "Apologies, blessed Keeper." He touched his forehead and looked down. Keeper? What was a keeper? Ben thought. Wasn't she an angel?

"This is not the Awakening you await," he continued. "I fear a Guardian has betrayed the Creator."

The angel's eyes turned stormy, shifting from lightest blue to deep green to nearly black, her hair snaking up and down her back as it transformed faster—curly to straight, brown to snowy white.

Nordale stepped toward her, stopping at the flame to touch his forehead and bow slightly again. "My lady, we are here to help preserve the sacred Treasure. These loyal Guardians have risked their safety to prevent the traitor from reaching it."

The angel turned her green/blue/gold eyes on Ben, her expression remaining curious through every shift. The impact of this odd gaze made Ben's knees shake, his stomach dropping like riding a plunging rollercoaster.

"Nordale," Tiernan took a cautious step forward, her voice filled with awe. "Who is she?"

The angel didn't give Nordale a chance to answer. "I am Kareth. Keeper of the Flame."

"Kareth?" Tiernan blurted, looked from the angel to Nordale. "Like, THE Kareth?"

"The first Dragon Guardian?" Willow cried. "Whoa, you must be really old—"

"Willow!" Tiernan snapped, whirling with a scathing glare.

"What?" Willow shot back as if she didn't understand what she'd said that was so wrong. Marcus sighed and shook his head. Tiernan closed her eyes and turned back to Kareth, who chuckled.

"I suppose I am old in your view of the world, child. But time does not exist in this realm," said Kareth. "To me, it seems like I said goodbye to my darling, brave Nordale just yesterday."

Nordale's crooked back straightened at her words. "It was a time when the world was in chaos. Without seven dragons, the Flame was dying," he explained, lost in memory.

"And it would have, if not for you, my love. Nordale sacrificed himself to become the seventh. To keep the dragons safe until the Guardians could return order." Kareth's smile was sad. "It has taken longer than expected?" Her question hung in the air.

Nordale nodded. "Much longer, it seems."

"Is that the Flame?" Willow asked, pointing.

Kareth's eyes flickered to Willow, then to Tiernan, her expression darkening. "I do not understand. You are Guardians, yes?" When Tiernan nodded, Kareth asked, "Yet you do not know about the Flame?"

Tiernan swallowed hard and shook her head.

"You have the Codices?" Kareth asked.

Tiernan brightened. "Yes, we study them as children."

Kareth frowned. "I wrote about the Treasure."

Tiernan shook her head. "I'm sorry, there was nothing about a Dragon Treasure or a Flame or anything like that. I mean, we've all heard legends about the Dragon Treasure, but we thought they were just … fairy tales." She faltered at Kareth's expression. "I'm sorry."

Kareth turned to Nordale. "If you are awake then the Treasure is already in danger. There is much these Guardians should know." She continued to shift her appearance as she explained. "There are seven Keepers who each protect one of the seven Soul Treasures. Those Flames both feed and are fed by the human essence. It is a circle. Give and take. The Flames are necessary for the soul and souls are necessary for the Flames."

Ben's mouth went dry. His knees wobbled and he really hoped he could stay on his feet. The meaning of those words felt too huge for his brain to hold.

"The Creator used a perfect balance of all seven to create the human essence: Creativity. Joy. Humility. Curiosity. Compassion. Love … and Hope. These Treasures exist within the heart of a Beast of the First Realm."

"Dragons!" Willow breathed.

"Yes, child. Dragons. And unicorns, griffins, fae, phoenix, mermaids, and centaurs," Kareth ticked off the legendary animals on her fingers.

"These seven beasts are sacred. Without them, the Flames cannot be. And again, without the Flames, the human soul cannot survive."

"Unicorns?" Willow squeaked.

"Mermaids?" Marcus sounded skeptical.

"Centaurs?" Ben cried, his heart racing so fast he thought it would beat right out of his chest.

Kareth turned to the Flame and let her fingers drift through it. It didn't seem to burn her or even hurt at all. "This Flame is the Flame of Hope. Of all the Treasures, it is most important." Kareth smiled, sadly.

Her words hung in the air, dramatic and solemn.

After a brief pause, Kareth shifted a dozen times quickly. It reminded Ben of thumbing through a flipbook, frames of animation passing by at lightning speed. "Without Mysendrake, it is weaker."

"Faylene must have found out about the Flames, somehow," Tiernan said in her pondering voice. "You say you wrote about all this in the Codex, but it is definitely not a part of anything we learned ... how did that happen?" Hands clasped on top of her head, Tiernan paced like a tiger. "We'll have to figure that out later. Now we need to figure out what she is planning to do? It's not like she can steal the Flame, right? And even if she could, what would she do with it?"

Kareth and Nordale exchanged a look. Kareth's voice was soft but there was anger there. "Does she have the Amulets?"

Tiernan stopped pacing. "Yes. Both of them."

Kareth closed her eyes like this was not the answer she wanted to hear. "Together, the Amulets' powers protect the wearer. They give her access to this realm. They would allow her to bond her soul to the Flame, as mine is. If she is one with the Treasure, she is one with the dragons."

Tiernan took a step back as if Kareth's words had shoved her. "What would that mean?"

Kareth hesitated. "She would control them completely, body and mind. If this is done with a dark heart, they would essentially be enslaved."

"She would be unstoppable," Tiernan moaned, sinking into a squat, her hands on her forehead. "I wish we'd never been given this knowledge," she cried. "Humans can't be trusted with power! Isn't that why you had to protect the dragons in the first place?"

Nordale's eyes sparked with indignation. "That blame is on my shoulders, and the shoulders of my brothers," he growled. He turned to face Marcus who shrank back under the intensity of his words. "Before, man worshipped and revered the Beasts of the First Realm. One night, a fire burned a village. A man there blamed a dragon although it was his drunken carelessness that started the fire. The lie spread. The men of the village feared for the safety of their families. Although their intentions were just, fear poisoned them against the dragons. The men took up weapons and began to hunt them down. With an army of hundreds, they defeated the dragon. Over the years, fear like this spread. Wherever people lived, fear took root and grew. Humans rose against the dragons, and with each death, the Flame diminished."

Nordale's eyes filled with tears but his jaw clenched with determination. "Kareth came to me after the death of the seventh dragon. I helped her hide the remaining."

"Why do I feel guilty?" Marcus mumbled.

"Men are responsible and we must always remember," Nordale nodded at Marcus. "We must stand by the women who saved us."

Marcus glanced at Tiernan.

"Seven dragon hearts were just enough to keep the Flame alive," Kareth continued. "Nordale sacrificed his life to become that seventh, but underneath he is still a man. Yes, a magical one, but his mark is not from the Creator Himself. Even so, his sacrifice kept the Flame from dying completely. Before, when humans lived in harmony with dragons, the Flame was strong and bright. The world was a different place. After the dragon hunting, the Creator called on the Keepers to hide all the Beasts. And they became secret. They fell to legend. As it must be."

"Why didn't the dragons just have baby dragons? It's not like they were extinct, right?" Willow asked.

"Dragons are not prolific beings. Offspring are rare and gestation can take decades. Also, dragons mate only for love. And when they do, it is for life."

Tiernan nodded. "Since Nordale isn't a dragon anymore, the world has only six dragons again," she said, her voice wary.

Kareth nodded. "I am afraid so. Nordale must return to his dragon form to protect the Flame." The sadness in her voice made Ben's heart ache. She took a step toward Nordale and they clasped hands. "You know this."

"I do. It has always been my honor to serve you," Nordale said.

Kareth reached out with her other hand toward Tiernan. "Nordale can return to his dragon form, but control of the Amulets must be returned to the pure of heart. My soul is already bound to the Flame, and so, with both Amulets, I also could control all the dragons. I can stop her."

Tiernan stared at Kareth, eyes brimming with tears. "I'll see to it."

Ben's stomach churned. "We should never have given Aunt Matilda's Amulet to the Guardians," he blurted. "None of this would have happened if we'd just kept it." His voice sounded rude, even to him, and Tiernan looked at him with high eyebrows.

Kareth released Tiernan's hands and took a step towards Ben, studying him curiously. She put her hands on his cheeks, closing her eyes. Ben felt her dipping into him, searching his mind, knowing him completely. It wasn't a horrible feeling. He didn't feel like he was being invaded, although he knew that's exactly what she was doing. Ben felt like they were joined, like she knew everything about him in an instant.

Kareth opened her eyes. "Without the seventh dragon, the Flame's weakness will soon be felt. You, most of all, must cling to hope."

Ben looked into her eyes and inhaled sharply. "Why me?"

Her constant shifting came to a sudden stop, pausing on the visage of a woman with pale skin, long black hair, sky-blue eyes, high cheekbones and a wide, bright smile.

A woman who looked exactly like his mother.

"Because, dear Benjamin," she said. "You can help."

"Help?" Ben squeaked.

Kareth smiled down at him with his mother's eyes. "Help wake the other dragons."

CHAPTER 38

BEN STAGGERED BACKWARD into his brother, who grabbed his shoulders. If he didn't know better, he'd swear his mother was standing right in front of him. But he did know better.

This was impossible.

"Mom?" Marcus whispered, his voice crackling with emotion.

"No," Ben shook his head. "It's still Kareth, but somehow…" He recovered his balance and stepped forward. "Somehow, it's Mom, too." Seeing his mother's face, so real like that, infused Ben with a peace he hadn't felt since the day his mother died. The effect was as if he'd just sunk his aching body into a warm bath. Every muscle in his body relaxed.

"Darling Benjamin," the vision of his mother said in the rich voice remembered so well. "You have a musical gift, do you not?"

Ben felt his backpack shift on his shoulders. Confidence bolted through him, blooming an idea. "Ohhhhh. I get it! They're drums, aren't they?" he asked.

Willow stepped to his side. "What are drums?"

Ben grinned as the concept solidified, so obvious now he couldn't believe he didn't realize it before. "The stones," he explained. "Stonehenge!"

Kareth/Mom smiled, her eyes shining. "Can you feel the call?"

"I … I think I do." He wasn't sure what it was he felt, but there was a rhythm thrumming in the back of his mind, a beat with a familiar, comforting sense to it.

"Use it," Kareth/Mom said, her voice dropping to a whisper. "Call the dragons home."

"But, I'm a boy!" Ben protested, looking at Willow and Tiernan. Why would he have the power to wake dragons? From what Nordale was saying, the Creator wasn't real happy with the guys of the world.

"You are Family," Kareth said, her voice sounding so much like his mother's that hot tears stung the backs of his eyeballs. "Family is a living thing, with roots that run deep and branches that reach high and wide. As part of the Guardian Family, you are connected to a powerful magic. Every face you saw were those who came after me. Some carried the bloodline. Some did not. Some were Guardians. Some served the family in other ways."

She shifted again; his mother's dark hair became blonde and streamed into a long braid. Pale skin darkened. Freckles popped up. Blue eyes deepened to green. "Some risked everything to protect it," Kareth said. Another shift, the change slight. The green eyes and freckled skin remained, but the hair took on a reddish hue, curling to her shoulders.

Ben had never known Aunt Matilda when she wasn't old, but the resemblance in this young version of her face was obvious.

"She was so pretty," Willow murmured, just as entranced by this glimpse into Aunt Matilda's past.

Kareth shifted back into his mother's face. "Marcus. Ben. Willow. Hanna made a sacrifice to uphold her promise. Through Matilda, you have inherited that promise. You are part of the Guardian family. A lost part. But now, you have found your way home."

A strange expression clouded Tiernan's face and Ben saw her cut her eyes toward Marcus. Before he could think more about it, Kareth went on. "Each Guardian has something special. Willow may be a Whistler, but Ben, the music lives in your heart as well. Boy or girl."

It was true. He felt it. His backpack shifted again and something about that sent a tingle of joy through him.

Kareth smiled. "Dragons are creatures of rhythm. Their wings move to a beat. It is their inner Fire that power the Flame of Hope and maintains the rhythm. The sacred stones of this holy place are infused with that same magic. Use it to draw the other dragons to the Flame."

"All of them?" The idea that he could summon three more dragons to them made his head spin.

Kareth nodded. "They will fight to protect the Flame. The magic that calls them may also sever the bond between the traitor and her dragon prisoners."

Ben grinned. "So if I can break the bond—"

"Faylene and Elsbeth won't be able to control the dragons anymore!" Willow finished his thought.

Under the beam of his mother's smile, Ben swelled with confidence again. And something else … hope. For the first time since they started this ridiculous mission, Ben felt like they actually might pull it off. And he could play a part in making that happen.

"What about the Amulets?" Willow asked.

Kareth's smile slipped a little. "The Amulets are earthen gems. Because they are from this world, chaos is part of them. Their power could prevent the bond from being broken, I do not know. If you get them away from the traitor, I can break the bond myself."

Ben felt his backpack twitch again.

He slid the pack to the floor and squatted, unzipping the top. He grabbed the fuzzy mallets, sliding the smooth, cool wood of the sticks between his fingers. Drumsticks had always felt natural in his hands, but now that feeling was more pronounced. Like they were made to be there.

He laced his fingers between them, crossing the sticks so that they formed an X. When he held them up in his hand, they felt like a weapon. "I'm ready," he announced.

"Yeah, I'm not sure I like this plan," Marcus said, wary.

Ben gave his brother a stern look. "We need the other dragons' help. Drynfyre can't do it all on her own. And if we can break Faylene's bond in the process, all the better."

"Hold on," Willow said suddenly. "What if that breaks the bond between me and Drynfyre?" Willow's eyes filled with tears. She turned to Ben. "I get it now. What you meant before about freaking out about the what if's!" Willow sucked in a breath, the tears spilling over. "I ... I don't want to lose Drynfyre."

As she burst into sobs, hands over her face, Tiernan immediately moved to hug her. "Hey, hey, hey, no crying," she said. "Do you really think the bond between you and Drynfyre will disappear just because magic doesn't make her obey you anymore?" Tiernan gently pulled Willow's hands away from her face.

Willow sucked in a shuddering breath, trying to regain control. "It's more than the control." She shook her head like she wished she could make us all understand.

"Can't you feel her love? Even now?"

Willow hesitated, then nodded, sniffling.

"Drynfyre loves you and not just because you're her Whistler. Can't you feel how much that's changed since you woke her again? You must be able to feel that, because I can."

Willow raised her eyes to meet Tiernan's. "You can?"

Tiernan nodded. "It's powerful. And wonderful."

"That's what makes it so horrible. What if that goes away?"

"This is about more than magic, Willow. It is about faith," Kareth said. Her shifting countenance paused on an older face with eyes bright and clear and intelligent. A slightly older Aunt Matilda than Kareth showed them before, but before disease stole her mind.

"Faith and love," the words came from Aunt Matilda's mouth, in Aunt Matilda's voice. "They are the two most magical things in the universe."

Kareth/Matilda's eyes locked on Willow. "Yes, your bond may break. But that will not change your hearts. The only thing broken will be the invisible chain that binds you to her mark."

Willow nodded, "The infinity mark?"

"Yes. That mark controls the dragons. That mark ... her heart ... it will guide you." Then Matilda's face slipped away as Kareth returned to cycling between faces again, faster and faster.

"We have to protect the Treasure," Ben said, setting his jaw firmly. "We have to save Drynfyre. And all the dragons. We have to stop Faylene." He looked around the white space and turned to Nordale. "How do we get out of here?"

Kareth lifted a hand, palm up. A ball of golden light appeared, swirling and warm. It floated up from her hand, then moved to the side, expanding into a shimmering rectangle. Ben didn't hesitate; he knew this was a doorway back. "Thank you," he said to Kareth, and ran through the glowing space to find himself standing in the middle of the Stonehenge circle once again.

On the motorway, a car sped off—the same car he'd seen just before they entered the doorway. It was as if no time had passed at all. They'd spent at least fifteen minutes in the white, wall-less room but it seemed like only seconds had gone by out here in the real world.

Ben's initial shock became relief. There is still time to stop Faylene. He scanned the monument, eyeing each stone and wondering which to use. He'd have to guess and hope his instincts wouldn't steer him wrong.

He ran to one of the fallen stones along the outer ring. It sprawled in the grass, an unconscious giant waiting for him to wake it. Dropping to his knees, he put his hands to the stone's surface. A tingle spread across his palms and crawled up his arms.

This is the one.

If he played from this side, he could stay inside the circle and its protection. A mallet in each hand, Ben closed his eyes and allowed his hands to fall. Where the rhythm came from, he didn't know. Everything he was doing right now was on instinct, and he just had to trust it. Have faith, isn't that what Kareth had said? Over and over, he brought the mallets down on the stone. Opening his eyes, he searched for a sign of the other dragons, but the only thing in the sky was clouds.

"Aw, man," Ben moaned, crestfallen. What was he doing wrong? Frustrated tears stung in his eyes. Then a thought popped into his head.

The diary!

The pattern along the bottom of its pages appeared before his mind's eye. Remembering it, the pattern took on a meaning it hadn't before. With a lurch, Ben realized what it meant.

He grabbed at his backpack, digging through the contents to find the diary, thumbing through its pages. "It's a rhythm!" he yelled.

Willow ran over. "What is?"

He didn't have time to explain. "Hold the book for me!"

Willow squatted down, becoming a human music stand as she held the book so it faced Ben. He played again, a deep vibration running through his arms each time he brought a mallet head down. Instead of hard rock, he felt the give of a taut drumhead under the mallets. He followed the pattern, seeing notes instead of random marks. The beat thumped slowly, then increased in intensity like a war cry echoing in his chest, energizing his heart, fusing with his pulse. After a few cycles, he'd memorized it, the rhythm programmed in his muscles. He allowed his eyes to drift closed, arms operating independently from the rest of his body, pounding the beat. Over and over. Never slowing. Never missing.

"Dragons!" Marcus screamed.

Ben's eyes sprang open. His eyes searched the sky and far off in the distance he saw it was true.

The dragons were coming.

CHAPTER 39

TIERNAN HAD CHASED Ben through the doorway of golden light, but as soon as she'd stepped back into the real world, her cell phone rang.

She screeched to a halt and dug the phone out of her belt. The caller ID read THOMAS. "It's Thomas!" Marcus and Willow stopped, too, but Ben ran ahead. Thumbing the speaker button, Tiernan yelled, "Thomas? Can you hear me?"

Her uncle's voice came through clear and strong. "Tiernan? Thank God! Are you all right?"

"Yes! We're at Stonehenge right now. Is Coreen okay?"

"She'll be fine. Had her appendix out, but she'll be okay. She's just worried about you."

"Oh, thank God!" Tiernan threw her head back in relief. Marcus and Willow grinned and hugged each other.

"I'm going to go tell Ben!" Willow ran after him.

"What's happening?" Thomas asked.

"We woke Mysendrake, but …" Tiernan put a hand to her forehead. Where to start? "Thomas, the Guardian at the English den is working with Faylene. We tied her up."

Thomas growled. "Unbelievable! Coreen has already called Belinda's sister; she lives north of the den, so at least she's closer to Stonehenge. She'll have to double back, but we'll send her your way."

A deep pounding beat filled the air. "What is that?" asked Willow.

Marcus grabbed her arm. "Look!"

Ben knelt beside one of the fallen stones, playing it like a drum. With each mallet drop, the air reverberated with a powerful pulse of sound.

"Dragons!" Marcus screamed, his extended finger pointing toward the horizon where two dragons flapped towards them.

"Uh, Thomas," Tiernan said, "I gotta go. Things are about to get a little out of control here." She thumbed the disconnect button without waiting for an answer, sliding the phone back into her belt. The next thing she knew, Marcus had scooped her up into a spinning hug, nearly knocking the arrows out of her quiver. He set her down, hands resting on her waist.

"Coreen's okay, and we're not outnumbered anymore," he smiled down at her.

Tiernan's heart hammered hard. No boy other than an uncle or cousin had ever hugged her before, and certainly not like that, with his face buried in her neck, his lips touching her skin. Tiernan's face burned with heat. She cursed the ridiculous blotches that she knew were spreading across her neck and cheeks. Marcus leaned closer and she realized what was about to happen. She pulled back.

"Marcus, no, we can't ..."

"What's wrong?" He gazed down at her, eyes wary. "I thought—"

"Well, yes, I did ... I mean, I do, I mean. Ugh." She sighed. "You heard what Kareth said. We're family. Your lineage and my lineage meet up back there a hundred or so years ago. So—what?" She balked as Marcus gave her a wicked grin.

"Tiernan, it's okay."

"What? No, it's not! Ew."

This time he laughed out loud. "No, we're not family. I mean, not by blood anyway."

Tiernan stared at him, confused. "But ... you and Ben are in Hanna Vorman's bloodline—"

"Actually," he interrupted, "I'm adopted. Mom and Dad thought they couldn't have kids. I was a baby in need of a home. When Ben came along ... well, let's just say he was a surprise." He grinned. "Let's discuss this later, okay?" He gave her a quick peck on the cheek and took her hand. "C'mon."

Ben's drumming had also summoned Drynfyre back to Stonehenge, with the red and gold dragons not far behind. Swooping low, Drynfyre circled the standing stones before coming to rest on top of one of the horizontal lintels not far from Ben. She spread her silver wings wide and balanced on her hind legs, snout pointed skyward. Fire burst from her wide nostrils as her front talons raked the air menacingly. The red dragon circled low and landed on a cross stone opposite Drynfyre on the inner circle.

"Völsendrake," Nordale whispered. The dragon's amber wings stretched wide and his explosive roar made them all clap their hands over their ears. Drynfyre bellowed in answer, pumping her wings and lifting off the stone only to settle back down. It was as if they wanted to fight each other, but couldn't move off the stones.

The golden dragon landed on the cross stone just above Drynfyre and Völsendrake. "Geldfyre," Nordale confirmed. Faylene glared down at them.

Tiernan stood paralyzed with awe and, if she was honest, complete terror. Ben's drumming stopped, the lack of sound bringing her back to her senses. Her fingers found the Pfife's cord around her neck and she yanked it free. "Nordale! Willow, we need the Song!"

Willow had already retrieved the sheaf of parchment from Ben's backpack. As she handed the paper to Tiernan, Geldfyre crowed, loud as a T-Rex. Willow shrieked. Drynfyre roared in reply to Geldfyre and then pushed off the stone and took to the air again. Völsendrake and Geldfyre did the same.

What happened? Tiernan looked around. Ben wasn't playing anymore. Had that allowed the dragons to fly again?

"Look out!" Marcus screamed. The enormous stone on which Geldfyre had perched toppled from its vertical pillar. As it tumbled down toward Tiernan and Willow, Marcus shoved Tiernan backwards across the grass then grabbed Willow around the middle, rolling with her as Ben ducked down behind his stone for cover.

The stone crashed to the grass, shattering in a spray of chunks. A piece the size of a baseball whizzed toward Marcus and Willow, knocking Willow on the side of her head.

Tiernan army-crawled toward Willow and Marcus. "No, no, no," she pleaded. Marcus groaned and rolled onto his back but Willow didn't move. On her knees, Tiernan smoothed the hair away from Willow's face, feeling wet blood along her temple where a deep gash oozed. "Please be okay. You have to be okay!" Sobs bottlenecked in her throat, clambering over each other to get out as doom settled in Tiernan's heart, so frigid that shiver bumps popped up along her arms.

In the sky above them, teeth and talons flashed. Fireballs blasted. Flame spewed. But none of that mattered, because Willow was dying. Tiernan could tell just by the look of her.

"Is she all right?" Ben scrambled across the grass to them. Tiernan knew he wanted her to tell him Willow would be all right. But Tiernan couldn't lie. The blood, the wound, the dull color of Willow's skin, all revealed the horrible truth.

"Wait ..." Nordale stood over them. Tiernan squinted up at him through the sunlight. He was a wizard. Did he have some magic or something that could help? His strange smile sparked a flash of fury in her. "Why are you smiling?" she demanded, her voice raw with fury.

"Watch," he said. "The bond was not broken ..."

Tiernan pulled her gaze back to Willow and what she saw made her grab Marcus' hand. "Look!"

He squeezed so hard she thought he might actually break her fingers. The gash in Willow's temple healed before their eyes. A healthy color returned her cheeks, her lips warming. She blinked and groaned. "Yeowwza, my head hurts," she complained weakly.

Tiernan erupted with joyful laughter, and then Marcus was laughing too, leaning back in the grass. Ben whooped with delight. "Yeah, I'll bet your head hurts!" he crowed. "Jeez, Willow! You were dead!"

Willow squished her lips together. "Ha ha. Very funny."

"I'm not kidding! You got hit in the head with a rock. You sure looked dead!" Ben laughed again but it was clear Willow didn't find it funny at all. Tiernan put a calming hand on Ben's arm, giving him a pointed look.

"Drynfyre's life force is bound to Willow's," Nordale smiled. "She healed her."

Willow's eyes found Nordale, her brows raised in question. "Is that what happened?" she whispered.

"Well, you were pretty much dead about thirty seconds ago and now you're not," Marcus said, a huge grin on his face.

"Was I really dead?" Willow asked Tiernan, skeptical.

"Or close to it," Tiernan nodded. "You healed all up before we could get a proper freak-out going. Much appreciated, by the way."

"The bond between dragon and Whistler keeps the Whistler safe," Nordale explained. "Sadly, that also means if a dragon dies, so will its Whistler."

Before any of them had a chance to truly digest the meaning of this, the dragon battle in the air above them intensified. The first of the other dragons arrived. With an angry screech, a deep blue dragon swooped in from the northern sky. Wings slapped. Roars echoed off the stones around them. Cinders rained down, littering the grass, burning tiny embers.

Tiernan's gut writhed as she considered what Nordale had said. If something happened to Drynfyre ... "Why doesn't the bond protect the dragon, too?"

"It does. A bonded dragon can withstand much more than an unbound one, but a dragon battle is another matter as the talon of another dragon is more powerful than the magic of the bond."

Tiernan wasn't sure why Ben's rhythm hadn't broken the bond when it had clearly summoned the dragons, but they were lucky it hadn't or Willow would have been lost. If something happened to Drynfyre, they still could lose her. But that bond needed to be broken, at least between Faylene and Geldfyre. It was the only way Tiernan could get the Amulets away from her. With them, Kareth would be able to put a stop to all this madness.

Suddenly, Tiernan knew what had to be done. It was something she never thought she'd be capable of doing, but there was no other way. If Ben's rhythm wouldn't break the bond, she'd have to do it herself. And there was only one way to do that.

She would have to kill a dragon.

CHAPTER 40

IT TOOK A MOMENT for Willow to fully grasp what had just happened. She remembered getting wonked in the head. It hadn't hurt, more just a flash of high-pitched exquisiteness that dissolved to nothing. The next thing she knew, a tugging sensation in the center of her chest pulled her back into the hazy morning light of Stonehenge's inner circle, and she was staring up into the concerned faces of her family.

So, that's what a near death experience feels like.

Thinking about the near miss made her woozy so she stayed seated, hugging her knees to her chest, as Ben plopped down next to her. "Where did Tiernan go?" she asked loud enough to be heard over the sounds of dragon battle above. Ben pointed to a spot behind her and she twisted around to see Tiernan gesturing wildly to Nordale, who shook his head, arguing with her. Then, a moment later, he seemed to reconsider, putting his hand solemnly on Tiernan's shoulder.

"Willow, are you okay?" Ben asked, the tremble in his voice drawing her attention back.

"I think so," she answered, gingerly touching her temple. She had blood caked in her hair. She could feel its stickiness on her forehead. "I feel a little funky, but mostly I'm worried about Drynfyre. What if something happens to her?" She jumped as a bowling ball-sized fireball sizzled across the dewy grass on the far side of the stone circle, quickly fading to embers.

"Nothing's going to happen to Drynfyre," Ben said, determined. "She'll be fine. You'll be fine. You are … fine."

If only speaking such wishes would make them true.

The sound of Pfife music somehow cut through the pandemonium. Willow and Ben whirled as a cyclone of mist enveloped Nordale, encasing him like a cocoon until his dragon head rose out. Nordale was Mysendrake again. He stretched his long neck, unfurling emerald wings that shimmered as they dispersed the cocoon of mist.

The next instant Mysendrake was in the air, soaring gently at first as if he needed to re-adjust to his serpentine form. Circling, he landed on the grass just outside the circle, his gaze locked on the battle above.

Tiernan ran over to them, handing the sheets of music to Ben. She adjusted the quiver of arrows on her back, slipping the bow over her head with the string across her chest, near where the Pfife hung. "Get into the circle," she ordered. Then, adamantly, to Marcus she said, "Make sure they stay there."

"Where exactly do you think you're going?" Marcus reached for Tiernan's arm. "You can NOT ride Mysendrake up into that mess!" He glanced upward. "Because, you know, that would be ludicrous."

"I've been called worse," Tiernan grinned, but the smile didn't reach her eyes.

"Marcus is right," Willow said, clambering to her feet, grabbing Tiernan's other arm as much to keep herself steady as to hold her back. "You can't do that!"

Tiernan's expression tightened and she looked over her shoulder at Mysendrake. He turned his gaze to her, bellowing as if urging her to hurry. "Make sure Ben keeps playing. We have to try to break this bond. Maybe he didn't play long enough before," she said. "I know what I'm doing!" With one last look into Marcus's eyes, she ran for the emerald dragon, Pfife to her lips. Again, somehow the Pfife music eclipsed the roars and screeches of the battle above as she played Mysendrake's Flying Song.

Marcus dragged Willow and Ben back into the circle, hovering near the edge as Tiernan scrambled up Mysendrake's gleaming forearm. Goosebumps rippled along Willow's scalp at how brave and fierce Tiernan was! Apparently, she wasn't the only one who was impressed. Marcus was just as spellbound, making a soft noise, a mix of disbelief and admiration, as Mysendrake took off with Tiernan on his back. Willow followed their flight, Tiernan settled behind his head, bow drawn and arrow at the ready.

"She is unbelievable," Marcus breathed. But he sounded like that was a good thing. A very good thing.

A roar trumpeted from the eastern sky where a huge black dragon plunged from the gathering clouds, adding even more fire and talons to the battle. Moments later, another dragon, this one dark purple, appeared from the south.

"That's all of them," Ben said.

Willow ticked them off on her fingers. "Yep, that's seven." She looked at Ben. "Why aren't you drumming?"

Instead of answering, Ben turned and ran for the fallen stone. He flipped the journal open, running his finger along the markings as he turned page after page, studying the line intensely, trying to find his place. Willow followed, to help hold the music for him again. Ben froze, leaning in close to the book, flipping back a page, then forward. "Oh my gosh," he cried with a jolt of surprise. "The rhythm changes right here. It's so slight I didn't notice it before. Do you think that's why it didn't break the bond?"

"Maybe. If so, we're lucky you missed it," Marcus said. Willow felt the goosebumps pop again. She had a feeling luck had nothing to do with it.

Ben handed her the journal and she held it out again as Marcus paced back and forth in the grass behind them, eyes on the sky. Ben drummed, careful to include the new syncopation. The hollow, deep thwonk of mallets on stone filled the air once again.

Two of the dragons immediately responded. The dark purple one and the deep blue one settled on the crossbeams of the circle as Mysendrake thundered past. Tiernan stood on his back slinging arrow after arrow at Faylene riding the golden dragon: Geldfyre, Nordale had called him. The arrows kept bouncing off the protective field around the dragon until, miraculously, one sailed through.

"Oh my gosh!" Willow cried. "Ben, keep playing! I think it's working! We need to make those dragons land on the circle again."

Faylene ducked down behind Geldfyre's neck, seemingly aware that something had changed. The red dragon ridden by Elsbeth—Völsendrake, Willow remembered—dove toward Mysendrake, but was intercepted by Drynfyre, who parachuted her wings, flipping her legs forward with talons extended toward the red dragon's neck. Völsendrake veered right, nearly colliding with Mysendrake who had twisted upwards to avoid a crash with Geldfyre. Twin screams pierced the air.

Elsbeth and Tiernan had fallen off their dragons.

"Tiernan!" Willow and Marcus cried at once. Mysendrake immediately changed course, swooping beneath the Guardian and catching her on his back like a seasoned circus performer. Tiernan threw her arms around Mysendrake's neck, clinging to him. Her bow tumbled away, landing on the grass beneath them.

But Elsbeth continued to fall. And scream. Before she hit the ground, the black dragon swooped in and caught her in its talons. The dragon's wide ebony wings kicked up clouds of dirt and grass as it gently set the woman on the ground just outside the circle. The black dragon looked down at Elsbeth's crumpled form, studying her. Willow wasn't sure what it was going to do. It had obviously saved her for some reason, but why? Maybe the dragon wondered the same thing.

Ben kept drumming the rhythm and the black dragon seemed to respond. It tossed its head like it was trying to resist, bellowing madly. And then it launched up, coming to a land on another of the cross stones.

Willow coughed, swinging her arms to clear the dusty air. She looked at Elsbeth, lying in the grass. "Is she ... dead?"

"I don't know," Marcus said, moving to the edge of the circle for a better look.

"The bond must be broken," Willow whispered. "Why else would they have fallen off?"

"Look!" Marcus pointed to the sky. Tiernan stood boldly on Mysendrake's shoulders, whirling some kind of slingshot thing over her head. A stone flew at Geldfyre, thwacking him in the eye. The dragon shot a fireball back and Mysendrake had to dodge it, but Tiernan seemed ready, holding onto one of his long, slender ears for balance, one foot against the back of his head, as if she did this sort of thing every day. For fun. "I don't think she'd be able to ride like that if it was," Marcus said.

"No, look, she's holding on. She wouldn't have to do that if there was a bond," Willow said.

Marcus nodded in awed agreement. "Oh my God, she's completely nuts."

Turning back to Elsbeth, Willow sighed. "We should get her inside the circle."

"What? No, way," Marcus said, holding her back.

"It's the only place she'll be safe," Willow countered.

A horrible screech interrupted them and they both turned toward it, just as the sun beamed out from behind a bank of clouds. The light blinded Willow and she sensed more than saw the two dragons hit the grass. They rolled as Willow shaded her eyes, squinting to see Mysendrake on top of Geldfyre, his claws embedded in the other's scaly breastplate. Tiernan must have jumped off his back at some point because she now raced for the circle as Geldfyre screeched again. It sounded like he was in pain.

Where was Faylene? Pinned beneath the dragon?

Ben dropped the mallets and scrambled to Willow's side to get a better look. Geldfyre let out a wretched wail as Mysendrake retracted his talons, settling on the ground beside his fallen brother. With a mournful cry, Mysendrake leaned down and touched his snout to Geldfyre's.

Cold dread prickled Willow's scalp. Had Mysendrake *killed* Geldfyre?

"Tiernan!" Marcus met her just outside the circle. "Did you seriously jump off a flying dragon? You are out of your mind."

"I thought we'd already established that. And besides, Mysendrake was landing at the time, not flying." Tiernan casually brushed flecks of grass from her thighs, moving tentatively like she might be more hurt than she was letting on.

Mysendrake gave a bellow so explosive and loud that they all jumped. Shafts of brilliant orange light burst from the spaces between Geldfyre's scales, puncturing the air with a high-pitched whine—each beam a different note in a tragic chord.

The remaining dragons settled into place around the monument. Drynfyre and the large black dragon perched side by side on a section of the outer circle where three horizontal cross stones topped four vertical ones. The moment stretched on, orange beams shooting into the sky, disappearing into the gathering clouds, the dissonant chord quieting as the beams faded and then finally went out altogether.

The dragons simultaneously dipped their heads, and the moment held again, the scene paralyzed, on the verge of shattering. The only sounds were the rumble of distant thunder and a morning bird's soft call.

With a scream of fury, Faylene rose up from the grass just beyond Geldfyre's still form, unsheathing a gleaming dagger from the belt at her waist. Her manic glare fixed on Tiernan.

CHAPTER 41

"TIERNAN!" BEN SCREAMED a warning, but she was already racing for the open grass beyond Stonehenge. Where was she going? There was nothing but land in any direction, nowhere to escape to, so maybe she hoped to lead the crazed woman away from the circle. Away from them.

If so, it worked. Faylene gave chase with a demented intensity and the speed of someone much younger.

"Tiernan! Wait! Come inside the circle!" Marcus screeched, turning to Willow. "Why did she run? She'd be safe here!"

"I don't think so, Faylene has the Amulets." Willow's voice sounded pinched and panicked.

"Stay here!" Marcus ordered and sprinted after Tiernan.

"Marcus, don't!" Ben screamed, but his brother kept going.

"Drynfyre!" Willow called. The dragon immediately left her perch, dropping to the ground just outside the circle. Willow gave Ben a hard stare. "Do NOT leave this circle, Ben. You hear me?" Drynfyre scooped Willow up onto her back and flew off with a mighty thrust of her wings.

"Why is everyone leaving the circle?" Ben screamed after her. What did Willow think she was doing? For God's sake, she'd been dead only a few minutes ago!

Those brief moments when he thought Willow had died had been so horrible. He couldn't lose someone else; he didn't think he could handle it. But Willow hadn't died. She was a Whistler. Unfortunately, it now seemed like the bond was definitely broken, which meant Willow wouldn't have that magical protection anymore. And what about Marcus? Tiernan? Everyone else was putting their lives at risk to stop Faylene.

Everyone but him.

Ben grabbed the binoculars and ran to the edge of the circle. He scanned the meadow, finding Tiernan as she scooped up her bow from the grass. That's what she was running for! He'd forgotten she'd dropped her bow when she'd almost fallen off Mysendrake. Now that she had it back, she plucked an arrow from the quiver on her back and whirled to face the oncoming Faylene, nocking the arrow as she turned.

Ben moved the binoculars to find Faylene. She'd stopped a few hundred feet away from Tiernan and stood inside a glowing ball of violet light. Tiernan's arrow just bounced off as if the bubble was made of rubber. Somehow Faylene had conjured the same bubble of protection that the dragon's Song produced. It must be the Amulets, Ben thought. How powerful were they? Ben couldn't imagine how Tiernan would be able to get them away from Faylene.

An explosion behind him made Ben drop the binoculars and clap his hands over his ears. A thick, orange pillar of flame spewed thousands of feet into the air from a short stone beyond the outer circle. The light looked eerily similar to the beams that had shot from Geldfyre's chest just before he died.

Mysendrake launched back into the air and headed for Tiernan. On the flat side of the tall stone beneath where the red dragon remained perched, a rectangle of ethereal light appeared. Kareth stepped out of it.

She wore his mother's face again. Pure joy jolted through Ben, forcing out a sob. His entire body was desperate to go to her, and whether it was that or something else, he was overcome with weakness. It required too much effort to keep standing and he fell to his knees in the grass. Clouds thickened in the sky overhead, completely blotting out the sun. In the filtered light, shadows softened and colors faded, making Kareth appear even more ethereal.

She wasn't actually his mother, Ben knew that, but Kareth had to be some kind of magical, heavenly being. Pure and good and full of love. Just like Widershins. Just like his mother.

Kareth stepped quickly to Geldfyre, kneeling beside the huge beast. She laid her head on his chest. It looked like she was crying. The orange beam of light thinned then sputtered, the roaring lessened, then petering out.

In the quiet that followed, Ben heard the Pfife music.

Ben scrambled for the binoculars he'd dropped. Drynfyre hovered in the air between Tiernan and Faylene. Willow sat on the space behind Drynfyre's head, between her wings, playing the Pfife. The tune grew louder and louder, as if Willow was playing through a loud speaker. How it was possible to hear her so well, this far away, was nonsensical, but it sounded like he was right there beside her. He swung the binoculars from Willow to Tiernan to Faylene, searching. Where was Marcus?

Ben adjusted the binoculars and found him, running, still a ways from the battle. What did he think he was going to do once he got there?

Swinging the binoculars back, Ben watched Faylene mold a ball of magical light between her palms, forming it out of thin air. She pitched it at Drynfyre and Willow with all her might. A flash turned the entire scene blazing white, the binocular lenses magnifying the brightness and searing his retinas.

"Ahhhhh!" Tears streamed and Ben dropped the binoculars again, hands over his eyes like his fingers could tamp out the pain. When it subsided and he was able to concentrate on something else, he strained his ears for a clue as to what was happening. He sure couldn't see at the moment.

He could still hear Willow's Pfife, but a frustrated, angry scream that he assumed was Faylene made him think that burst of light didn't do whatever she'd hoped.

There were explosions. Tiernan hollered. Drynfyre roared. Willow's Pfife music played through it all. Ben squinted through tears, unable to open his eyes enough to see more than blurred images and flashes.

It took him a while to feel his way back to the fallen stone. If he hadn't left the mallets on the ground, he'd never have found it. Kneeling again, he focused on Willow's tune, letting the mallets fall, allowing a rhythm to well up from somewhere deep inside. This felt right. Powerful. It wasn't like he was accompanying Willow, but that his beat and her melody were the same. He played. She played. He heard nothing but the Pfife and the thump of mallet against stone.

The next time he opened his eyes, he could see again. In fact, he could see all the way to the meadow.

All the other dragons had left the circle, and now hovered in the air beside Drynfyre, wings moving in time to Ben's rhythm. Six sets of wings beat the air, up and down, swirling clouds of dirt. Safe from the cyclonic debris inside her bubble, Faylene just laughed.

The sound was closer than logically possible. Whatever magic was happening between Willow's Song and Ben's Rhythm, it allowed him to see the distant scene clearly and hear every wing-beat. The blindness he'd experienced a moment ago was completely healed. The cloudy morning seemed surreally crisp and clear; his thoughts sharp and full of energy.

Tiernan stepped up until she was standing beneath Drynfyre, bowstring pulled taut. She had nocked an arrow, but there was something extraordinary about this one. It shimmered with white, electric magic.

"I grew up cursing Hanna Vorman for betraying the Guardians," Tiernan barked. "We all did! All this time you knew the truth."

Faylene scoffed. "All these years, we've been prisoners of Kareth's legacy. And for what? The Guardians were never going to wake those dragons! Not ever! You saw how the world reacted to Drynfyre's accidental Awakening. Presidents and Generals, men supposedly so strong and brave, they cowered with fear! They wanted to destroy her! Men are just as afraid as they've always been. The world needs a woman to lead; one who isn't afraid of the gifts the Creator gave us. I am the only one strong enough to wield this kind of power!"

"The dragons aren't your personal army," Tiernan protested. Ben could see the muscles in her bow arm shake. "You don't get to decide who is in charge. What do you think Kareth would think about what you've done?"

"Kareth is most disappointed," said a voice. Ben almost stopped playing, but forced himself to keep the Rhythm going as Kareth materialized next to Tiernan. She no longer looked like Ben's mother. But whoever she did look like, Faylene sure recognized her.

"No … you don't understand," Faylene croaked. "The world will never be ready the way the Creator hoped, don't you see? We have to be the ones to change it. I can do that!"

"Not like this," Tiernan said, flatly. "People are getting hurt. Your sister is hurt, don't you care about that? Now stop this insanity!"

Faylene's face turned a furious red. "This. Is. Not. Insane!" she screamed, forming another ball of light between her palms.

Willow's melody hit a high, dramatic peak. As if on cue, Ben let both mallets drop at the downbeat and Tiernan released the bowstring. The glowing arrow flew, rupturing Faylene's protective bubble, producing a wave of light and sound that flowed across the grass. It knocked Marcus off his feet just as he reached the meadow. It rushed toward Ben, blowing him backward. He landed hard, smacking his head on a stone.

The world fell silent.

When Ben opened his eyes again, he wasn't sure how much time had passed. He got to his feet and looked around, feeling stunned and shaken. The strange super-human sight and hearing he'd experienced before was gone. His ears felt like they were filled with cotton. His head swam. Queasy, he sank to the ground with a moan.

Thwunk, thwunk, thwunk.

In unison, the dragons returned to perch on the circle's cross stones, save for Drynfyre. She landed softly, placing Faylene on the grass next to Elsbeth. An arrow protruded from the middle of Faylene's chest, just beneath where the two Amulets lay dark and still.

Marcus and Tiernan ran in from the meadow as Willow slid off Drynfyre's back. Ben lurched toward her, stumbling into her hug as soon as she reached the ground. "We did it!" he sighed. "It's over."

"Yes," Willow said, her words cracking with emotion. "I wish I felt happier about it."

He realized creeping tendrils of darkness had wrapped around his heart as well. "I know, me too. It doesn't feel right to celebrate someone dying, even if that someone was trying to do something bad," he said.

Willow turned and threw her arms around Drynfyre's thick leg. The dragon lowered her snout to nuzzle Willow's cheek.

"I can't hear Drynfyre anymore!" Willow wailed, tears spilling from her eyes.

Ben swallowed hard. "I know, I'm sorry."

Marcus put a hand on Ben's shoulder and squeezed, his eyes on Tiernan. "You okay?" he asked her.

Tiernan nodded, but she couldn't look at him. Tears ran down her cheeks.

Ben's eyes were heavy with tears, too. A lump clogged his throat as an icy sense of doom slunk through him, coating his insides with dread. He'd never felt so horrible in his life. Was this some sort of post-traumatic stress, like soldiers got after war?

Marcus studied them, swallowing hard like something was caught in his throat. He turned to Tiernan. "What is going on? Tiernan!"

"Tell them, Tiernan. You made this choice, you need to be the one to tell them." They turned as Kareth approached, once again wearing the face of Ben's mother. This brought on a fresh surge of despair for Ben, deep and hollow. It wasn't fair! He wanted his mother to be really alive. He missed her desperately, and wished he could go to her for comfort. He felt like he'd never feel happy, ever again.

"With Geldfyre gone, there are only six dragons again," Tiernan said softly.

Kareth placed a hand on Tiernan's shoulder.

"You must finish what you began."

CHAPTER 42

THIS WAS WORSE than when her parents told her they were separating. It was worse than when her puppy Chi-Chi ran away when she was six. Worse than when Aunt Matilda died. This was like someone had poked a hole in her heart, letting all the love and wonder leak out, leaving behind a mess of misery that stuck to every fiber of her being.

Willow couldn't stop crying. Drynfyre stretched her head down and nuzzled her cheek and she looked up into those amazing purple eyes. If only she could hear what Drynfyre wanted to tell her.

"What choice did you make?" Marcus asked, looking from Kareth to Tiernan. "What does she mean, Tiernan?"

Tiernan's quiver and bow slipped from her shoulder and fell to the ground. "Marcus, I'm sorry. It was the only way," she murmured.

Kareth shifted, changing, cycling through various Guardians. "Tiernan," she said, with soothing forgiveness. "Just as Hanna did in her time, you made a sacrifice. For your friends, your family, the world."

"Sacrifice? What sacrifice did you make?" Marcus demanded, his voice tight as if he was choking back tears.

Kareth smiled sadly at him. "Is it as I said. Hope is essential to the human soul. Without it, humans could not face the challenges life presents. Without hope, people would not have the strength to persevere. And, my dearest children, the world must go on."

All the pieces fell into place in Willow's mind. Of course. There had to be seven dragons in the world. That was the rule. There was power in that number. That was why Mysendrake volunteered to become the seventh dragon all those hundreds of years ago. Kareth had said the Flame weakened when they had Awakened him. Yes, he was now back in his dragon form, but with Geldfyre gone ...

So what sacrifice had Tiernan made?

Oh no.

Willow turned away from Drynfyre. "Tiernan? What did you do?"

Tiernan put a trembling hand to her mouth. "It was the best thing I could think of at the time," she whispered. Kareth smiled the warmest, most loving smile Willow had ever seen.

"Tiernan. Please!" Marcus sounded so desperate.

Her cheeks wet with tears, she lifted her chin, finally looking at him. "Marcus, it's the only way. I have to take Geldfyre's place."

"No! You can't!" He pulled her away from Kareth, fingers tight on her upper arms. "That's ridiculous!"

"What are you talking about?" Ben asked, but it was confirmation for Willow and brought on a fresh wave of tears.

"I'm a Guardian," Tiernan explained, and her words seemed to calm herself. "It was my responsibility to stop Faylene. Now it's my responsibility to set things right again. I knew what it would mean, to kill a dragon. But it was the only way to break the bond. To get the dragons out of her control. Nordale agreed with the plan. He understood. No one else would understand but him." She pulled her arms free from Marcus's grasp and wiped the tears from her cheeks. She'd seemed afraid before, but now, she was determined. "There must be seven dragons or the Flame will die. Hope will die."

Marcus pulled her into a hug and she pressed her wet cheek to his t-shirt. "Let me be the one," Marcus blurted.

Stunned, Tiernan pulled away from the hug, staring up at him. She opened her mouth and then closed it again. A red flush crept up her neck, blotching her face. "What? But ... why would you, I mean, that's—"

Marcus cut her off with a kiss.

Ben and Willow looked at each other, their eyes wide.

Marcus leaned back and gently wiped the tears from Tiernan's cheeks, replacing them with a kiss to each cheekbone. "You can't go," he said. "Not when we haven't even been out on a proper date."

Tiernan stretched up on her toes to kiss his cheek. "I wish more than anything we could have that date, believe me. But this is my responsibility." Marcus closed his eyes in resignation, chin trembling.

"Marcus, I always dreamed of doing something more than babysitting a sleeping dragon," Tiernan sniffed and wiped at her cheeks. "I never thought I had a choice about being a Guardian, but maybe this is my real choice. I want to make the right one." With a sad smile, so like Kareth's, Tiernan put a hand against his cheek, then turned to where Faylene and her sister lay side by side. After studying their still forms for a moment, she squatted down and unclasped the Amulets from around Faylene's neck. Brilliant purple shards of sunlight glinted off the dark gems, but no glow shone from them. When she rose, she took one long look at Marcus, and turned toward Kareth.

"Okay, I'm ready."

Willow threw her arms around Tiernan's waist, and Ben did the same from the other side. "Oh, Tiernan. You are so brave," Willow sobbed, the desperate sadness worsening with the realization of what their friend was giving up.

Tiernan put her arms around both of their shoulders and kissed the tops of their heads. "You two are the brave ones. Besides, if Nordale was willing to do this fifteen hundred years ago, then I can do it now." She suddenly looked at Kareth. "Wait, will this still work if two of us aren't real dragons?"

Kareth's face continued to cycle through the Guardian faces. "Yes, but it will be different. We cannot return the dragons to their dens."

Willow dropped her arms from around Tiernan's waist and turned to Kareth. "But where will they go?" The idea of never seeing Drynfyre again was just too horrible to bear.

Kareth looked down at her, smoothing Willow's hair. "They will need to remain together. With only five organic beasts of the First Realm, it will require their combined magic to secure the Flame." Kareth looked up at Mysendrake and he dipped his head in answer, as if he agreed. Then she addressed the dragons assembled on the cross-stones. "When I called upon my sisters to hide you all, I believed your protection was more important than anything. I believed separating the dens was best, so that if one were compromised, the others would still be safe. The Guardians dedicated their entire lives and the lives of their families for centuries to uphold this task. And you were safe. But from the moment I stepped out into this world, into the now, I sensed how much it has changed. There is more power in staying together. Instead of hiding alone, let us show this new world what the human soul truly needs. Let us show how hope can be strong. How it can be a foundation to build upon."

Kareth turned her gaze to Tiernan, stepping toward her. "Your willing sacrifice, like Nordale's, is proof of that. Proof that what is here," Kareth put her hand over Tiernan's heart, "your hope for the world ... that is the true treasure.

"Now, we must begin. The Flame weakens," Kareth said, looking at Willow and Ben. "What you feel, people all over the world are also feeling. It affects the young first, but it will spread. Some, who are already vulnerable, will act on this sense of hopelessness, doing things they might have never done. The more hope fades, the more repercussions will unfold."

"Then no more talking, let's do this," Tiernan held the Amulets out.

Kareth looked into Tiernan's eyes, then up at the dragons again. "Have no fear, I will not leave you vulnerable." As Kareth took the Amulets, the gemstones glowed to life, shedding an amethyst glow over the scene. Kareth raised her palms to the sky, turning as she addressed the dragons. "*Draconia regnum*, the true Keepers of this Soul Treasure. Today you are called to a noble purpose. What say you?"

Six roars shook the air; the sound filling Willow's head until she thought it might burst. Fire spouted to the sky from the dragon's mouths like multicolored fireworks. Mysendrake and Drynfyre took their perches on the cross-stones of the inner arches. They settled, wings folded on their backs. Kareth smiled up at them like a proud mother, but tears glistened in her eyes. "Drynfyre," she said and the silver dragon dipped her head, respectfully. "Völsendrake." The red dragon did the same. Kareth named them all in turn, first looking to the large black dragon. "Wyndrake." She turned, addressing the deep blue and purple dragons. "Edenfyre. Bryndrake." Lastly, Kareth touched her forehead with her fingers and lifted them to Mysendrake, whispering his name. After a long moment, where she stared at the dragon, and he right back, Kareth turned to Tiernan and took her hand.

Marcus had moved to the other side of the monument where Willow couldn't see him. She wondered if he didn't want to watch.

As Kareth led Tiernan to a stone outside the circle in the back, near where Geldfyre had fallen, Willow was struck by a sudden exhaustion and her legs folded beneath her. She lay back, staring up into the sky. She should be standing with Tiernan, but she couldn't make her body move. Ben crumpled next to her and she heard him begin to sob. "Hurry, Kareth," she murmured. She couldn't think of anything else but sleep now. It was all she wanted. To go to sleep … and never wake up.

CHAPTER 43

TIERNAN HAD NEVER been so sure and so unsure about anything in her entire life. When they reached the stone, Kareth asked her again, "Are you absolutely certain you want to do this?"

Tiernan squeezed her eyes closed. No, she wasn't certain but what choice did she have? Marcus' kiss was almost enough to make her change her mind, but of course, she couldn't. Seeing what the loss of the seventh dragon was doing to Willow and to Ben was enough to convince her what she was doing was the right thing. She felt the dread and hopelessness herself, creeping into her own soul. Knowing the entire planet would soon be infected by such a feeling—she had to go through with this.

But as she approached the stone, all the nevers piled up in her mind. She would never crush on another guy. She'd never turn eighteen, or twenty-one, or get married or have children. She'd never do all the things she always thought she'd grow up to do.

She also never got a chance to say goodbye to her family.

But if she didn't do this now, the world wouldn't be the kind of place where any of those other things would matter anyway.

A strange calm settled over her. "Yes, I'm sure." The lump in her throat loosened. Her heartbeat slowed.

Kareth took her hand and held it between both of her own. "Brave and noble Guardian," she said. "You have answered a call to serve the Creator in a way most humans never could." She held up one finger, correcting herself. "In a way most humans never *would*. You make a sacrifice that will never be forgotten."

"Maybe people will write songs about me," Tiernan cracked, half sob, half laugh. Kareth smiled and placed one of the Amulets around her neck, the other around Tiernan's. She held the gem over Tiernan's heart. "May the power of these two blessed stones make this sacrifice true."

She chanted words in Illian, but Tiernan couldn't follow along. She'd never been all that good at translating the language on paper, and hearing it was even more difficult.

Then a tingling sensation began in Tiernan's toes. Kareth removed the Amulet from Tiernan's neck, then her own. Dangling one from each hand, she stretched her arms wide again. The tingling spread further, up through Tiernan's body, sparking a burst of heat in her chest with an intensity that made her gasp. Kareth brought her hands and the Amulets together forming a single necklace, which she held high. Her chanting grew faster and more insistent; and the heat in Tiernan's chest cranked up.

It was happening.

Tiernan turned and looked out over Stonehenge. The dragons all watched reverently.

She found him at the far side of the circle, leaning against a stone. Their gazes locked. Her vision shifted, like a powerful camera lens zooming into his face. Tears glistened in his eyes. Then his lips turned up at the corners, just slightly.

For a moment, eyes on him, Tiernan felt the loss of what might have been. But then pride swelled and a deep sense of purpose drove everything else out of her mind.

BEN SENSED THE CHANGE the moment Kareth's voice fell silent. In an instant he went from unbelievably miserable to normal, the misery a dream he couldn't quite remember. The threads of it slipped away like spider parachutes in the wind, wisp by wisp, until they were gone.

Next to him, Willow popped up from the ground like someone had released the spring holding her down. Her eyes were misty and red-rimmed. "What happened?" she asked.

"I don't know." Together, they looked to the other side of the circle. Kareth stood by the short stone near where Geldfyre fell. A cool breeze snatched the tendrils of Willow's hair pulled loose from her ponytail, but Kareth's robes didn't billow or move. She held her arms above her head like she was offering the Amulets to the sun. The dragon before her was the color of spring grass. Twice as tall as Kareth, yet considerably smaller than the others, the new dragon spread her wings and stretched her snout skyward.

Ben and Willow scrambled across the circle toward them. The dragon's ears were long and slender like Nordale's, her snout broad and flecked with black. Golden scales formed a mask around her amber eyes. At her heart, a red infinity mark glowed.

They stared up at her in awe. "Tiernan?" Ben murmured.

"Terrwynfyre," Kareth said, with a nod. "It is fitting."

Willow gently stroked the dragon's foreleg. "She'll always be Tiernan to me." Willow's chin quivered and she heaved a great sigh. "I already feel better. Thank you."

"Me too," Ben confirmed, looking to Kareth. She nodded at him. Tiernan had saved them. She truly had.

Sadness snagged Ben's heart again as the enormity of Tiernan's choice hit him, but this wasn't the darkness of before. This sadness didn't threaten to drag him under and drown him. It was more like a smoldering grief, something that would probably never leave him. Something mixed with respect and love.

Dipping her head, Tiernan nudged Willow's cheek. Willow rubbed her hand along Tiernan's jaw, like you might pet a horse. Ben reached up and did the same on the other side of Tiernan's long snout.

Marcus came up behind them, his voice tight. "I feel it, too. We all owe you, Tiernan."

Tiernan remained still, her eyes locked on Marcus. Then she made a soft sound. A sad dragon sigh.

"Together, the seven are powerful, but as I promised, I will not leave you vulnerable to those who might covet your power," Kareth said, gazing up at the dragon audience above. She reached out for Ben and Willow's hands, pulling them away from Tiernan as the newborn dragon extended her wings, lifting from the ground and alighting on the short, round-topped stone behind her. One of the larger dragons couldn't have balanced on its slender crest, but she fit perfectly.

Kareth continued. "The Amulets will make you one with this holy circle of stones. It will not be a hibernation, merely a sleep that will protect you. And I will always be nearby." She moved into the circle. Marcus followed, glancing over his shoulder as if unable to look away from Tiernan for too long.

The wee-wah of an English police car siren wailed in the distance.

Whatever Kareth was going to do, she'd better do it fast.

Ben and Willow followed Kareth to the center of the innermost circle. The dragons, perched on the cross stones all around them, peered down like giant vultures. "It is time to say goodbye," Kareth said, looking at Willow.

"Goodbye?" Willow exchanged looks with Ben and Marcus, confused.

Kareth smiled sadly.

"Why goodbye?" Willow demanded. "What do you mean *they'll be one with the circle of stones?*"

"I will join them with earthen properties so that they are stone, like the circle."

"WHAT?" Ben and Willow exclaimed at once.

"You're going to turn them to stone?" Ben cried.

Kareth held up a hand. "Not permanent, but important. The dragons will not hide any longer, but their form will ensure the world will not feel threatened. They will become a monument to what happened here. A way for all to remember that hope deserves a second chance."

Willow looked up at Kareth, fighting back tears. "If you say this is what needs to happen to keep them safe, then it must be right." Then she turned to Drynfyre. "I hope we will see each other again someday."

Willow sniffled, her voice cracking. "I know you can't hear my thoughts anymore, but I think you still know what I'm feeling, don't you?"

Drynfyre snorted, then made a strange sound: part coo, part purr. She dipped her head toward Willow and blinked her eyes slowly.

Ben stepped forward. "You helped us even though we were the ones who got you in such trouble. Thank you for protecting us." He smiled as big as he could, despite his trembling chin. "I'll never forget you."

Marcus cleared his throat and paused for a long moment. "I, uhm, it was … an honor … to meet a real dragon."

Ben turned to Mysendrake. "And you! You're the coolest wizard-hiding-in-the-form-of-a-dragon ever!"

Willow took a deep shuddering breath. "Thank you, Nordale!"

Mysendrake dipped his head in response.

Kareth hugged both of them. "You should be very proud of yourselves."

Willow shook her head. "If I hadn't woken up Drynfyre in the first place, none of this would have happened."

Ben pulled himself up to his full height. "No, we're both responsible. And we both tried to make it right."

Kareth put her hand on Willow's cheek. "There is a reason all this had to happen. Remember, there are no coincidences."

There was that line again. For some reason, hearing it now made Ben feel better.

"Have faith, children. Of all the magic in the world, faith is, by far, the greatest." Kareth brushed her fingertips across the surface of each Amulet, then touched both Willow's and Ben's foreheads. Her expression shifted through dozens of faces, dozens of pairs of eyes, dozens of smiles, but behind them all Ben finally saw only Kareth. The way she looked on the outside wasn't really who she was, he could see that now that he knew her better.

The doorway of light opened up in the stone, and Kareth turned toward it. Her hair shifted from long, blond and straight to short, brown and curly, then spiraled down into luxurious red ringlets. She stepped into the light and disappeared with an ethereal sizzle, leaving only crusty, weathered stone behind.

Shafts of red light shot from the dragons' chests, as if their entire soul shone through their infinity marks, even Tiernan's. The seven beams met in the center of the circle, and then, with a slow, deep crunching sound seemed to come from all around them, the dragons transform into stone as solid as Stonehenge itself.

CHAPTER 44

GOOSEBUMPS RIPPLED ALONG Willow's arms and legs as Drynfyre's shimmering silver scales turned stony grey. Her eyes went flat and lifeless. The only color on her entire being was the infinity mark on her breastplate that remained volcanic red.

Willow pulled Drynfyre's Pfife from inside the collar of her shirt. It felt cold and dead in her hand. Thunder rumbled from the clouds as misty rain started to fall. Rain splattered down, running along seven stone chests, sizzling against seven blazing infinity marks.

A car door slammed behind them. "Hullo there!" A middle-aged woman with short, spiky black hair and bare legs raised a bright red umbrella as she rushed toward them across the wet grass. She wore a blue bathrobe tied around her thick middle and black fuzzy house slippers. She held her robe together like she feared it might pop open and reveal the pajamas Willow suspected she wore underneath.

Willow, Ben and Marcus jogged across the circle to meet her near the bodies of Faylene and Elsbeth.

"Hello children!" the woman said, her thick English accent straight out of Harry Potter. "Thomas said I would find you here. Are you all right?"

Before they could answer, she went on. "I understand Gerta joined the traitor, hmmm? Never right with the Family, that one," the Guardian wheezed, her blue eyes twinkling with tears. "Oh, where are my manners? I'm Georgiana Kindleman, Gerta's second. She and I watch over sweet Mysendrake ..." Her gaze crept toward the monument, taking in its new dragon adornments. "At least ... we did. Perhaps you could enlighten me to what happened here. But on the drive home." She jerked her head in the direction of the ever-closer sirens.

Willow's heart clutched. Did Georgiana know Mysendrake was really Nordale? How much should they tell her? Could they trust this woman?

The siren grew nearer.

"Time to go," Georgiana said, turning on her heel.

"Wait! My backpack!" Ben cried before they'd gone ten steps. Georgiana paused as Ben rushed back through the rain to retrieve it. "What about ... them?" Willow asked, nodding at the Guardian sisters.

"We'll let the Constable handle them," Georgiana said, glancing down the long road to where an ambulance and half a dozen police cars had appeared at the top of a hill. Without waiting for Ben to catch up,

Georgiana grabbed Willow by the hand and ran for the car. Marcus screamed at Ben to hurry. Moments later, they'd all piled inside Georgiana's little car.

Willow pressed her forehead against the window for one last look at the dragons on their monumental perch. Seeing Tiernan on her solitary stone, away from the others, made her heart ache. She felt horrible leaving them all behind. Her gaze locked on Drynfyre and she reached out to the dragon with her mind, wanting to feel her one last time, but she could sense nothing. "Good bye," she whispered.

Georgiana punched the gas pedal and the car sped away. In the front passenger seat, Marcus nervously glanced behind them at the approaching police cars. Ben reached over and grasped Willow's hand.

She kept her eyes on Drynfyre's stony form until the road veered and Stonehenge disappeared behind a hill. Eyes heavy with tears she didn't want to cry, Willow turned around in her seat and met Ben's gaze. He looked like he felt much the same way.

"Now," Georgiana said, her voice calm and smooth as if running from the police was no big deal. "Would someone like to tell me why our dragons seem to have migrated to Stonehenge?"

THE THREE POLICE CARS pulled to the side of the road. Their drivers rushed across the grass to where the single victim lay. One of them swore he'd seen a woman stumbling across the meadow beyond the ancient circle of stones, but when he and his partner went to investigate, no one was there.

CHAPTER 45

WILLOW WOKE WITH a start, the sensation of riding Drynfyre so real that for a moment she believed they were airborne. Disappointment brought her crashing back to earth.

Just another dream.

It had been so good to see her parents when the huge military transport plane landed at the Air Force base near Denver. Willow's dad had sobbed like a baby when she walked down the back loading gate, grabbing her up in his arms and hugging her. Mom joined in and they had the first family hug they'd had in a long, long time. Ben and Marcus did the same with Uncle Josh. It was quite the reunion. And nobody was even mad that they'd flown overseas on a dragon.

Thomas was there, too. He said Coreen was still in the hospital. Georgiana had called him from her house and relayed the story they'd told her. Thomas had told their parents, more or less. But he hadn't told Coreen yet. He wanted to wait until she was stronger. Hearing about Tiernan would be too hard right now.

From the base, they'd had gone to a hotel in downtown Denver where they'd met with Belinda and the other Elders to tell the story again and answer more questions. By time that was done, and they'd driven home, it was almost midnight.

Now, although it seemed like it should be morning already, her bedside clock read 1:11. Only an hour had passed since she'd fallen asleep, but she'd had so many dreams about Drynfyre that it felt like she'd been asleep all night.

Willow sat up, snapping on the light to chase away the unsettling darkness. Sweat dampened the back of her nightshirt and stuck her hair to her forehead. Throwing back the sheet, Willow moved to the window. She needed some fresh air. She slid up the sash and let the crisp night breeze flow over her. It filled her room with the smell of rain and wet pine needles. It was good to be home. And yet ...

Something was missing.

The Pfife sat on her dresser, a souvenir from their unbelievable adventure. Willow ran a finger across its delicate length. The energetic thrum that used to run through it during her bond with Drynfyre was gone, another absence leaving her feeling empty and incomplete. She hadn't been able to bring herself to try to play it.

How would her life ever be like it was before all this happened? How could she go back to just being a kid who liked to dig through trash cans and play the violin? Everything was different now and not just because the world knew dragons were real. So much had happened that the world didn't know. Would *never* know.

The Guardians would make sure of that.

Her violin case leaned in the corner by the window. Placing it on the bed, she took out her violin and bow, adjusting the chin rest. It seemed like forever since she'd played, but she needed to feel the music right now, like it would give her some kind of connection to Drynfyre. Willow pulled the bow across the strings, keeping the pressure light and the sound soft. Her fingers moved, finding the notes, recreating the tune. It sounded different played on a stringed instrument, but it was definitely Drynfyre's Awakening Song. Willow didn't think she'd forget that melody, ever, for as long as she lived.

A tap on her bedroom door startled her. The bow squeaked across the bridge. Willow chuckled at her jumpiness. "Come in," she stage-whispered.

"Hey," said Ben, easing into the room, the door clicking shut behind him. He padded over in his red and green tartan bathrobe, hands behind his back. "I heard you playing. You okay?"

"Yeah, I just really miss her is all."

"I know. Me too." Ben sat on the edge of her bed, revealing what he held in his hands. The sheath of music. "I thought maybe you should have this. It kind of goes with the Pfife. I'd like to keep Matilda's journal, if that's okay with you."

"Of course, I mean, she put your name on that list of Guardians. You should definitely have it."

Willow took the music and spread it out on the bed, each song's title now unreadable in the script of Kareth's ancient language. Willow couldn't tell which Song was which, but maybe if she played the notes she would recognize the tunes.

"Why do you think Matilda did that, anyway?" Ben asked. "Added me to that list?"

"Maybe she trusted you to keep her secrets. She always liked you. More than she liked me, that's for sure."

Ben shrugged. "Maybe, but it's weird. I mean, it was a list of girls."

Willow thought for a moment. "But just because someone was a girl didn't mean they were trustworthy. Nanette and those other Guardian traitors sure proved that to Hanna. Faylene and Elsbeth sure proved it to us. Maybe Matilda was trying to make a point. Maybe it shouldn't all be just about boys and girls. Just because way back then men were running things, why should men be blamed forever for what those guys did?"

Ben gave a contemplative nod. "Like Thomas. I bet he'd make a great Guardian. It seems unfair that he can't be one."

"Just being a girl shouldn't automatically make you worthy, you know? Just being a guy either. It's who you are inside."

They sat quiet for a moment, and then Ben gave a chuckle. "Sometimes all that's happened the last few days doesn't even seem real. I think maybe that's why I can't go to sleep. Like I'm afraid if I do, I'll wake up and it will have all been a dream." He looked at Willow. "I don't want to go back to the way things were before."

Tears burned at the back of Willow's eyes. She knew what he meant, and even what he wasn't saying. He didn't mean just the adventure, or even the dragons. He was talking about the two of them. They were different now, as cousins. As friends. "I don't want that either," she said, and returned his smile.

A loud thump sounded from outside the window, rocking the house with a slight tremor. "What was that?" Willow and Ben scrambled off the bed and ran to the window. Marcus burst through the door wearing grey pajama bottoms and a dark green Lucky Charms tee shirt. "Did you see? Wow, did you? You aren't going to believe it!"

"Tiernan!" Ben cried leaning out the window. The green dragon sat on the front lawn, a dark-haired young woman on her back. Willow snatched up her robe and raced downstairs, Ben and Marcus right behind her.

Tiernan took up most of the front yard, her green scales shimmering dark in the moonlight. "What are you doing here?" Willow cried looking up at the unfamiliar Guardian on Tiernan's back. "Who are you?"

The girl raised a hand in greeting. "Don't worry, I'm one of the good guys. I'm Sophie, the second at the Maryland den. Kareth sent us." Tiernan extended her foreleg and Sophie slid down like she'd done it a hundred times. She had long, straight hair woven into a thick, dark braid. Her deep brown eyes smiled with friendliness, as if she had known Willow for years. She wore an outfit similar to the one Tiernan had worn; a long khaki colored tunic belted at the waist, slim pants and boots. Around her neck hung a leather cord and from the cord hung a Pfife.

Marcus and Ben hovered a few feet behind Willow. She turned around and beckoned them closer. "These are my cousins, Ben and Marcus. Guys, this is Sophie." Willow turned back to Tiernan. "How is this possible? What about the Treasure?"

Tiernan stretched her neck out long and high and Willow could see her red infinity mark. It flared red, then turned silver as brilliant lights streaked around her, covering her in sparkles. Then, just like with Nordale, three loud pops and flashes transformed Tiernan back into her human form.

"Tiernan!" Marcus ran for her, scooping her into his arms. She held onto him as he spun her around.

"Whoa, take it easy Romeo," Sophie warned. "That transformation can mess with her head. Give her a moment, will ya?"

"It's okay," Tiernan laughed, her voice scratchy and hoarse. "I don't mind."

And then, there was kissing.

Willow and Ben rolled their eyes at Sophie, who just grinned coyly. "She was pretty excited to get to see him again." Sophie said, quickly raising her hands. "You two as well, of course."

"But I don't understand! If she's here, then …"

"It's a long story, and there will be plenty of time for me to explain on the way. All you need to know for now is Elsbeth is not out of the picture after all. It looks like she and Faylene had plans to steal the Nirvana Gem. Plans that Elsbeth intends to carry out. One of the Fae Guardians in Texas got wind that someone was asking the wrong kinds of questions to the wrong kinds of people. But at least we know what she's up to."

"But, I still don't understand, what does that have to do with us?" Ben asked.

"Well, isn't it obvious?" Sophie asked. "Kareth gave us one week to find Elsbeth and stop her before Tiernan has to be back at Stonehenge. As long as she stays in dragon form, a week away should be okay." Sophie cleared her throat loudly. Marcus and Tiernan looked at her and Tiernan's face went red.

"Kareth said a few minutes wouldn't hurt," Tiernan explained.

"What is going on out here?"

Everyone froze, turning toward the porch where Willow's mom and Uncle Josh stood in their bathrobes, stern looks on their faces like perhaps they knew exactly what was going on out here on the front lawn. "Ummm," Ben began, but Marcus broke in.

"Dad!" He pulled Tiernan toward the porch. "This is Tiernan! I never thought you'd get to meet her but here she is!" Marcus was giddy, a stupid grin stretching across his face. Willow had never seen him like this.

"I thought you said Tiernan was …" Uncle Josh swallowed. "A dragon?"

"She was! She is, I mean, not right now but she can change back, do you want to see? It's SO cool, but not yet, okay?" Marcus grabbed Tiernan's hands. "Just a few more minutes before we go, okay?"

"Go? No, no, no, you're not going anywhere," Willow's mom said, coming down the steps and pulling Willow away from Sophie. "They just got back, safe and sound, and they aren't going anywhere with any of you dragon people. Ever again."

214

"But Mom!" Willow whined, not realizing how much she wanted to go on this new adventure with Sophie until just that moment. "Elsbeth is still alive and trying to get another of the Soul Treasures." Willow looked at Sophie. "That's what it is, right? That Nirvana Gem you mentioned? Which Beast of the First Realm are we talking about here? Unicorns?"

"Centaurs?" Ben asked, hopefully.

"Fairies, actually," Sophie said.

"Fairies?" Willow crowed. "See? Mom, we have to go. The Fairies need us!" Her mom kept pulling her toward the porch. "Mom, please!"

Sophie stepped toward them, raising her Pfife and playing a few notes into it. Willow's mom froze on the spot, her expression melting from panic into something soft and pliable.

"It's all going to be fine, Willow will be safe with us. You won't need to worry."

"We won't need to worry," both her mom and Uncle Josh said, robotically.

"Whoa," Ben marveled. "I didn't know Pfifes could do that."

"Just a little something I've been working on," Sophie grinned. "I wasn't actually sure it would work. I discovered some new note combinations that affect humans instead of dragons. This one is like hypnosis. Makes the target susceptible to suggestion." She looked at Willow. "I mean, if you're okay with this? It'll just keep them from worrying. No permanent damage. At least, I don't think so."

"Should they be worried?" Ben asked sounding rather worried himself. "I mean, if Elsbeth is as dangerous as Faylene was, we aren't exactly going to Disney World."

"Are the Fairies at Disney World?" Willow bounced up and down on her toes, hands clasped together.

Sophie shook her head with a laugh. "No, they're at a Renaissance Festival in Texas."

"Of course they are," Marcus grinned.

"Texas? We're going to Texas?" Ben pumped his fists in the air. "We're going home!"

Tiernan moved toward Willow. "You guys know what we're up against here, but we need all the Guardians we can gather if we're going to stop that woman."

Willow's heart raced at the word. "Guardians?"

"But we're not Guardians," Ben shook his head, confused.

"According to Kareth, you are. You earned it after all that Flame of Hope craziness," Tiernan grinned. "Besides, if I have to stay in dragon form, Sophie here is going to need some help. So... what do ya say?" Tiernan looked from Willow, to Ben, to Marcus. "You guys up for another adventure?"

"I'm in," Marcus said right away.

"Me too," Ben agreed, but cast a wary look at his dad, who stared into space like someone had pushed pause on him.

Willow thought about what Tiernan had said. She and Ben were Guardians now. Trusted to watch over the Beasts of the First Realm. It didn't seem real. It didn't seem possible. Yet, according to Tiernan, it was true.

The idea swelled inside Willow's heart. Who was she kidding? There was no way she could turn away from this invitation. She grinned. "I'm up for it. But first, we probably should change out of our pajamas."

The End